BIMINI AND OTHER STORIES

FRANK BUCHAR

ISBN 978-1-4357-1216-4

Cover Design by Ward Shipman
www.guyinaboat.com

ABOUT BIMINI AND OTHER STORIES

In these ten carefully wrought stories, set in the Caribbean, Canada, Tibet, and other exotic locales, surprise is a constant element. Covering a wonderful selection of tales and a sparkling novella, this volume encompasses magic realism and other genres with a deft, sure touch for the magical, the bizarre, the humorous, and the tender. Many of the stories explore the mysteries of love and desire across time and place.

Bimini follows the search for the fountain of youth in the Hemingway Caribbean with some unpredictable results.

Medicine Bag presents the extraordinary adventures of a magical Cree medicine bag on a spree in Northern Ontario.

The Undiscovered Country is a bizarre romp into the afterlife where a star and a rock kiss, and Che Guevara is remembered as a Bolivian plumber.

Margarita is a tale of escape, reflection, a cockfight, and returning home.

Second Chance probes the raw and curious aftermath of a broken relationship and the brutal honesty of a man determined to move on despite untoward apparitions in the night.

Katrina offers a glimpse into the psyche of a middle-aged woman who ostensibly has it all- two loves and a comfortable lifestyle in two different worlds, Bali and Canada. A chance encounter and a modern menace probe the mysteries of life and love, and gratuitous choice.

Leonard takes a modern look at love and will in Toronto's Beaches. Existential questions abound in this comic narrative that celebrates love and friendship.

Mystic Stallion features a lovesick Yale University student and his strange encounter with an old man and the lost journal of the sixth Dalai Lama, the Dalai Lama that no one talks about because of his all-too-human loves.

Canadian Club provides a startling and arresting glimpse into the lives and loves of Canadian consultants in Bangladesh. The meaning of beauty and truth becomes entangled in harsh political and human realities.

Past Reason Hunted is a novella of the future probing the intersection of two vastly different civilizations, long after a nuclear holocaust has taken place. Technologically advanced dome worlds and lush underground colonies collide as a result of human emotions that remain immutable despite the lessons of time.

For Lara

BIMINI AND OTHER STORIES

CONTENTS

BIMINI

If you would've asked me a few years back, say even five, about my going off on a search for the fountain of youth, I would've called you crazy. Completely loony-tunes. But that was a few years back, and things have changed. Melody's forty -five now, and just beginning to look it. And so am I, looking my age that is, when I'm brave enough to take a good, hard look in the mirror, without sucking in my gut and flexing. What I do see when I'm honest enough to just plain *see* is a balding, overweight guy named Vernon with wrinkles beginning to take over most of my face. Amazing what you can pretend isn't there. I don't have a painting in my closet that gets older while I stay forever young, like that guy from a story. I just want a few more good years with her, prime years, with everything looking fairly good and working the way it used to, and maybe Melody loving me the way she used to. We've had our share of troubles. So that's why we're here in Bimini- to search for the fountain. Melody doesn't know that yet. I want it to be a surprise. I've done my homework on this thing. After all, you've got to remember they once sent a real live expedition in search of this fountain of youth. Ponce de Leon was the Spanish conquistador who organized the expedition. Oh sure, there's not too much to go on, but enough. An old Indian woman, by the name of La Viega, led them there, to Bimini, and things just sort of trail off from there, with no real records or anything. But why should there be? Can you imagine the rush there'd be if the whole world knew? It'd make the Klondike Gold Rush look like a picnic in a closet.

Just think about all those filthy rich people who'd give a fortune to turn back the clock. The one thing they can't buy- that's the part I love. They can't buy youth. And then, just think about what would happen if governments knew about it. Maybe Spain would want a piece of the action, being the first, and all. I'm sure the whole island would be cordoned off faster than you could say Mick Jagger.

So my plan was a simple one, and with a bit of on-line Googling, we were off. The first few days we just laid back at the hotel, and didn't do too much of anything. Just drank a few cool ones and ate some cracked conch. Sat under swaying palms with coral white sand between our toes. Hemingway liked it here, right here in this very bar, on this very island. It's a pretty lively joint on the weekends. I don't know if it's the same way it was when Hemingway stayed here, but it feels like the kind of place he could booze up in. He sure had a great life in spots like this around the world when he was younger. Now I'm a retired postie, early retirement, but I can get into this kind of lifestyle, no trouble at all. Sure doesn't take long to get into the rhythm- just a few days and you're as relaxed as can be.

I met one of the locals in the bar, a guy named Curtis Brown, who said he'd show me the place where the fountain was supposed to be, near the little airport on South Bimini. So I said why not. It's as good a place to start as any. I pretended it was just a bit of a lark for me, nothing more. Melody was kind of lukewarm about it when I told her. She didn't quite believe in it, but we were in Bimini, and that was enough for her. She said she didn't want to lose an afternoon when she could be sunning at the pool by the resort nearby. Melody's still got her figure, thin, but with curves. She's still a looker, and even the young guys give her a second glance.

So that's how I got there, to the fountain site, the first time. Curtis hired a cab from a friend of his and we were there. A sun-bleached and battered "for sale" sign marked the spot. Not much to look at since it's all dried up ground, with nothing but scrub brush around. "Yeah mon, the place where the fountain used to be, here," he said. Melody sure was happy when Curtis gave her a pair of black conch earrings. The guy sure has a lot of jokes. He's got a space between his two front teeth that you could pass two quarters through sidewise.

Now I didn't mind so much that Curtis charged me fifty bucks for taking me to a dried up piece of scrub land. It's a tiny island and everybody's got to make a living somehow. I knew where I was gonna be looking, but there's nothing wrong with a bit of company. Besides, he's a real charmer, always talking with Melody, and making her feel good. The whole place here though, looks and feels seedy, a little rundown. The kind of place you know where things are happening on the sly. I'll betcha more drugs are shipped out of here to the mainland than you can shake a stick at. Funny, that expression, about the stick I mean. You see, that's what I plan to do. Shake a stick.

When I told my brother Wesley about dowsing, he laughed real good. He lives up there in New Hampshire in the hills outside of Concord. He's not a redneck though. Just a tough, wiry son of a bitch that likes to be left alone except for Wednesdays when his poker buddies come over for a sauna and a few cold ones. He's as mean as a mongoose if you cross him. Anyway, when I showed him my divining stick, you'd a thought he'd swallowed laughing gas. It's a real beauty, made out of witch hazel. He took it up in his hands and walked like a zombie right up to his kitchen sink. I noticed his grip on the stick wasn't right, but I didn't say a thing. I'd never seen Wesley laugh like that since we were kids back in Poughkeepsie. He told me he could use a bottle or two of magic water himself, but that if I couldn't find any, to bring him back some dark rum. "Dahk rum", he called it. He's lived there going on thirty years now, and my brother's getting old, like me. I'd sure like to surprise him with some magic "wadda." I love that New England accent of his.

An old guy from upstate New York taught me how to dowse with a stick. Dowsing, as he explained it to me, is the art of finding water with a stick. He took a shine to me because I never laughed at him like the other kids. Said I had the gift. Dowsing works, though most people don't believe it. They don't believe in a fountain of youth either which is just fine with me. I don't need the extra competition. Funny thing, you know. Most people say they believe in a god, and some kind of afterlife, but when you think about it, that's a lot more fantastic, and more unbelievable, than a magic fountain right here on earth. Go figure.

So I went back a few days later, by myself, to the place Curtis had showed us, near Cavelle Pond. Nobody was around. Took out my dowsing stick but nothing was happening. That's when I went for a long walk till I got to the end of the makeshift road and just kept on walking. I'm used to walking from my years with the post office. Only, in the last couple of years my left hip started to go, osteoarthritis the doc said. I saw a mongoose as I was walking about, and I thought of Wesley then. I remember Wesley saying that my Melody had been around the block a few times. Now what's that supposed to mean? Funny I thought about that, but when you're alone you think about all kinds of weird things. After I wandered around for a long time, I sat down. A beautiful spot it was too. After a while, I tried the dowsing again, and you'd have thought I had the Parkinson's, all the shaking that was happening. I felt a jolt like lightning move down my spine. The forked stick I held was jumping in my hands and then, suddenly, went down like a lead weight. It sort of stabbed the ground hard, and it sure surprised me. I walked away from the spot to check if it was like that all around there, but it wasn't. I'd found underground water, but I didn't know what kind. It was a real lonesome spot though, that's for sure.

When I got back to the hotel, Melody and Curtis were having a drink in the wraparound porch which overlooks the courtyard bar and the street. I walked through the bar with its fishing photographs everywhere. I mean the walls are plastered with them. It kind of makes you feel sorry for marlins. They're a pretty fish, and if fish could fly, they'd be the ones to do it, shaped so nice they are. Curtis was telling Melody a joke or something, but he sure stood up in a hurry when he spied me. So polite a guy. Melody had a smile on her as big as Texas. Curtis started talking about Andros, his home island, saying how special it was, saying we'd really like it there, it being really cheap to live there and all. Melody had been telling him how we planned to find a place down here to live, if the price was right. I don't know where she got that idea.

Well, the next few days I thought about how I was going to dig. I mean I didn't want anyone to follow me or anything. And, with Melody, I just had to come up with the real thing, or forget about it. She's a tough one. I needed time, time to work and really check things out. I needed a sledgehammer, a drive point, enough pipe to get down deep, and a few tools. So I told her I was going to try some fishing, just like Hemingway. And, when Curtis offered to show her Andros, I thought it was a good thing. Why not? She said that she'd be staying with Curtis's sister, Laila, in Nicholl's Town, for a few days just to get a feel for the place. Curtis said he'd get her settled and then be back the same day. Simple, just like that. I couldn't believe how everything just dovetailed into place.

The next few days I worked like a trooper. I was lucky to find the pipe and stuff I needed in town, and made do with a few tools I scrounged up around the hotel to make the job easier. I had to do everything real quiet like, going here and there for this piece and that. I was real excited when I got back to the site. I started up right away. I walked forwards with my stick about twenty-five paces, and then she came down hard on the ground like a lead pigeon. I felt that strange and familiar jolt of electricity run through my body again. I reckoned I had her, dead centre, and her depth to boot. I made a few more passes from different directions with my stick, and those places where it pulled down strongest, I put in a stake. The centre of the stakes marked the spot where to dig. I hammered in the drive point with the sledge, making sure I put a driving cap on the threaded end where I was gonna put on my couplings for the pipe. Once I'd got a length of pipe in, I threaded on a coupling with another piece of pipe, put on the driving cap to take the sledge blows, and kept on driving until I needed another extension pipe. It didn't take long to get down deep, where I needed to be.

Not a lot of water came out at first, but enough, a trickle. It was kind of muddy brown at the start, and then clear, as clear as dripping tap water back home in Chicopee, Massachusetts. I was able to fill four bottles, empty Captain Morgan rum bottles. It sure was exciting. I didn't drink it right then and there. I wanted to do it back at the hotel, in style, on the wraparound porch, sipping at it like one of Hemingway's heroes. So, I stopped up the water flow, packed up my things, covered up all my traces as if I'd never been there, and was gone.

Curtis didn't show up that night. I started asking around the hotel and found out that Curtis planned to stay a few days on Andros himself. They said he had a lady friend with him. I started worrying and couldn't sleep until I decided to head over to Andros in the morning. I drank a few shots of dark rum with some of my Bimini water to try to get some sleep.

Curtis's sister's place was real tough to find. When I did find the house, two really big guys said that Melody and Curtis had gone jigging for fish. They kind of smirked when they said it, and that bothered me. I waited there for a long time. They didn't invite me in. When Melody and Curtis got back it was real late, and they were both high on something. Melody seemed real surprised to see me, and then she turned real mad and said that if I didn't trust her, she didn't want to be with me for a while. I tried pulling her away, but then the two big guys were in my face and started pushing me away. Melody had this real weird look on her face. She said she needed some time alone and for me to go. I got real mad then and tried to make her come with me. She pushed me away and went inside. Curtis just stood there with a big wild grin on his face. He nodded to the two guys, and they just went crazy then and started into me hard. That was the last bit I remember. The next day I was in a ditch by the side of the road with my face all puffed up and bloody. My jaw felt broken. I tried to find a cop, and when I finally did, and we went over there, Melody said that she didn't want to go home with me. She didn't seem to care what happened to me. That was the tough part. She looked real cold and hard. She said to go home, that she was staying, and that we'd work something out. She said she'd call me.

The policeman just shrugged, and I could see he felt kind of bad for me but couldn't do anything about it. The feeling in my stomach felt worse than my face looked. So I left. I got back to Bimini the next day. Sure didn't feel good, inside or out, for about a week. Melody called and said she'd taken the money in our joint account. Said to keep the house. Said that it was over. Said she wondered why I couldn't see it coming. Said she hadn't been happy for years.

When I got to Wesley's place no one seemed to be home. I could see two of his turkeys in a low coop to my left. I left my luggage inside his porch, and placed a bottle of my Bimini water together with a bottle of dark rum on his kitchen counter. I felt great and even my jaw was all healed up. Funny thing was, I was looking great, years younger already, and tiny dark hairs were starting to sprout on my bald spot.

It was the second last day of December, and it was bitter cold, with hard packed snow everywhere. The New Hampshire sun was brilliant, the air fresh. Bimini seemed like a different world away. I walked around to the back of the house, and I saw a small trail of smoke coming from the sauna at the bottom of the slope behind the house. I sprinted down the hill fast, and I mean real fast, with an effortless stride, and I didn't slip once. I could see Wesley looking at me from the small verandah attached to the sauna. He was looking at me real puzzled like. I could see by his eyes that he knew something was different about me.

I've always thought, if you've got it, flaunt it. I told him that he had to believe. He asked me, "What do you mean *believe*, Vernon?" I just felt so good then that I sprinted away, laughing. I wasn't even breathing hard. I ran around the pond just off the sauna deck and towards the woods. I could see a goldfish in a hole cut in the ice of the pond. I could see everything so clearly. The scales of the goldfish were luminous and it seemed to be casting the brightness off from inside itself. The sun was everywhere, on everything. I felt so strong and young. It was only late that night after a few rum drinks chased by Bimini water that I realized I didn't even miss Melody anymore. I knew where the conversation would be going after a few more drinks. I wanted to talk to Wesley about investing in some real estate down south, way down south, in Captain Morgan country.

MEDICINE BAG

Some things resent being noticed. Some things, like some people, enjoy being in the limelight and when they're not, well, then they're just waiting in the wings for the right moment. The right moment is always synched with benign rays of light. The same law applies to a thing as it does to a person. All things being equal. That's why the right moment is always filled with pearly, radiant light. Light as rich and creamy as the floor of heaven; light as pure and pampered as the ceiling of a brothel. The medicine bag had found the right moment. It came in the form of an exuberant Ukrainian. Ukrainians are known for their exuberance. This particular Ukrainian was particularly exuberant. Light was spilling out around him like an evangelist on Sunday TV. Peter Shevchenko synched with the right moment.

The medicine bag had been the spiritual and physical property of Martin Spence. Martin Spence lived in a small Cree village on the shores of James Bay. He lived there with his wife and two small girls. His daughters smiled whalebone smiles. The only things really re-markable about Martin Spence were his possessions: he owned a beaded, deer-hide medicine bag and an espresso-type coffee machine with a steam attachment for making cappuccino.

The medicine bag came to him from his paternal grandfather who was known to be the first man from the reserve to have seen an automobile. The automobile in question was a Model-T Ford that had belonged to a second generation, Italian hog-butcher from Detroit, Michigan. When Martin's grandfather saw the Model-T, it barreled down on him with its curious cargo of hog-butcher and bootlegged wine until it left him with an undeniable impression. The big toe on his right foot still showed a slight depression where Ford's genius had rested. And the cappuccino machine: it was the sum total and symbol of Martin Spence's achievements in white society. Not necessarily polite society, but white society.

As far as the outside world went, Martin Spence had worked for three months in an automobile car lot in Oakville in exchange for his room and board and the cappuccino machine. The salesman in charge of the car lot also owned a franchise for selling espresso coffee machines imported from Milan, Italy. His brief stint as a carwash attendant had left him with an undying respect for all things native and a marked disdain for an impolite society. Even the cappuccino impolitely gurgled and spewed muddy waters into his coffee mug. The coffee fainted away in his mug like a Victorian lady in a drawing room. But Martin Spence swallowed her down nevertheless, petticoats and all.

The medicine bag was a good thing in Martin Spence's life. Literally. Benign rays of light connected him up with the light and made him happy. His life was as rich and juicy as the first dark summer cherry. And his family was notorious in the village for their whalebone smiles. And so it went. Until Peter Shevchenko came along looking for arts and crafts: inexpensive gifts for friends. He filled his packsack tight with moccasins, mitts and all sorts of beaded souvenirs. He would have taken more with him but he ran out of money.

The night before he left the village, Peter Shevchenko stopped to see Martin Spence. Shevchenko, a lifer with the Department of Indian and Northern Affairs Canada, wanted to leave him with a message for the Chief. Martin Spence was well respected in the village, and what's even more important, Shevchenko thought, reliable. He wanted to make sure the Chief got the message. On his way there Shevchenko saw the silhouettes of some geese flying in the night sky, moving gracefully across the moon. Some people by the riverbank pointed at the sky while the birds measured themselves against eternity. The horizon stretched out over the waters like the arms of Franklin's widow draped across Hudson Bay. But Shevchenko was oblivious to all of this. He was thinking about money. He knew he was going to make a bundle when he left the Department. With his contacts he'd make a fortune selling dry goods to the different reserves. Only the things people really needed. Cash and carry. That was the ticket.

Shevchenko prepared himself for the role he was going to play. He cleared his throat, set his jaw and squinted his eyes. He liked to appear direct-the square shooter approach. His life was really made up of little acts he was always performing right in front of his own eyes. He was his own best audience. If you could've cloned Shevchenko and set him apart in a world peopled with Shevchenkos just like himself, he would have thought himself in a blessed utopia. He was knocking at the door. Martin Spence wasn't fooled. But he liked Shevchenko anyway. Exuberance goes a long way.

"Well, Peter, hello," Martin said. The two men looked at each other and smiled. Martin saw the thickset man with the large nose he had come to like while Shevchenko took in Martin's ample form, his bright, piercing eyes, and the raven-black, luxuriant pony tail that set the gold standard for pony tails in the village. Martin was standing in front of the doorway with one of his little girls leaning against him and staring up in wonder at Shevchenko's wide, bright face. She peered up at him through her telescoped fingers.

"Martin, sorry to bother you, but could I come in for a minute," Shevchenko asked.

"Sure," Martin said, "c'mon in." They went over to the couch and sat down. The little girl ran to the kitchen where her mother and sister were beading deer-hide moccasins. She kept on stealing glances at Shevchenko from around the corner. Whenever Shevchenko winked at her, she giggled and turned her telescopes into fists, and then she was gone.

"Gee, you've sure got a lot of nice things here. I didn't know your wife made them." Shevchenko picked up a pair of duffle-lined mukluks. He liked them better than the ones he had just bought. He whistled softly in appreciation. It was a low arching can-opener kind of whistle.

"Nice job, Martin. She's really good."

"Yeah," Martin said.

Martin pushed away a heap of moccasins and mitts that his wife had been working on. The deer-hide that she used in making them was another offshoot of the great American machine. American sportsmen on vacation, working in conjunction with American express cards and bazooka memories from Vietnam, bagged the deer. The skins were flown up on government planes in neatly-tied bundles.

Shevchenko handed Martin the note as he explained what he wanted to say to the Chief. He looked like a square shooter when he said it. Suddenly, out of the corner of his eye, he noticed something. Or was it the other way around? The right moment was coming into synch. The medicine bag waited in the wings. Shevchenko couldn't help what he was feeling. It wasn't a very nice feeling. The feeling had a dark, exciting edge to it. Not like the packaged, deer-hide feelings that came to him along with the ballpoint pens, Big Macs and scented glad bags. This feeling was different. He wanted to steal the thing in the corner just behind Martin's shoulder on the top shelf: the medicine bag. Following Martin to the door he did the one thing he feared most. He wasn't acting; it was for real. Giddy with excitement, he snatched at the bag and shoved it under his armpit. The feeling he had was almost sexual. It was a secret, hard feeling. The right moment flooded Martin Spence's home in wave after wave. Shevchenko synched with the medicine bag and benign rays of light. It happened without anyone really being aware of it. It was an historical event in the order of Stanley meeting Livingstone. But no one knew it.

The Bluebird taxi that had brought Shevchenko home from the airport stopped once en route. The cabbie stopped to pick up a pizza for his radio dispatcher, Darla. He turned off the meter when he ran in for the pizza. Darla was not one of his favourite people. He said so to Shevchenko.

"That slob, that big, fat slob always gets us to pick her up something...and she needs it all right, boy, does she need it."

Shevchenko wanted to be agreeable.

"Pretty fat, eh?"

"Fat, is she fat?" he asked grinning. "She sits all day in a lazy boy she brought in to the office, and let me tell you she barely squeezes that lard-ass in. She's always chewing on something, chocolate bars, popcorn, pistachio nuts. And they're just to tide her over until the troops get in with reinforcements: pizzas, burgers, fried chicken." The cabbie hated fat. He particularly hated Darla because she brushed against him whenever he happened to be in the tiny office. Darla rubbed her hips against him shamelessly, muttering "excuse me," and smiling. It was like being shoved around by a waterbed. The other cabbies teased him about it. One of them, a part-time psychology student, told him that, secretly, he probably wanted Darla and that that was the reason for his despising her so much. The cabbie didn't tell Shevchenko about the free analysis. By the time he got home, Shevchenko was salivating like a Pavlovian dog from the smell of pizza. It was driving him mad. Meanwhile, the medicine bag bided its time at the bottom of Shevchenko's packsack.

Shevchenko didn't bother to unpack his packsack. That was the last thing on his mind. He was making last minute plans for the log house he was going to build. A dream home in the bush for himself and his young bride-to-be. He studied house plans, read all the latest log-building books and looked for the ideal chainsaw. He forgot about the medicine bag. While Shevchenko poured over loan interest tables and new insurance rates, the medicine bag gathered more and more power to itself. Its power grew like a snowball tumbling silently down Mount Everest. A snowball that grew to astronomical proportions. Invisible atoms of power stuck onto the beaded medicine bag. Benign rays of light disguised as shadows hid within the folds of Shevchenko's packsack.

The land that Shevchenko chose to build upon was nine parts bush and one part abandoned farm. The bush parts were as untamed and unruly as old brillo pads. The abandoned farm sat on cleared ground that was as hard and obvious as a fist. Rusty traces of agriculture could be seen lying discarded near the blurred edges of the farm where the brillo pads began. Shevchenko's fiance, Madelaine, looked at the land and then at Shevchenko, and then back at the land again. She wasn't quite sure what to make of it all. She was a little intimidated by his friend, Abe Saunders. Abe owned the adjoining property and was a curious kind of latter-day pioneer. He was a little too enthusiastic and hopeful about the land, a little too exuberant in the wrong kind of way. He didn't seem to notice the broken pitchforks or the warped barn-boards that were just a few feet in front of him. He was talking to Shevchenko about forming a cooperative. He was wearing his treasured antique buffalo coat.

"You see, the way I see it, we can't go wrong if we follow the co-op plan. We have to pool our skills and resources together. Now I'm thinking long-term. This isn't going to be a fly-by-night operation. This is for our kids and grand-kids, get me?"

"Gotcha," Shevchenko said. He was wondering about what Madelaine was thinking, standing beside him quietly, listening. He felt very manly and important. He picked up a stone and threw it high into the sky. The stone was half stone, half dream. It landed with a thud and then whispered through the dry grass to a stop. He turned to Madelaine.

"Honey, what do you think?"

Madelaine looked past Abe Saunders into Shevchenko's eyes. She thought he looked very manly and important.

"It's good country," she said demurely. Abe Saunders went to his van and brought back two bottles of beer. He opened one of them prying it loose with the other bottlecap. Foam garlanded the neck of the bottle. Shevchenko took the bottle from him and then winked and toasted him at the same time.

"The co-op plan is good. I've got my eyes on a little portable sawmill down the road, you know, one we can dismantle and rebuild over there on the land. It'll be my contribution to the co-op. Just the thing we need for log-cabin building. What do you think?" he said, turning to Abe who was opening his bottle of beer with his belt buckle.

"Terrific," Abe said. He said it loudly as if he were trying to make a point in an argument. Madelaine smiled and walked over to Shevchenko putting her hand on his. She didn't like the smell of Abe's buffalo coat. It was an old, dank, almost-extinct kind of smell. The coat had once belonged to an RCMP corporal in the days when young boys dreamed of being mounties and wearing bright red tunics. The coat was disappointing now. It was all shaggy, loose, and worn. It was pitiable to see it now and think of how fine it had once been.

The three of them walked over to the small lake and sat on a poplar log that had been felled by a beaver. The chips were still a bit moist. Abe returned to the van for a few minutes. He came back with two more beer and two old .303 rifles. They spent the rest of the afternoon drinking beer and taking pot shots at shadows under the water that looked like swimming beavers.

It wasn't long before Shevchenko set out to build his log house. He spread the house plans on the kitchen table in the apartment that he shared on weekends with Madelaine. Madelaine was taking a short nap before the two of them went out to a movie. Shevchenko loved moments like this when he had something he really wanted to do while Madelaine lay asleep in her bedroom. She was a kind of security to him. He pored over the plans and decided he'd better use diagonal lines to show where the mud room was going to be. He liked the idea of a mud room. It sounded rich, as if there was a place for everything in his home, even mud. He remembered he'd left a ballpoint pen in his packsack; so, he went to find it. He hadn't bothered to unpack since his trip up North. Rummaging through his things, he came across the medicine bag. He'd forgotten about it. He wished now that he hadn't stolen it, but there was no use in thinking too much about that. Martin Spence would never miss it. Anyway, he'd make it up to Martin somehow, and, besides, Martin's wife could make another one easily enough. All of the leather crafts he'd bought there would make great gifts for Madelaine's family. Maybe he'd even give the things to them before Christmas. After all, they were going to be family. Why not, he thought, why not.

Atoms of pure energy danced between the tiny spaces of the beaded design all over the medicine bag. The atoms shifted restlessly across the tight network of blue, green and black beads changing places with each other in a cosmic leapfrog. Shevchenko, his mind distracted by the thoughts of a log house second to none in Northern Ontario, absently fingered the beaded design oblivious to the reality of the swimming, tumbling atoms beneath his fingers.

Shevchenko heaved the butt end of the log down from his shoulders to the second tier of logs that Abe and the boys were helping him with. Abe pushed the log into its notch and then slapped it decisively with the palm of his hand.

"Good honest sweat, eh!"

"You betcha, Abe, you betcha," Shevchenko said.

"You know," Abe said, "this is what the co-op idea is all about-everybody pitching in and making it happen. Here, in this place. If we're smart and keep the creeps out of this part of the country, it will really be an OK place, get what I mean?" Abe prodded, smiling.

"Sure do," answered Shevchenko. "I've got two hundred acres, Sam and Bill have another three hundred between them, and you're the kingpin Abe, you've got four hundred acres. The group of us make up a little empire. Why, I'll bet you, the bunch of us are bigger than one of those European countries that's so small you only hear about it on rare stamps. Don't worry, nobody will get a piece of things out here unless they're invited. If ever I decided to leave and had to sell out, you fellows would get first crack at it. I mean money isn't the most important thing in the world. I'd have to think about you guys too. There's no way I'd sell to a creep."

All the boys nodded in agreement. They were all shirtless and sweating heavily from working on the logs. Sam suggested a beer break but Abe said that that could wait until more of the logs were up. Madelaine and the women were making sandwiches for the men. Tied to Madelaine's apron string was the medicine bag. She had worn it to impress the other girls. It fit in with the new image she had of herself as Shevchenko's wife-to-be. It was a nice touch to add to the log house. The medicine bag swayed to the rhythm of Madelaine's hip movements as she sliced the pickles. It liked to be in the limelight.

By nightfall the boys had raised the seventh tier of the logs. Even Abe was ready for a beer break around the campfire. All of a sudden a tremendous crashing noise caught everyone's attention. The sound of logs pummeling onto the ground gripped Shevchenko in fear. He turned and saw the last of the logs tumbling from its position.

"What the hell is going on?" Shevchenko screamed. Abe raced past Shevchenko to the house site.

"No, no, it just can't be!" Madelaine cried out. Sam and Bill gaped in wonder at the scene. Abe and Shevchenko looked at each other and then at the logs.

"But the notches we made were as tight as vises," Abe said.

"I know...I know," Shevchenko said.

No one knew what to say. The logs were down and everyone seemed embarrassed by it all. After an awkward silence the group decided to leave the site and return home. Abe and Shevchenko agreed to meet the next day and go over everything they'd done, step by step. Abe took one last look at the logs and shook his head like a confused buffalo.

Nothing seemed to go right regardless of what they tried. There was no logical reason why the logs should have fallen. But they did.

And there was no reason why they should fall a second time. But fall they did. Abe and Shevchenko couldn't understand it. The fresh water supply became fouled somehow. The septic system didn't meet local regulations. And to top it all off, Shevchenko learned that an insurance company had a lien on his property. The old wheel of fortune was spinning around wildly with benign grace at the wheel. The kind of benign, mischievous pent-up grace found in Martin Spence's medicine bag.

Shevchenko was crestfallen. He was puzzled by his bad luck. Sitting on his peeled, grounded logs, he played with his Swiss army penknife, throwing the blade into the wood again and again, fascinated by the sound of the knife as the tip of it penetrated the wood. He stopped when he saw Madelaine running towards him. She was laughing and waving a letter.

"Peter, Peter, it's good news- your uncle died! I mean, no, he left you something in his will."

"What?" Peter exclaimed. Madelaine's excitement was contagious. Peter snatched the letter from her hands and read it quickly. "Madelaine...you won't believe it. An uncle of mine that I didn't even know I had left me a warehouse full of some kind of machinery. It doesn't say what, but the letter says it's 'a considerable stockpile of equipment'!"

"Wow," Madelaine said, "our luck's changing at last!"

"You're telling me... I'm going to call up the lawyer right now. He'll be able to tell me what kind of machinery it is, and how much it's worth. Boy! Maybe it's a warehouse full of tractors or stereo equipment. Geez! We're rich. I knew our luck had to change. I just knew it!"

He squeezed Madelaine's hand and then started running for his car. He was going into town to make a phone call. He had just opened the car door when suddenly he saw someone coming up the graveled bush road on a motorcycle. There was a cloud of dust trailing the rider. Shevchenko couldn't make out who it was. They waited to see who it might be. The rider was wearing a white helmet with a black visor that covered his face completely. When he stopped the bike and took off the helmet Shevchenko couldn't believe his eyes.

"Martin...what are you doing here?" Martin smiled a gap-toothed whalebone smile. He looked over to Madelaine and seeing the medicine bag tied to her belt he started chuckling.

"Thought it might be here," he said. He spoke very quietly and the inflections in his voice sounded strange to Madelaine's ears. Shevchenko followed the gaze to where it rested on Madelaine's hip. The medicine bag! He felt guilty and embarrassed.

"Martin, I didn't mean to take it really," Shevchenko said. Madelaine didn't know what they were talking about, but she could feel the concern in Shevchenko's voice.

"The bag was a gift from my grandfather," Martin said, "but a strange gift. It's a bad bones bag for strangers. That is why it must be held by a member of the band. If I hadn't remembered your visit, the medicine bag would've teased and troubled you forever. It's a spirit bag." Martin started chuckling again, wondering what the bag had been up to since it had left the house. Shevchenko didn't understand. Without saying a word of explanation to Madelaine, he asked her for the medicine bag and then gave it to Martin. Once the medicine bag was in Martin's hands benign rays of light were scattered and dissipated in the late afternoon sunlight. The atoms of pure energy dancing across the beaded design stopped in their cosmic tracks. After a few awkward moments Shevchenko and Madelaine left to make their important telephone call. Martin sped ahead of them anxious to make it to the airport in time to leave for the North and his village. A friend of his would be waiting at the airport for the borrowed motorcycle.

Shevchenko's inheritance left him very disappointed. After several time-consuming long-distance telephone calls to Toronto, Shevchenko learned that he was the sole owner of a warehouse full of defective espresso machines imported from Milan, Italy. According to his uncle's attorney and creditors, the machines would not be legally his until he had paid several large and outstanding bills, bills of course, that ran into hundreds of thousands of dollars, not to mention the warehouse storage costs that had accumulated.

And the medicine bag. Well, it had synched with the right moment and was anxious to be back in Martin Spence's happy home after an exhausting, madcap holiday.

THE UNDISCOVERED COUNTRY

I died today. Maybe it was yesterday. I'm not certain just when. Time slips away here and doesn't seem to matter the way it did once. I am at home, my old home, where I lived as a boy and young man. Why this should be so I do not know, but I am here and see the town all around me as I hover about the place like a refugee from a Chagall painting.

Spirits move and glide here like silken scarves on a gentle wind. I've discovered things I never dreamt were possible. I've already made friends with a rock through a kind of dreamy communing. My friendly rock has a placid sentience, an inviting inclusiveness about it. A concentrated force, an imprisoned power that makes no demands.

The rock I came to know was a rough, sloping piece of the Precambrian Shield about a hundred square feet in mass. I melded into it and found it to be comfortable without the slightest trace of self-pitying sentimentality for having been stuck in one place for eons of time, for eternities of stillness.

It seemed to suggest to me, and there were no words passed, that I needed to curb my ... flippancy. Oh yes, things are different here. I drifted through its pyrite veins and lost myself for a time in what I can only term its immutable stability. Its only longing as far as I could make out was its love for a distant star, and as love matches go, I've never beheld anything quite as moving as the way the star left its silvery sheen, its sweet, eternal kiss, over the rock's surface without trespassing on the rock's deep, dark crevices.

Thirty-Eight First Avenue, Schumacher, Northern Ontario. So this is my soul's local habitation. Odd. Seems to me that I spent most of my early youth trying to escape this place. And now, here I am, posthumously feeling a tie to the place I never thought possible in my old form. The place is changed, altered, at first glance. But with a slight, deft maneuver, I find I can get back to different periods of my life and beyond. Even the times before my birth, and the eons before that, when my rock was but a Precambrian infant.

I am troubled by my exit from life. I'd like to find out how it happened, but on that point I feel like an amnesiac. It's a complete blank, apart from a searing red tear and then a sudden rupture in white spilling into this place, the undiscovered country, which I'm discovering in spurts, in rushes, in flashes of recognition that move like northern spring sunlight across the darkened contours of a strange, dream-like terrain.

I can only now just remember things. Odd, how it is. When I was living and woke up in the morning, trying to remember a dream, I would concentrate on fragments, shards from my unconscious, that I would catch pieces of, like a fish's slippery tail. I would grasp the slithery, jumping nature of a dream memory, and then slowly, gradually, I would have the whole fish, the whole dream, or as much of it I guess as you can get in the bright light of conscious day. But if you didn't make the attempt, you would have nothing left, not even the slime of a pike's tail, or the stardust residue of a dream's escape upon you.

But now the images from my actual life as it was lived, barely intrude, or sometimes, just fall into my awareness without any effort at all- like drops of water dripping from my old kitchen faucet, my washer-less kitchen faucet that may still be dripping its way to watery oblivion. Ah, how I miss that faucet. So recalcitrant; so impervious to the wishes of the home handyman in the new millenium.

That faucet reminded me of Che Guevara. I would replace the old, corrupt rubber washer, the Batista of decay, and the new washer would be ok for a time, like the post-revolutionary Che in Cuba, and then it would change, wistful and quiet for a while, and then it would begin again, persistently dripping and pining away for some Bolivian dream of gushing revolution, never able to stop the drip, the dripping of the possible, until the children's stomachs were full, and they could dream dreams that caused them to laugh aloud in their sleep to their fathers' unmitigated delight. Ah, how I miss that dripping faucet.

Once, my spirit came across Shakespeare playing in a meadow with his son. I heard their laughter before I saw them. They were running under the branches of a huge oak tree, playing a game of tag on the sun-dappled grass. Their laughter mingled with the sounds of a stream, sun-bright and silvery, a short distance from the oak. There was a magic about the place and a soft green-golden sheen on the surface of the grass that was even richer and darker on the great oak's trunk. Two skylarks flew high in the sky as if drawing an arc in a happy conjunction of earth and light.

I don't miss drink much. Mind you, I'm still able to enjoy the odd nip. Guinness is my favorite. It's the capuchin foam at the top I crave. I move with the lips of the drinker and leave my imprint there, a slight indentation, the displacement of spirits with spirit. No one seems to mind. After all they think it's their own lips that are doing it. The lips of the dead do not impede their progress. We're very circumspect, we, the drinking dead. Everyone needs a vanguard of some kind.

I do enjoy floating about the hotels and beverage rooms of my native place. Drinkers, I've come to understand, are a very spiritual lot, no pun intended. The mundane act of drinking alcohol is a search for the ethereal, a ring toss into the unknown, spiritual world. Certainly, it's the easy way. There are no rigorous, monkish practices in the fluid art of the imbiber, and that's perhaps why there are so many failed mystics in the pot. But all the markings are there, no doubt, of intense, unrequited longing for the gods on the periphery of their consciousness.

I miss my body- muscular, quick to anger, quick to lust, quick to the quick. This bodiless existence is frustrating at times. I miss the feeling of the sun on my skin. If I could only recreate myself, for one day, one final day, I would give all. But what do I have to give now?

It's an odd, singed freedom I feel. I'm not lonely at all. There are souls around me, essences that ride the winds in this strange place above or below the life I knew. They move quite quickly. Most are friendly. Some, not many, are wild, dark things howling in anguish, but not to be feared unless you let them. Fear doesn't really have a place here. It rules life so ruthlessly that it's expended by the time it collides into fearless death. Small victories, I guess.

Suddenly, like the old, familiar experience of waking from a sleep, I am conscious of watching my former self. He is dressed in a white terrycloth bathrobe and walks to the sliding glass doors leading to a patio balcony overlooking the sea. He opens the doors wide, and a light tropical breeze fills the suite, billowing the curtains momentarily. The smell of the sea is in the air. The swells of the curtains envelop him and for an instant shroud his body in its white, caressing outlines. He can see splashes of red hibiscus blossoms through the transparent gauze-like material. He feels the warm, morning sun through the curtains. He doesn't move. He enjoys the experience.

He hears a light knocking at the door behind him, and a waiter enters the room with a breakfast tray of fruit, croissants with marmalade, and coffee. The aroma of the coffee falls sweet upon him as he moves to sit in a white, wicker chair by a glass-topped table. The waiter hovers discreetly for the usual morning tip, and then is gone, like a ripple in the ether, in the air's memory. He enjoys the coffee, savors it in fact, while he dreams of future glories. Such a fool he is. Such a fool I was.

But strangely, I feel compassion for the man. Especially now when the gaunt shadow moves towards him as swiftly as a swallow. On the tail of his vision he catches a glimpse of her dark, wild hair, just a glimpse, before she falls upon him with a knife and a screech such as he had never heard before. And then the coffee is everywhere, and he pushes her away, his forearms cut and bleeding. She bounds back at him, stabbing, stabbing, with a demonic fury. He cries out, and then the woman reels back, shocked at the strange voice. The woman screams out the name of someone. There is confusion; blood melds with coffee. The woman shrieks, as I leave my body. I do not know her. She looks violently distraught for an instant, and then flees. I hover about the body as the waiters rush in and cover the wounds with thick white towels that become red in spots that grow larger and larger in blotchy, uneven circles. Who'd have thought there'd be so much blood, rich, red blood in me: the blood of a prince, almost purple. Ah, egotism, even in death. Someone is working very hard at stopping the bleeding.

I am running very fast now on the back road of my hometown. It is a brilliant summer's day and grasshoppers are everywhere. There are tiny pin-cherries on some of the wild trees. The sour taste of them is in my mouth. I try to spit out the tiny pits. I am running faster than I have ever run before, stopping only once to kick out the front teeth of a dead beaver's skeleton on the road. The sound of the thousands of grasshoppers is deafening. The beaver's incisors are orange-yellow and curved like a mandarin's fingernails.

I feel a breath moving into the body below me. I am no longer hovering; I am descending. My compassion falls into the living body, wounded but still quick. I am unconscious lying in a pool of blood. I can faintly smell fresh coffee on the periphery of consciousness. Ah, yes, yes.

MARGARITA

He wondered why whenever he felt lonely, he felt it in his stomach and in his chest. Here he was, walking along one of the most beautiful beaches he had ever had the good fortune to walk upon, and here he was, miserably lonely. Would he ever change? Could he ever change? Did he want to?

His loneliness crowned the way he walked upon the beach. Despite the Latin beauties, the wonderful pounding surf, the brilliance of the white sands, despite this, despite all of this, he felt lonely.

He wanted a beer. He barely knew ten words in Spanish, but cerveza was one that he picked up immediately. Necessity is the mother of language he mused. He found a spot where he could sit and drink his beer, a thatched roof affair that cost him three hundred bolivars for the beer, and included a beach chair, and service for the

day. The beer's label read Polar. A Polar beer by the Caribbean Sea.
He liked that.

He watched a pelican glide by across the blue expanse of sky
above him. His spirits were starting to improve. He needed this place,
this time. Toronto was another planet away. Marissa was an alien
being. He needed to get away from her. When he had left the apartment she had told him not to come back. So be it. The sound of the
door slamming behind him was a relief to him. It was like the taste of
this cold Polar beer in his hand. It was all so easy. A telephone call to a
last minute travel club, a short call to his office, and it was done.

The parade stopped all traffic on the main thoroughfare, Quatro
de Mayo. Luke smiled at the marching bands of children, the gold-
satin costumes of the little Indians following a replica of Columbus's
ship, the Chinese dragon float with a young girl tossing single candies
into the air above the crowds thronging the sidewalks.

He wondered how his own son, Stevie, was doing. He remembered the curiously tentative way Stevie had looked when he learned
that Luke was going away for a while. And then the sudden generous
way Stevie had thrust a Mars bar in his hand just before the door had
slammed closed behind him. When he unpacked his bags in the hotel
room, the chocolate was partially melted. Luke had sat on the side of
the queen-sized bed and eaten the chocolate, so grateful for the gift his
son had given him.

The balcony of his eighth-floor room was a tiny, pie-shaped affair. Just a bit of a leap and it would be all over. Luke pushed himself away from the railing and locked the sliding glass door behind him. Odd, he thought, how he could never get away from the high-rises. Toronto… Porlomar… he was always several floors above the ground. He poured himself a duty-free shot of Teacher's Scotch and took it neat, savoring the way it burned the back of his throat.

"You can't always do what you want, you know! Try to be a little less selfish, and maybe, just maybe, this marriage will last."

Luke regarded her words from a still center deep within himself. Marissa used words the way a Spanish picador used lances: a jab here, a jab there, not enough to kill, but just enough to inflame, to incite. Luke just stood there, feeling the weight of his body pressing down upon the parquet floor of their apartment, wondering for a moment if he would be able to move away from the spot he was standing on, and get away from her.

"Well, can't you say something? Or do you want to save it all for that bitch?"

Stevie was crying, sobbing uncontrollably, his little body hunched in upon itself, trying to draw itself clear, the child-soul crying out for deliverance, for everything to be the way it was when there was just an uneasy, taut silence over packaged gourmet dinners.

"Do you think you're a man? I've had better men than you. I took pity on you, you fucking asshole!"

"Marissa, that's enough… Stevie's here."

"Stevie, Stevie… if you cared so goddamn fucking much, why did you take up with that slut?"

Stevie tried to get to his bedroom. Marissa yanked him up hard by his forearm, lifting him off the floor.

"Oh no, you don't. You stay right here. This is still a family, and you're part of it you little brat."

Stevie wheeled under her in pain. Luke grabbed Marissa's shoulder. A hot, searing, flashing feeling tore through his consciousness. He wanted so much to stop this, to stop her. He checked himself.

"Oh, so now you're going to hit me! Just try, you bastard! Just try. I'll kill you if you even touch me. Let go! Let me go!"

There was a touch of fear in her anger now. He could hear it. She knew just how far she could go. She stopped. Luke took Stevie in his arms and left the kitchen.

"You can run, but you can't hide, asshole!" Marissa screamed after them.

This world was different here, Luke thought. There was an ease to things here. A fluid grace, a dark and open-handed grace, penetrated things. In one of the cabs he had taken to town, he saw a picture of the Virgin affixed to the dashboard; beside it, a few inches away, there was a photo card of Hugo Chavez: icons of this time and place, complementing each other.

A few days passed and the tight ball within his gut had already begun to dissolve. He began to look around more, seeing past the confines of his own situation, the high-rise nightmare of his own life with Marissa. But for Stevie he would have left long ago. The ties that bind. He ordered a beer by the poolside bar and sat under a glorious palm. He should have brought Stevie, but he knew Marissa would never allow it. How Stevie would love being under a palm in February. The sun and the breeze felt good against his skin. He laughed. He'd forgotten how good it could be.

The man was so gentle, so careful, as he set the bird down. The other cock raised its head in readiness. It had only one eye. The back feathers of both birds were shaved clean. Each of the cocks had sharpened metal spurs attached to their claws. Earlier the men had watched the birds walk about with their spurs. Around them, men, only men, Luke observed, were gambling at various games, all of them strange to Luke.

The cockfight arena itself was sheltered by a great, circular tin roof supported by poles. There were numbered seats around them. Off to one side of the arena, a man and a boy sold beer at fifteen bolivars a bottle. Business was brisk, particularly as the first fight drew near. Men started to fill in the lower seats closest to the pit.

These were the gamblers Luke thought. They needed to be closest to the action. That's what the numbers were for, to identify the gamblers. Luke smiled.

The cocks began pecking at each other, hard, thrusting pecks. One-eye's beak was already bloodied. The other cock seemed to be taking advantage of One-eye. He would swoop up, strike, and then fall back. One-eye's neck feathers were up. He leapt high and pounced on the cock. Again and again they clashed, beaks and spurs tearing wherever they could. The men around the pit were doubling bets, crying out to each other in growing excitement.

Two men, the owners, moved around the outer, higher circle of the pit soliciting more bets. The noise grew louder as One-eye gained the advantage. The other cock was losing ground and would spin off, trying futilely to win some temporary respite, some pause to collect itself again.

But One-eye pecked and cut... short, sharp jabs, and swooping thrusts that hit their mark. The noise of the place was deafening under that tin roof. The other cock lay on its side panting. One-eye stood triumphant over the tired bird. One-eye's back twitched in victory: he crowed, the sound carrying high above the din.

The referee with the careful, gentle hands took the downed cock and placed it in a section of a small, double-sided, wooden coop that was lowered from the ceiling. The man extended his arms wide and placed his hands softly around One-eye, ever so careful to avoid the sharpened spurs. He set One-eye down on the other side of the coop. Luke watched as the referee brought still another cock from outside the ring. Then, he released the first cock from the shelter of the coop.

He seemed passive now, the fight out of him. The referee slapped the beak of the visiting cock and set him upon the tired one. The referee held the visiting cock all the while, cradling him in his hands as he pecked away at the bird. The tired one roused and fought back, enough to cancel any loss for the moment; it was still game, a contender. The referee gently placed him in his coop again. The same ritual was repeated for One-eye. There was no mistaking it. One-eye tore away at the visitor. In turn, One-eye was set down once again in his coop, and the visitor carried off and put into a burlap bag, the specialty of his service acknowledged by the applause of the gamblers. The fight would continue. There was still fight in both birds. The double-coop was raised by a rope and pulley high above the pit. The other cock seemed to be revived. He fought back gamely against One-eye but soon, he was downed again, the side of his head and beak exposed to One-eye's vicious thrusts.

The bird was still alive when the referee carried it to its owner. Perhaps he would fight again another day. But not now, not with One-eye. It was over. One- eye was carried triumphantly to his owner, a man all smiles and pride. The game was over. The men left in groups for beer and card games nearby. Another fight would begin soon. Luke went for a beer, glad that the cock he favored, One-eye, had won.

He smiled, remembering episodes in his kitchen with Marissa. How nice it would have been, he thought, if there had been a referee with careful, gentle hands who could separate them. A few girls were selling food by the entranceway. Luke departed from the place and headed back into town, taking time to pee before he flagged down a bus.

Luke glanced out of the airplane window. Below him was Puerto Rico. His holiday was winding down. Next to him, on the extended tray of the adjacent seat, was a glass of dry red wine. He sipped carefully. There was turbulence. He hadn't accomplished very much. The holiday had not engendered any brave solutions over the ruin of his marriage. And there was Stevie. He would do what he had to do to make a better life for the boy. On that point he was clear and focused in his thinking. He knew he had to be careful. Marissa would do whatever she could to hurt him, and that meant hurting Stevie. He was glad to be home, in a way. The old life was over and done. This new one was already difficult, but that was the nature of new beginnings. He'd had a few days in the sun, and it was enough. Things would be better now regardless. The past was prologue.

He could see the Caribbean Sea far below him, and above it, the broken clouds marked his return. He felt better. In his luggage he carried a hand-carved red flute for Stevie, and a bold Caribbean promise in his heart that he was not yet aware of. He smiled and settled comfortably into his seat. Below him the sea was covered by pearly clouds that stretched as far as he could see and beyond. He glanced at his watch and set it back one hour. Now he was on Canadian time.

SECOND CHANCE

Perhaps things would change, Richard thought. He knew it couldn't go on like this. It had to change sometime. It couldn't go on indefinitely. He prided himself on having some good sense. He knew there had to be balance, and in his usual quirky way, he said to himself that if ever he began to spend more time drinking than exercising, he'd be in trouble. And for him, there was a thin line between the two. And so he would exercise, keeping his body fit with light jogging and free weights. He'd push himself, doing that last extra chin-up before finishing his workout. He'd use imagery too, visualizing a smaller, more compact version of himself.

Afterwards, after alternate hot and then cold showers, he would set off for his pub. He'd order two drafts.

"Two big ones please." The first was so cold, so desirable after the workout, his muscles still pumped from the exertion. He felt great.

Had only a year passed since he'd made that fateful drive north to the church, a renovated red brick church that had been their home for a preciously short, careless year? He wondered at that. At time passing in the way it had. The draft was going down so well. He didn't recognize anyone in the bar yet, that is, anyone he'd care to sit with before his friends came. It was nice to have the cool drafts alone.

He remembered coming into the church the time after they had left, the profound silence of the place. He knew they were gone. It was the strangest feeling for him to see the letter she had written. He even smiled at the spelling mistakes contained in the message that changed his life forever. He admired the letter, in a way. It was confident and resolute, so unlike her. At least she'd done that. He felt a little death growing inside him. It was too early yet for him to know the numb pain that he would feel in the small morning hours, the savage sense of loss and betrayal that would be his and his alone. He could not know yet that he would weep quietly into a pillow offered by a friend. Only the tears were his.

He remembered too, the weekend morning that he had found the note from his daughter. He was at the Church alone and about to shave. The night before he had drunk his home made wine alone, long into the night. He had felt rough. Opening the cupboard door above the sink, he reached for a new razor and found the note. It was written in sprawling, juvenile handwriting.

"I love you dad." He smiled at that, the remembrance of that. He drank his second draft, his drifting memory tender now, no longer raw and open. He had left the note there in the cupboard. One weekend a friend of his had chanced upon it and had wept, touched by the piercing simplicity of the penciled note. He wondered now about the note. Had he left it there deliberately, for someone to find? Or had he left it for himself as a curious kind of cupboard treat? In creating the new man from the ashes of the old, had he cunningly set bait to attract sympathy? It was all so strange, like a past life.

But the Church, in his time of need, had been his. It was like Superman's fortress of solitude, he mused. No green kryptonite there. Only the memories were like kryptonite and could hurt, but only when he let them, only when he was self-indulgent and sentimental, and altogether too stupid, an emotional fool. He steeled himself against that. He made himself tough.

"No mercy given, none taken." That was his motto, his creed, as he set about putting the past behind him and putting new women in his bed.

He would sometimes wonder at his callous lust, but not for long. He had to be busy to forget his past, and the best way was through the intimacy of strangers. It took up a great deal of his time and energy when he wasn't working. Nothing else seemed to matter. The iridescence of his lust delighted his eye, and he held it to the light to capture the evanescence of its colours. He even studied the Karma Sutra and practiced Hatha Yoga for greater flexibility.

Times there were that he would go to the Church alone for a weekend. The drive north was an escape for him, leaving the grit of the city and heading north through small rural towns that were made of brick and stone. And then off the main road and on to the graveled one that ran between corn fields and low-lying cedar swamps and then finally on past the solid sugar maples to the Church.

When he opened the great wooden doors of the Church, the loneliness of the place gripped his heart for a few seconds. They were gone. He shook the feeling off- not for him the melancholy ruptures of the heart and mind brought on by brooding over the losses of the past. He steeled himself. He wasn't always successful in being strong. Sometimes he would see in the mirror the hurt in his eyes, the glints of light in them sharpened by his recent experience. But that would pass. He knew he would have to remake himself, and he was determined to do just that.

He made his supper. Scrambled eggs with chopped up green onions stirred in during the cooking, and some brown farmer's bread, and a glass of dry, red wine. He sat on the stool beside the sturdy butcher's block he used as a table. He straddled the seat of the stool with his legs on either side, his knees pressed up against the massive block. It had been sanded and restored by his father-in-law. Even that relationship was changing fast he considered. It always came down to taking sides after all was said and done. It was the old thing about blood being thicker than water. The wine tasted good. Bacchus was alive and well.

Removing his shoes and socks, he stood up and stretched. He then walked across the large open space of the kitchen-living room area. He enjoyed the sensation of his bare feet moving across the smooth, worn, wooden floorboards. He imagined that it was like what a sea captain must feel walking across the deck of a tall ship. It gratified him. He was home. Home alone, but he was home.

He poured himself another glass of wine and then placed a disc in his stereo. He exercised to the first two songs and then took a sip of wine. Afterwards, he stretched, taking care to push his muscles only so far, just enough to make headway against the tightness. He only went a little into the pain, just a little to build upon, only enough to make a small difference in his flexibility. He drank a large glass of water and waited for the next song. He was ready to dance. He didn't think about anything else. He pushed the memories away. He had thought and rethought the emotional pain until it was just circling in his mind. He didn't want to be caught in it anymore. The song began. He moved into it embracing the rhythm alone.

The music was loud. It filled the space around him with pulsating sounds. He moved into the dynamics of it. He wheeled and turned and jumped like a centaur. His face was flushed. Beads of sweat fell across his forehead. Whenever the music sped up, he went with it, eager for it, trying to anticipate it. It was joy for him, almost ecstasy. He exulted in it. And when it stopped, he stopped for a moment and rested. He sipped some more wine and toasted the still air around him.

And then it began again. He leapt like a cat. His feet moved easily across the wooden floorboards, keeping the beat, feeling the smoothness of the floor that seemed to come alive with the dance. He tossed his head back and let out a wild yelp, a strong, piercing cry that signaled his vitality. The music continued and then there was another song to dance to, and another. It went on and on until finally, he fell to the floor exhausted, laughing. He took another glass of wine and sipped at it, listening to the way his heart pounded within his chest. And when he grew quiet, and the wine was finished, he turned off all of the lights and went to bed, falling instantly to sleep.

In the morning he made coffee. It was about eleven o'clock when he took his coffee with him to the bit of a yard just behind the Church. A couple of whiskey-jacks were flying overhead making a racket. The neighbouring cornfields were a sea of green, tall and abundant. Barefoot, he walked between a few of the rows that paralleled his yard. The thick foliage almost upset the balance of the coffee cup in his hand. The soil was rough and lumpy beneath his feet. It was a fine day with a cool breeze coming from the hills to the northwest of the Church. He felt fresh and invigorated, with barely the trace of a hangover. He knew it was good wine he had made. He held his face up to the sun, feeling the warmth of it on his skin.

He decided to cut the grass. While he mowed and trimmed the lawn, he speculated on whom he might invite to the Church the next weekend. The anticipation of a romantic interlude here at the Church warmed him as much as the sun on his back. He smiled at the thought.

His thoughts danced like a smooth flat stone skimming the surface of a shining sea. He remembered women he had met in the previous week. He savoured the memories, remembering details, the silky sheen of auburn hair, earrings shaped like Turkish scimitars, fair hands that Botticelli would have admired and loved. He remembered too, the anxiety of trying to find a way to introduce himself to a woman who caught his fancy.

"I'm curious to know how I can get to meet you." Smiles or shrugs followed: an invitation or a summary execution, all of it done with the eyes.

He walked around the Church running his fingertips against the bricks every now and then. He loved the fine, simple brickwork resting on the old-style concrete blocks that had been laid in 1909. He wondered what it must have been like when it was in its original form, a log Church on the same site, one that was built in 1857. And then he imagined how the huge draught horses must have looked as they hauled the earth from the space that was now the basement living-quarters. The Church: the focal point, the spiritual heart of a small hamlet, now a bachelor's retreat. He fancied himself a spiritual bachelor, smiling at the irony of change. And then he remembered.

Was it his imagination at work, that night when he thought he had seen a ghost? Or was it an apparition? He wasn't sure of the distinction between the two. He remembered how he had exercised and drank to the point of exhaustion, and then he had fallen like an axed Douglas Fir onto his bed. He had been awakened by a kind of light hovering at about waist level in front of his bed. It was something roughly circular, the size of a fist, that glowed. It caught his attention, and when he roused, it turned out not to be a light but an old woman, an old woman with wire-rimmed glasses, hunched over and admonishing him with her forefinger. Later, he fancied she must have been a Presbyterian ghost from bygone times, times that didn't approve of his brand of spiritual bachelorhood.

Was she offended at him for his passing ladies, for the priest's robe he wore on special nights for that woman of high imagination whose required fantasy was that of him enrobed by a priest's habit and encompassed by the flying buttresses of a solid church surrounded by the pagan spears of a thousand stalks of corn thrusting up into the open, soft vulnerability of the night skies? Whatever, the old woman faded into the luxury of the velvet night, and he would never see her again.

When he related the incident to his grandmother, she couldn't help but laugh with delight. She believed him. She believed that he had seen a ghost, and she herself believed in such things. But she also loved him for being open to such experiences, even while to herself she acknowledged that he deserved such a wagging finger.

The things of the night are different from those of the day. Not original, he thought, but once someone grasped an idea, it was as much his as the person who originated it. He believed that. The Presbyterian ghost belonged to the realm of night. The Church was as much hers as it was his, and he was willing to share it with her. There was plenty of space for all, for the creatures of the night, and the creatures of the day. And why shouldn't there be bridges between the two? The sun of this day felt so good upon his body. His coffee was almost cold. He went in for a second cup.

He slid the huge wooden latch to one side to open the front doors of the Church. He loved the sound the sliding mechanism made as he pushed it hard to the left. His father-in-law had made it for him in happier days, days when they had done a bit of work together. Andrew would call him aside for a belt of scotch that he had tucked away in his Honda pick-up or in one of the outbuildings on his own property a mile away. Andrew's wife was a prohibitionist as far as Andrew was concerned and wouldn't tolerate the stuff in her home. Take it or leave it. And so Andrew left it, nicely tucked away in low buildings among the cedars. Ambrosia for the pagan, rural gods, and for Andrew.

Ascending the stairs he slid his hand along the polished wood of the banister and opened the swinging inner doors of the Church. And then the great arched space of the Church enveloped him, held him mute for a moment. Alone, he surveyed the place, the flotsam of piled boxes that still remained for his wife to collect and transfer to some new warehouse facility, manic collector that she was. But the cynic in him dissolved at once in the inviolate, healing space of the Church with its curving, sun-bright walls and the small library that he and Andrew had built there, right there upon the altar. He felt a surge of elation in knowing that this space was his, for this time, now, here and now. He let out a barbaric yawp, in triumph, in appeasement to his raging, wounded spirit, a spirit that was already being healed in the sweet, enclosed balm of this space.

He set the empty draft glass on the table. Even in his lust he would often feel lonely. The intimacy of strangers struck him often as being a merely athletic encounter, competitive and carnivorous somehow. He often felt it soon after he had made love to a woman. Something lonely and cold would settle into his soul, and he would dismiss it, discount it. He would affect a tenderness, caress a bare shoulder and then kiss it, lingering there, making the moment tender, knowing it wasn't true. He would rise from the bed and make his weekend beloved and himself a snack, perhaps a bit of cheese, a tart apple cut up skillfully, some farmer's bread, and a little jam. He would serve it to her on a wooden cutting board, placing it on the bed covers atop them, his thigh touching hers as they ate.

Only in the night, asleep, he would awake slightly fearful, and know he was not alone, and then he was grateful and suddenly aroused. The warmth and voluptuousness of a friendly body at his side ignited the fires within him, and then he turned towards the generous, softly sleeping form that consumed him as eagerly and wantonly as he consumed her.

As he began to drift off into sleep, a telephone rang. Suddenly from far away, he heard a ringing sound. He was at the Church. The sound was just at the edge of his awareness. He rose quickly, leaving behind an uneaten snack in an unmade bed.

"Hello," he said. There was a pause, and then he heard his mother's voice.

"How are you doing Richard?" she asked, her voice warm and careful.

They chatted about trivial things, both skirting the obvious: the break-up of his marriage, the painful sense of loss and suffering. She talked about people he knew and who had died. Finally, just before she said good-bye, she mentioned a friend of his had wished him well and had left her with a phrase that had lingered in her mind.

"Oh by the way," she said, "Milan said to me that you had something special now."

"What's that?" he asked, a little curious.

"A second chance," she said, and then gently bid her son good-bye, suggesting by her tone that she would call again soon.

KATRINA

So, so odd, to be half in Bali, with the other half in Canada, but a woman does need her distractions. You know, as soon as I'm installed in the one place, I begin to long for the other. I've lived like this for three years now. Six months in one place is just right. November to April in Bali, and May to October in Canada. The best of both worlds, as they say. These past six months have been a dream. Jeremy made these earrings for me. Isn't that a fine little gold dragon? He has his little shop and makes these beautiful things for sale. All of it handcrafted, though it's harder and harder to find the right help. I do think he's more Balinese than anything else. The Balinese have an artistic soul, just like Jeremy. It's the most difficult thing, leaving Jeremy, but knowing that I'll return in six months makes up for it. As soon as I leave Bali, and I'm in the air, I'm in a different mode. Here we are just a few minutes from takeoff, and I feel so alive. Don't you love the ensemble that the stewardesses are wearing? So chic.

En route, I'll be preparing for Richard. For Richard, and six months in Canada. Every parting becomes a welcome, a delirious, delicious welcome that I love. I couldn't live in just one place. It would mean giving up Jeremy or Richard, and I can't dream of a life without the two of them. It's certainly not conventional, but then I've always abhorred conventions, particularly political ones.

Richard's a journalist. An outspoken man in public, but very private in himself, and as gentle in his own way as Jeremy. He has a wonderful old home in Ottawa. He e-mailed a picture of the peonies in our greenhouse last week. They're in bloom, heavenly pink blooms that I can almost smell. Peonies are such gorgeous, reckless floozies. Maybe that's why they don't last.

They've never met, you know, Jeremy and Richard, though they know of each other. It's not as complicated as you think. Not at all. Once I'd decided on how I wanted to live, I asked them, each of them, if they could deal with it. Richard was very surprised, and hurt, at first. I remember we were listening to Vivaldi's Four Seasons, on the verandah. We were drinking chilled Veuve Cliquot. His great spaniel eyes filled with tears. Poor Richard. I think he thought I was trying to say goodbye, but when he realized I loved him, and will love him always, he went silent. Mind you, he brooded for a few weeks, and once, he asked me how I would feel if the situations were reversed. He looked so intense and fragile at the time. I held him for the longest time. I remember he was trembling so. I said I'd feel the same way as he did. But I was set on telling him the decision I had made. I wasn't about to defer living my life once again. I'd done that for decades when I was married with the twins. And that was another life. I'd made up my mind. I can love more than one man. And I have.

Jeremy was amused at first. Yes, amused, as if I'd surprised him, at something he thought I was incapable of. Odd, but I think it excites him sexually. My arrangement, I mean. He tries to be innovative, even unusual in his approach. And sometimes I just wish he'd stop trying so hard. So insatiable, with his costumes and all, but so very tender.

I love the tenderness of my men. Richard will sometimes take me into the garden, ask me to close my eyes, and then shower me with rose petals, just as he's kissing me. He's very tall and regal-looking, a bit like a younger Prince Philip, but only in looks. He's very tactful and truthful. Once, when I had just returned from Bali, he told me that he had had an affair with a junior correspondent at his paper. One of those intense young women with a penchant for absurd weekend activities like skydiving or spelunking. It didn't last very long. He said he was ashamed to think he had done it out of spite, as a way of "getting even," he said, for my "lover in paradise." I wasn't surprised. Richard dislikes letting his passions or lusts control him, but he detests anyone who doesn't allow him his solitude. He's quite impassive and cold if you don't know him. He likes to initiate things, from rose petals to lovemaking. And that's quite alright with me- as long as I get to finalize them.

Just before I left for the airport this evening, Jeremy showed me a wonderful necklace he's working on. So intricate and detailed with interlocking silver birds and garlands. He wanted me to choose the stones. He said it would be ready when I returned. When he said that, he nodded and smiled that wry smile of his, and I could tell he was feeling a bit sorry for himself. For all his sophistication, Jeremy is like a child. A precious, thoughtful child.

Odd, how he's tall, almost as tall as Richard. I must have a secret obsession for tall, elegant-looking men. Jeremy has this shock of thick, white hair, like the old photos of Mark Twain. I don't expect either of them to be celibate when I'm away. But I do expect, no, I demand that they be careful and very, very smart in their choices. I don't begrudge them their dalliances, but I do not want to experience any, any residue of their passions. I have made that crystal clear.

Most men, if you'll allow me, are like, well, like dogs. Forgive me, but it's true. They don't always think with their heads. But they must be corrected if there's to be a relationship that's built on tenderness and consideration. Jeremy is probably feeling very much alone right now. He'll be sad like a puppy dog for a week. But after that week, his eyes will begin to wander, I'm sure. He'll start by being ever so solicitous towards some sweet young thing in Denpasar who's caught his eye. And you can imagine what follows, in due course. I know him too well, bird dog that he is. I've told him not to get entangled and to keep the nest clean, and he knows exactly what I mean. Exactly.

There's a special Balinese dance, a dance called the *kebyar* that is danced by a grown man. But the dance is about the moods, the temptations of a pubescent boy. The dancer mimes and gestures while sitting cross-legged on the ground. Quite remarkable. The interesting thing is that the dancer dances only with his torso, and his arms, and his hands. It's really quite beautiful. And it made me think about men.

I think most men are like pubescent boys throughout their lives. All of their impetuous desires, their quick lusts, their follies, stem from that period in their lives when they're suddenly, deeply aware of their sexuality, pulled by it every which way, and puzzled by its power. Once you realize that, it's an immense leap in understanding them. Having that knowledge, and using it, is like knowing how to use the little iron ring in a bull's nose. Imagine a huge bull, susceptible to a tiny tug on that little ring. Think of the great bulk and mass of a stupendous bull moving on command by the barest pressure of your little pinky.

I'm so looking forward to Ottawa. Richard and I will meet for lunch at Byward Market, at one of those smart little outdoor cafes where the world passes by. Later, we'll walk up to the National Gallery to see my favorite painting. It's called Eiffel Tower. Such a wonderful little piece by Chagall where lovers are floating in the air, floating like silk scarves around the Eiffel Tower, and the colours are the colours of love, of love and tenderness. What a lover Chagall must have been.

Oh life is so good once you decide on how, *how* you want to live. It's far more important than what you do, because what you do always becomes what you did. I wish it could last forever. I'm so tired of people who just give up, who resign themselves to being old. It's as if they're just waiting to die. My father, after he retired, just sat in an armchair most of the day, absentmindedly dropping his forearm and striking against the arm of the chair with his fist, raising his arm, and then dropping it, again and again. So irritating. I'd rather he had drunk himself to death rather than bore himself to death. I can still see him doing that without any rhyme or reason.

The one thing I missed most from back home, Richard was able to supply me with. Every other month I'd receive a parcel of DVDs, and I'd be ecstatic. Bali is wonderful, so exotic, but I missed Nigella. She does things so very well. The nice little things that make life worth living. I love seeing an accomplished woman making her mark in the world. It's the added touch of class she brings to even preparing a chocolate dessert. I like to think that I have much the same flair in what I do.

Richard loves my vichyssoise. He's often said that it melted his heart. Such a wit. I have this little ice cube tray that makes miniature cubes, and I surround the bowl with them. A few light touches, and a sprig of parsley, and it's done. Presentation is everything. Do you know, I remember the first bowl of vichyssoise I had. It was at the

Chateau Laurier, my first stay there, in the days when it was *the* place to stay. I was enchanted by the high ceilings and the billowing curtains with the windows open. I remember a Sinatra tune that was big then- *Strangers in the Night*. That certainly dates me, doesn't it?

Everything was cushioned, carpeted, and clean. That moment in time... the taste of vichyssoise, the soft sounds of the music, and the feel of the breeze through the curtains, that will last forever. That's what life is- a series of moments, big moments- the rest is just filler. That's why you have to choose what you want. Otherwise, your life becomes just filler. Nothing but filler. And that is tragic.

It's so important to have something to look forward to. I love being busy with Richard, with Jeremy, with my two lives. I can't imagine how I could have lived the other life so long. It was so dreadfully boring. And my husband, well, that was the usual story of a man without a single redeeming passion. But as a stockbroker, I must say he was at least mildly successful. Thank God for that. Oh I don't regret having the twins. They were no trouble to raise, and they're both the kind of women that have bold dreams. They're both financial people in this new e-commerce business. About your age. We'll be going to the theatre and dinner, my girls and I.

The girls quite like Richard, but I prefer to keep things separate if you understand me. I feel it's better that way. I'm so looking forward to mornings in the garden. I've always thought the morning sun is most pleasant. I usually start very early with some yoga. Really, that's how I keep slim and agile. And then I putter about in the rose garden before Richard joins me for breakfast on the terrace. He's always especially tender in the mornings, my Richard.

Do you know, I love surprises, even the ones that are a little odd. Who knows why people do what they do? W. H. Auden said that the desires of the human heart are as crooked as corkscrews. I love that image. It's so apt. I don't really think people know why they do what they do. In fact, they may not like what they're doing, but they continue to do it anyway. It's all so odd to me, but very, very human. I can appreciate someone who does a thing out of passion. I've always thought a woman must be proactive in protecting her relationships.

The important thing I've discovered through experience, and I am much older than you dear, is balance, life balance. Regardless what comes your way, you must somehow find a means of countering it. If you can do that, and do it consistently, you'll be ok. And sometimes fate steps in to assist.

You know, there was a time when I almost lost Jeremy to a svelte redhead from Adelaide. Fortyish. She had, I remember, the most marvellous teeth. That was Jessica. Jeremy was smitten. I knew it by his eyes. I knew right away I might lose him, and if I lost Jeremy, I would lose my balance in life. Richard and Jeremy together, they're my balance.

For weeks I was miserable. I didn't even exercise. On a whim I saw a fortuneteller I'd noticed before in a tired looking storefront by the market. Near the mosque. Now, I'm not at all a believer in that sort of thing, but I thought the experience would be amusing. It's so inexpensive an entertainment. But I have to tell you, what happened was most curious.

I paid her five times what she asked. A pittance really, and it made her so happy, so grateful. Her specialty was palmistry, and she gave me a wonderful reading, a long life and a great love. But she wasn't very accurate. She said there was only *one* great love in my life. She didn't fathom that I have two.

But just as I was leaving she suddenly cautioned me from attending any nightclubs in Kuta, the tourist district, particularly on the twelfth of October. She was very specific I remember, even giving the names of places. I don't like bars, and I never have. I'm past all that, so I told her there was no worry about that.

A few days after my reading I went to visit Jeremy in his shop. Jessica was there. Jeremy's eyes were tango dancing all over Jessica, and that infuriated me. She was teasing him and flirting with him, right there in front of me. Oh, she didn't know that Jeremy and I were an item. How could she? Jeremy's about as talkative as a clam but charming in an understated way nevertheless.

Jessica asked him for suggestions on places to visit, or anything he thought that she and a group of Aussie friends might enjoy. In point of fact she even asked him to join her and her friends for a few days. He politely said that he couldn't afford the time away from the shop, and then he retreated for a few minutes into his back storeroom to fix a broken link in the gold anklet that Jessica had brought in for him to repair.

Now, you have to know that I'm not at all superstitious. I've broken several mirrors in my lifetime, and I step on cracks in the sidewalk all the time. My dear mother may have had advanced osteoarthritis, but she didn't have a broken back.

Without even thinking, I blurted out the name of the bar my palmist had mentioned, Paddy's Pub on Legian Street, and said that the twelfth of the month promised to be special. Jessica looked at me then and gave me the warmest smile you could imagine. Such magnificent teeth. She jotted down the information I gave her on the back of one of Jeremy's business cards that were on the counter by his cash register.

Jeremy returned with her anklet, and she beamed with gratitude. Jeremy, darling that he is, refused to take any money for the repair work. He said that a tiny bit of soldering had made the anklet as good as new. Jessica kissed him lightly on the lips, and Jeremy blushed then like a horny adolescent. I remember that.

Stewardess, may I have another glass of champagne please.

You can imagine how I felt when I heard the news. Who'd have thought that terrorists would bomb Bali, bomb Paddy's? I still don't believe it. I can't.

LEONARD

I have reached the point where I do not wish to do anything at all. The least effort is tedious to the extreme. A chore and a bore. I've just had enough of doing things. I spent the best years of my life working at a job I hated: employment counselor for the government. For me, it was hard time. I did it because, like most people, I had to. I had to make a living, and I needed the money to finance my freedom. Now, that I've got a bit of money tucked away in retirement savings plans and a modest pension, I've had enough. I'm forty-five, and I'm free. I saved my money to save myself. My condo is paid for, and I like the Beaches, not the Beach as some would have it, here in Toronto where I live. Now, I don't want to do a thing, I tell you: nothing. I've paid my dues.

Everything that I have to do, like shaving or paying my credit cards, is a bore. I don't like facial hair, so I shave. I have to shave every day. To make it less of a bore, I've tried changing the sequence in which I shave parts of my face. I usually start with my chin, move to my cheeks, and then on to my sideburns, and finally, under my nose. But, when I begin shaving in any other order, it seems strange and unnatural. So I revert back to the usual order of things, and it's a slow torture.

My girlfriend Moira says that a person without a purpose is like a boat without a rudder. When she says that, she always looks at me meaningfully with her mouth a little open and a silly look on her face that is meant to be profound. She doesn't even sail. She comes over to my condo whenever she feels the itch, she says. I wouldn't put up with her at all, she's so opinionated, but I get the itch too, so we put up with each other. Afterwards, we watch TV in bed and snack on sardines in hot sauce with crackers. She always brings the snacks, and I supply the wine. There is one thing though: I hate it when she tries to take over the television remote.

Perhaps that's why I haven't had any permanent relationships of the live-in kind. They always end up in a hassle of some sort, a money hassle, or a control issue hassle, or a habit hassle, to name a few. Take the habit hassle. I have a habit of sleeping with a foam pillow between my legs. I use a down pillow for my head. One of my ex-girlfriends, Sharon, said she found it disgusting when she found out that that was the pillow she used when she was staying over. It was ridiculous. I mean, I bathe every day, sometimes more often than I need to, and besides, it was my place, my bed, my pillow. That didn't last long I can tell you.

Now, I choose never to hassle. I'd rather forget about the whole thing and try again. Once, when I thought I'd met the perfect woman, she destroyed everything by a habit she had of mouthing "tsk...tsk...tsk," unconsciously. It drove me crazy. How can you develop a relationship with someone who "tsk's" you to death? I couldn't tell her why it had to end. I mean it sounds so silly, but it's the little things that get to you. So help me.

Moira decided one day that she was going to help me by en-gendering a sense of purpose in me. I remember the way she stood in the nude with one hand on her hip, looked me fiercely in the eye, a little cockily, and said,

"How can you live with this colour white everywhere? You need passionate colours on your walls. Something Santa Fe, American Southwest style. What do you think? Painting has a clear purpose and almost immediate rewards, don't you think?"

At least she never bores me. She's thirty something, thin, with delightful handfuls of flesh in just the right places, and with silky auburn hair and green eyes.

Her posture and stance, with its accompanying vocals and nuances of tone, told me that our relationship had progressed to the stage where criticism was no longer veiled. I don't mind veils. I've always thought more women should wear them. I lay back on the bed, looked at Moira against the backdrop of familiar white walls, and smiled.

"Let's say we did and don't. I mean once we start we'll have to do the whole place, because everything is white. It'll be such a hassle. Besides, everything will be everywhere, or covered under a tarp for weeks. I hate chaos."

Moira sniffed at me, tore a sheet from the bed and draped it around herself. "Oh, c'mon Leonard, we can finish in three or four days, and that'll include everything, even with a different colour for the trim in each room. You know it needs it. Besides, the important thing is to do something, anything, with a sense of purpose in it. You have to exercise your will, or it atrophies. I know you. When it's all done, you'll feel great. What do you say?"

When she left I stayed in bed for another hour. There were a few cracker crumbs under me, but I was too busy thinking about the paint job to get up and brush them away. I was thinking about my condo: two bedrooms, a kitchen, a dining room, a bathroom, and closets, plenty of closets.

Everything white. And miles and miles of trim, like architectural intestines. I pulled a bedsheet over my face. I didn't want to do all of that, but I knew she did. I mean, when I suggested getting it done professionally, she winced, she actually winced. For her, the whole thing was more about purpose than about paint. Money would ruin everything she said.

The thought of taking on that paint job really bothered me. It could never be just a simple paint job because there was more to it than just paint, a roller, and a brush. There was the cleaning, the taping, the moving of furniture, and the trim. Baseboards, and doorways, and window sills. This growing complexity bothered me even more than the crumbs under me. After all, you can brush away crumbs, but the painting was not just a simple flick of the hand. It was hundreds upon hundreds of strokes and touches and stretches in order to get at out of reach pockets of space that were probably never meant to be accessed.

The more I thought about it, the more I dreaded it. It seemed to me that it was becoming a control issue, like the remote. I should be able to flick my remote whenever and wherever I choose. Men fought wars for that right, the right of freedom of action. I should be able to leave my walls white without compromising my sense of purpose. After all, it was Moira's purpose, not mine. I called her cell number.

"Oh, hi Leonard. I was just thinking about when you wanted to start. I'm free tomorrow. What did you say? Stop for a minute. Stop. What do you mean a 'control issue'? This is about painting a few rooms that desperately need painting. It's about getting you to do something with purpose in it. It's not for me or about me. It's not my condo, it's yours. And you have the audacity to tell me that it's a control issue! I can't believe you. Hold on for a minute... stop it. Now stop! Leonard, you are incredibly lazy. You just want to sit and rot. You're just like the rest of your generation... the... the laziest, most self-centered, selfish generation that ever lived. Here I am trying to help you, to get you out of the rut you've been in, and you... you...what? What do you mean I'm fulminating? I don't even know what that means, but I can assure you I am not fulminating. You're a very sad person Leonard. I don't know why I even bother. I could do a lot better than a middle-aged paranoid with the beginnings of a paunch. Leonard, you're a sorry excuse for a man... like all the rest of your sick, sorry generation. The only one of your friends who's the exception to the rule is Luka, and he wasn't even born here. Goodbye Leonard, goodbye and get a life, for Christ's sake!"

I was stunned. The first thing I did after the call was strip. I couldn't believe what Moira had said, and I didn't believe it. I stood naked in front of my full-length hall mirror and looked for a paunch. She had said, "the beginnings of a paunch." I couldn't see a paunch. I tried to be very natural without holding anything in. Sometimes, in front of a mirror, you can just see what you want to see, but I wanted to see a paunch, if there was one. The things she had said to me were in anger, and I knew she had just meant to hurt me. And all the talk of my generation: my generation, as if I were an over-the-hill, self-centered, lout. I looked hard in the mirror. I saw a lean, fit, circumcised middle-aged man. A man with curly brown hair with a few flecks of grey sprinkled through it. There was no paunch. How could she have said such a thing?

My face is still good, not handsome, but decent. I'm not jowly, and if my nose is maybe a little too big, it's a reasonable fit for my face. It's clearly an anglo-saxon face with the ruddy traces of the British Empire in it. She knows that I workout at least three times a week and go jogging at least once a week.

I put on my bathrobe and decided to watch some TV. I kept flicking through the channels, not really seeing anything. When I finally called Moira, I just got her answering machine. I told her I needed to talk. She had been so cruel. Why did she have to use a bazooka when a pea shooter would have done nicely?

The next day I was about to go for a run when I almost stumbled over twelve gallons of paint outside my door. There were two gallons each of brown, blue, green, red, pink, and yellow latex paint. They were piled neatly in twos, and in the middle, in a huge plastic bag, I found two paint roller trays with extra rollers, and six brushes of different sizes. No note was attached. Not even a receipt. I called Moira. No one else but Moira knew about the painting issue. I hung up when I got her telephone answering machine. I'm so sick of talking into a void. The sight of all that tinned paint put me off running, so I stored the lot of it in my hall closet and watched Oprah.

At lunchtime I walked down to Queen Street for some sushi and noodles. When I returned, there was a message on my answering machine. I wondered if anyone ever spoke to anyone live on the telephone these days. I thought it had to be Moira, but it was Luka.

Luka's a good friend. He's only been in the city for a few years now. I helped him with his English when he did some odd jobs around the condo. A refugee from the Balkan wars. About my age, tall and dark with thick, brown hair and the best and thickest moustache I've ever seen. It glistens like an otter's fur. Luka's a great guy who somehow managed to keep sane through some really bad times. I tried probing him about it once or twice, about what he'd experienced over there, but he just shrugged, winked at me, and said,

"Sheet, sheet, Lenny. War is sheet."

There was a long pause before Luka's message started.

"... Lenny... is Luka here. *Dobar dan*, hello to you. I bring paint. Moira is call me yesterday. She tell me you need paint your house, or she go. Lenny... I tell you... Moira is good girl. Make good wife for you. Me think you must paint place. Make Moira happy again. I no mind help you. Is easy job. Finish fast. I buy paint from big sale. Is good price and is best paint. I bring you bill. Hope is ok. I know you like Moira. Is no good not paint. Is easy. I come see you tomorrow. *Laku noc*, good night my friend."

I was in a daze when I hung up the phone. Things were escalating. I was stunned. I had a closet full of paint that I didn't want. Moira was as mad as a snake bit dog. Luka was playing the peacemaker. And I wanted to keep my white walls. Things had just gotten so out of control. So I did what I what always do when I'm up against a brick wall: I went to the cineplex.

The movie was a bore. I sat there long after everyone else had gone. I didn't feel like moving. My body was slouched down, a part of the contours of the seat. I felt heavy and inert. The weight of my own body kept me there like the gravitational pull of some far-flung planet.

I couldn't move a finger. I sat there for the longest time until one of the movie attendants cleaning up asked me if anything was wrong. I shook my head, somehow willed myself out of inertia, and left.

Back home, when I opened my closet door, the paint was still there, stacked like munitions. Moira's idea had taken on a life of its own. I took out one of the frozen dinners Moira had prepared for me, and put it in the microwave. I sat at my kitchen table and looked at the bare white walls: to paint or not to paint. The easiest course was to paint. It would solve everything. Moira would be happy, and things could go on as before. But on the other hand, it was one more brush stroke against my independence, against my preference not to paint. I would prefer not to. So I sat there eating some of the best cabbage rolls I've ever had, and stewed in my own juices.

I was thinking, just thinking. I thought about Everest. A lot of people love the challenge of climbing Everest. They spend thousands and thousands of dollars and risk their lives to meet that challenge. A lot of people set themselves up for success or failure to meet the challenge that drives them forward. It may be Everest, or it may be painting a condo, but the driving force has to be theirs, not someone else's. My preference is not to climb Everest, and it's certainly not to paint a condo. Motivation can't be force fed like the way a goose is force fed before Christmas. The more I thought about it, the more I was sick and tired of being forced into something I didn't want to do. I ate the last of Moira's cabbage rolls and went to sleep.

The next morning, around six, I awoke to someone hammering on the door. It was Luka.

"What for you stay in bed so long?" Luka was dressed in old clothes, paint-stained old clothes.

Bleary-eyed, I motioned for him in come in. "It's Saturday. If you're dressed like that to paint, forget it. I'm not going to do it for love or money."

Luka offered up that roguish Croatian smile of his and shrugged his shoulders. "Why not you paint for love, for Moira? No big thing to throw paint on walls. *Lenitsa, molim te*, please make some coffee, and then we paint. Take easy make nice, you see."

I shook my head and told him he was nuts. I told him flatly, between coffees, that I was not going to paint anything. He just chuckled and said I was crazy, that it was just a small thing, not important.

"Just paint, little colour. Sheet, we take few days, then fineesh. What for you so stubborn, my friend?"

Half the morning passed before Luka left. I can still see him shaking his head and laughing as he walked out. "Lenny, my friend, you be real tough man, stubborn, like Croat. You sure you not have Croatian blood?"

I knew where he was going. He spent hours there every Saturday. Luka decided to stay in Canada for a very simple reason: Canadian Tire. From the first day he had walked into one of the Canadian Tire outlets in Mississauga, he was smitten. Luka fell in love with the glittering aisles and aisles of power tools, plumbing accessories, lighting fixtures, and gadgets of all kinds and sizes. I would have liked to have been with him on that first day. I can imagine his look of surprise verging into wonder when he realized the scope of retail in this country. In the rural Croatia he had left there was nothing like it. Croatian Tire didn't exist, and if it did, its parts paled in comparison: little more than a few bolts and screws, and with extraordinary luck, some Lada parts.

One bright, shining morning in a Canadian Tire store had cleansed Luka of any trace of socialism with all of its misguided idealism and had rendered him a consumerist, a capitalist, and a Canadian Tire devotee. I'd often seen the rapt look on his face as he pored over Canadian Tire flyers and catalogues. In fact, I used his passion to help him with his English. I'd point to an item in the catalogue, and he'd tell me what it was. Today his parts vocabulary is far greater than my own, greater even than Shakespeare's could have been.

I envied Luka. He worked as a janitor, diligently sending a portion of his pay back to relatives in Croatia each month, and lived quietly with his two great passions: Canadian Tire, and European soccer. Most Sundays, he'd come over to my place and watch Dinamo Zagreb games on my satellite TV. When his team scored a goal, he'd leap up and shout like a man possessed. I don't have anything that I'm all that excited about. Passion takes up too much energy. I just want to do what I want to do, which is nothing. Like I said, I've paid my dues. And now Moira spoils everything with this painting crap.

I decided to go out for a short run, and when I returned there was a message on my voice mail from my sister Caroline.

"Hi Leonard, it's Caroline. I know that it's short notice, but I wanted to invite you up to our place for a couple of days. James and I are going to be renewing our marriage vows, and I wanted you to be there. You were at our side ten years ago, and I thought it would be wonderful to see you here. After the ceremony we're planning a little party. I'm sure you'll enjoy it. Please come. We've plenty of room. I'll look forward to seeing you. We're expecting you. Bye, love."

Caroline. It's her second marriage, and she's determined to make it work. She's always loved ritual, and I guess the vows are what she needs right now. She loves the drama, and I guess the renewed sexuality of it. I mean, why renew your vows unless you feel sorely tempted and need to reassure yourself of the sanctity of marriage? I can just see my brother-in-law rolling his eyes. James, a civil engineer, is one of the biggest bores I've ever met. He once cornered me for an afternoon bemoaning the fact that engineers do not command the same respect in our society that doctors do. His point was the invisibility of infrastructure. Without roads, bridges, and telecommunications, he argued, modern society could not work. But because they're functioning and in place, he said, they're taken for granted. Doctors get all the glory when they're really nothing more than "body mechanics," as he put it. He sprays when he speaks, so I was desperate to get away and dry my face. In James's company, I've become adept at enduring a shower-like facial assault until it reaches critical mass, and then I cough, mutter some desperate excuse, and flee to the dry, shameless freedom of the nearest linen closet.

I e-mailed Caroline that I was coming, fearing that if I called I might get James instead. Even without spray and spittle, James is a formidable bore. I called Luka and left a message for him saying that I was leaving for a few days, and that he could watch the latest satellite soccer at my place. I told him where he could find the key. I knew he was still at Canadian Tire wandering the aisles like an acolyte, fingering the duct tape, and Swiss Army pocket knives, and assorted packages of Robertson screws that he believed to be the strongest fasteners ever made. The recessed square socket shape, he once explained to me in a kind of confidential whisper, is superior to the standard slotted version, and also superior to the cross of the Phillips model which strips too easily. Luka has provided me with more trivial information on parts and tools than I could ever hope to remember, or want to remember.

The ceremony was all that I expected it to be. Caroline was all tears and gushing sentimentality while James tried to look indulgent but was in fact a tad overwhelmed at all the flowers, good wishes, and toasts. I put in my appearance and managed to avoid being cornered by James during the whole time I was there. I noticed that the two of them were beginning to look alike, puffy, and formless, like a Herman cartoon. James hugely enjoyed himself at the party in the company of a self-effacing intern who simply nodded in agreement with everything James was saying about the failures of the medical profession.

On my way home from Caroline's place in Hamilton, I started thinking about Moira again. I missed crackers in bed. I decided to call her when I got back in. I was not going to paint, but surely she'd let that go. I was going to suggest a trip, on me, to Niagara-on-the-Lake to see a few plays and indulge ourselves with late breakfasts and wonderful marmalade.

I didn't know what I was going to do if she wouldn't let the paint issue go. I just wanted to see her again, the way things were.

The first thing that struck me when I opened my front door was the smell of fresh paint. The place was transformed. The halls were warm earth tones. The kitchen was royal blue and bright yellow like the colours on the flag of Sweden. The trim everywhere was in different complementary tones, with just the right accent. The living room was pure American Southwest, Santa Fe, right here in the Beaches of Toronto. My bedroom was the real surprise: red and rose colours like hot peppers and hibiscus melding into something indescribably delicious and wanton. I loved it.

A yellow post-it note on the TV caught my eye.

"Lenny. *Jebate*. I paint for you. Is easy sheet. You owe me couple case beer. Luka."

There was a knock at the door. I opened it and saw Moira standing there with a smile, a bouquet of yellow roses, and a bottle of chianti in a basket.

"Lenny, I missed you," she said sadly, just as she caught sight of the painted walls. "Oh Lenny, you do love me! You do love me!"

She quickly placed the roses and the wine on a side table and embraced me like we hadn't seen each other for a year. I stuffed Luka's
note into my back pocket and felt all at once the magic of colour, of
gratuitous friendship, and of Moira's moist, green eyes.

MYSTIC STALLION

I

It started out as a bit of a lark. Like most adventures, I guess. I'd just graduated from Yale, and wanted to take the rest of the summer off, staying on campus and reading what I'd never gotten a chance to. It left me plenty of time too, for long weekends at the Cape at my mother's cottage at Gloucester. I just wanted to take it easy and think about what I really wanted to do in September, to go after a law degree, or an MBA, or whatever. I'd already applied to all of the right schools, Mom made sure of that, but I wasn't really sure about where I was headed, or why.

Besides, I wanted to kick free for a while, and maybe even take a trip or two. It bothered me a little that I was the only one in the group

I hung out with that didn't have a clear focus on the future. All of my friends began to nauseate me with their plans and lock step ambitions. I felt out of it, and stranded on the empty campus, as if I'd been left behind, caught in some evolutionary backwater, where toads have gills. But once I got over that feeling, I started reading about Tibetan Buddhism, really big on campus that semester, and became fascinated with it all. It's amazing to me how much you can learn when you don't have to worry about grades.

During the Spring Break I'd been fascinated by **Seven Years in Tibet,** the book, not the movie. The movie was terrible. But the book, the book was a real find. It was the greatest true adventure I've ever read. I've never liked fiction. I prefer the real thing. And Harrer's book is as close as you can get. Especially the part about the Dalai Lama and the way he's chosen, and his fascination with tinkering. There was just such a magic to it all. I remember reading it non-stop at the cottage the day Susan called.

Mom gave me an odd look when she saw what I was reading. She was heading out to the tennis court and gently bouncing a tennis ball on her racquet as she spoke to me.

"Balance is everything Ben. Well, that's a retro thing to read. Funny, isn't it, how everything old is coming back? You would think, wouldn't you, that there has been a failure of creativity or at least originality in today's generation. Oh, by the way, Susan Schlossberg-Clarke called for you- something about a sailing regatta. You remember Susan, don't you? Oh, damn! Watch it!" The ball bounced off the rim of her racquet and then on to the coffee table in front of me, landing with a big, wet splash into my coffee, catapulting the coffee across the pages of my book.

Mom hates Susan. I know she's just trying to be protective, but I wish she'd just leave it alone. I loved Susan. I think I still do, but I know it's all over for her. We were so in love in our freshman year. Or maybe just I was. When she left to study in France, it was as if someone close to me had died. For her, it seemed to be no big thing. I remember seeing her off at the airport. I could tell she was put off by how devastated I was. She seemed annoyed as I fought back my tears. I watched her as she took her bags through. She didn't look back.

My mom and hers had been very tight. They played tennis every morning at ten, and they looked as if they could have been sisters: lean, tanned women with angular features and auburn hair worn in a wedge style. The Schlossberg-Clarkes owned a summer place a couple of miles away from us. It was a big, rambling seaside cottage like ours. After Susan left, I really felt clinically depressed. Mom knew about it, but she didn't say anything. She stopped playing tennis with Susan's mom though. She tried everything she could to cheer me up. We even went to a dude ranch in Wyoming, but I just sat on an old horse with my insides kicked out. I felt better after a few months, but I still didn't want to see anyone new. It took me a long time to get over it, but I realized I was back to square one when mom said she had called.

When I returned her call and heard her voice, I couldn't say a word. I was frozen. What can you say when you hear a voice that seems to touch every part of you, every part that's ever been alive and warm and filled with joy. I stammered something about being glad that she was back. I don't remember what else I said. I was just glad she was on the other end of the line. Nothing else mattered to me, and she knew it. She laughed and gurgled delight from the back of her throat. I remembered her laugh.

"Ben, I've missed you. How have you been? I've got friends with me that I'd love you to meet. Yes, there's a sailing race, and we need an extra hand. Glad you got the message. Your mother sounded so distant, as if she didn't remember who I was. You will? Yes, we'll meet there. At eight. It's so good to hear your voice again too. Bye."

I'd kept some photos of us together that I pulled out from the back of my closet. I'm not sure, but I think Mom got rid of all the others in one of her great housecleaning frenzies that usually coincide with something that she's upset about. That's the picture I love best. Susan is standing by their boathouse, blonde, tanned, and leggy, in a pink bikini. The white clapboard of the boathouse behind us highlights everything. She's eating a peach and smiling, and some of the juice is visible on her chin. It's glistening. She looks like a young Gwyneth Paltrow, but just a tad shapelier with curves to die for. I'm standing next to her, grinning like a Cheshire cat with dimples, a gangly six footer with a tangled shock of curly brown hair. My arm is around her waist. I wish I could remember how it felt, that sensation of my forearm against the small of her back. If I could remember that, maybe I could remember the joy I felt then too. I'd never been happier.

Susan introduced me to her friends, Jean-Paul and Monique. They spoke English well enough and looked to be a handsome couple. Monique was lithe, dark, and mischievous with huge eyes that always seemed incredulous at everything I said. She was very European in her manner, or what I took to be European manner, touching me on my arm when she spoke and very animated all the time. She was watching me and smiling as I tied a reef knot.

"Ben, you are very clever with knots. Can you do that with your legs?"

Jean-Paul was darkly handsome with a model's aloofness and the barest hint of cynicism when he spoke. His smile was halfway between a smirk and a pout. It probably takes a while to get to like a person like that I thought.

The morning was sharp and bright, and the spray thrown up from the racing was refreshing when it struck us. The sailing went well enough though my mind wasn't on racing. I loved watching Susan, her agility when she moved to reef a sail, or the way she leapt over Monique to shift her weight to starboard. Sometimes she'd look at me out of the corners of her eyes, a secret, special look that buoyed my spirits, and made me think I still had a chance.

That night we went out to dinner, and then to a seaside pub outside of Gloucester. Monique sat very close to me and patted my thigh under the table every now and then. She didn't seem to be paying any attention to Jean-Paul at all. Susan seemed to be enjoying a huge private joke with Jean-Paul that confused me until I figured things out. I guess I'm pretty slow at times. I was the joke. Pretty funny. Monique wasn't with Jean-Paul at all. Who knows, maybe Susan had planned to set me up with Monique all along, to give us both some international experience I guess. And Susan, well Susan was with Jean-Paul. That was becoming painfully obvious to me. I did my best to act nonchalant and laid back. I don't think I succeeded.

Later that evening they said good night to me and boarded a tall ship anchored not too far from the pub. The figurehead was a carving of a wonderful bare breasted goddess of the sea. The ship belonged to one of Susan's father's friends.

"A not so liquid investment," Susan had quipped. They were staying there overnight and expected me to join them, but I just didn't feel like it. Monique gave a long, sad face and brushed my cheek with her hand. Her lips were locked into a mock pout.

"Too, too bad, Benny, too, too bad." I watched Jean-Paul walk up the gangplank, followed by Monique, with Susan trailing a step or two behind, her fingers running along the guide rope. She didn't look back. It seemed to me that I could as soon expect the wooden figurehead to glance at me as Susan. I was glad mom wasn't awake when I got in. She's able to read my face so easily.

I didn't sleep very well. I left for Yale early the next morning, leaving behind a note for mom. I tried to sound as cheerful as possible in the note because I knew she would be interested in how I was feeling, and I didn't want her to worry. I went to the Head, the Wolf's Head, a private club on campus that I belong to. During the school year we'd meet on Thursdays for a special sit down meal with all fifteen members singing Egyptian chants. It's exclusive and exotic and a trifle odd with a trophy room featuring the mounted heads of big game, Hemingway style, a Great Room with authentic Egyptian artifacts, a library with false walls, and even Nazi dinnerware from World War II. I hoped that the plates had been wartime booty.

For me it's a walled getaway, with no windows, right on campus: a private place where I can be alone on one of the special little balconies, and read, or talk to someone, or have a steak and a cold beer.

No one was around. I went into the games room to find something to do and to get Susan off my mind. It's a big room, about sixty by thirty feet, with several vaulted, arched ceilings, a bit like a honeycomb, and all of it made of stone. The acoustics in the room are fantastic. It's the kind of place that if you wanted a feeling of real power, you could raise your voice and hear thunder. Usually I'd have shouted out a word or two, but I was feeling lousy and the sound of hearing my own voice magnified wasn't on the agenda.

About an hour after I was there, a couple of seniors came in to play some pool. I nodded to them and then decided to throw some darts. They were at the far side of the room, but in a spot that carried their voices to me very clearly and distinctly, as if they were sitting next to me. They couldn't have been speaking much above a whisper. They began talking about Tibet, and that naturally caught my interest.

"You see, the fifth Dalai Lama, the one who rebuilt the Potala, died before it was finished, sometime in the early 1680's. One of his ministers, Sanggye Gyatso kept his death a secret for nine years so that the work on the Potala could be finished. Rumor has it that this Sanggye was also the Dalai Lama's son and deeply committed to seeing his father's work completed. It's quite amazing when you think about it, keeping the Dalai Lama's death from leaking out for that long. I mean the guy was way more important to his people than a President."

"How'd they do it Max? There had to be a lot of people who knew what the Dalai Lama looked like. Nine years is an incredibly long time to stay in a closet."

"Well, for starters, he encouraged people to believe that the Dalai Lama was so deep in a profound meditation that he couldn't be disturbed, and then he found a monk that looked like the Fifth, one with the same piercing eyes and features that could pass for him in a pinch. It gets even better Jamie. When the Fifth died, Sanggye set about performing all the necessary funeral services at all the great monasteries across the country, but he had to be really careful not to let the cat out of the bag. He had to take great pains not to let anyone realize who the service was for. He used ambiguous poetic language to conceal things. But one of the monks caught on to the trick and started crying foul. So Sanggye took him aside and let him in on the secret. It didn't stop there. He was also obligated to consult a famous oracle to find out about the reincarnation of the next Dalai Lama, the Sixth. And he did."

"So what happened? Did the oracle keep the secret too?"

"In a manner of speaking he kept the secret, to the death, his death. Sanggye, ever afraid that someone would spill the beans, disguised himself as a beggar, and returned to the oracle's house, where the oracle's mother lived. He hung around begging until the old woman let it slip that the Fifth was dead. That convinced Sanggye that the oracle knew what had happened even out of trance. So he did the expedient thing: he had the oracle and his mother assassinated. Oh what a tangled web we weave."

"Jesus, what a story."

"And that's not the half of it. The Sixth comes into the picture when he's about twelve. Usually, they're much younger, maybe three or four, when they're found to be the reincarnation of the Dalai Lama. So here's this kid who hasn't been raised like a monk and who suddenly finds himself studying and preparing for the highest office in the land, a very celibate office, I might add. But the Sixth is decidedly different from any Dalai Lama before or after. The Sixth is a great lover and a poet. His name is Tsangyang Gyatso, and he is one of the most remarkable holy men who ever lived. He embodied within himself the highest forms of the spiritual life and the sensual life."

"What happened to him? Did people accept him the way he was?"

"From the little I know, I think his songs are still popular. The people loved him, and it was auspicious to have your daughter sleep with him. In fact, fathers often painted their houses yellow to commemorate the fact. Imagine that! He left his mark, but what happened to him in the end is shrouded in mystery. They say he could be in several places at the same time. Well I don't know about that, but it sure is intriguing. During his time as Dalai Lama certain factions plotted to overthrow him, and in the end they did. But legend has it that he didn't die when he was twenty-two. Some believe he survived, became a wandering beggar and lived to a ripe old age. After he died there were reports that he was seen and recognized at the big religious festivals, but no one knows for sure. They say he kept a journal and that's been lost. Quite a mystery isn't it?"

"Uh-huh. Say, after we finish this game, do you feel like heading out for a pizza?"

"Sure thing. I hope you like anchovies."

I sat back in my chair and gazed up at the stone honeycomb ceiling above me. I wondered what it would be like to be in Tibet. The more I thought about Susan, the more I wanted to get away, as far as possible from where I was, to find some way of escape from the numbness I was feeling. I don't know what I was thinking when I went sailing with Susan. Was I hoping she'd want to be with me again, the way it was? Or was I trying to test myself, to see if I was over her, over her smile, over her hair, over her legs, over her breasts, over the nape of her neck, over everything.

I lazed about for the next few days. Just enjoying the early June sunshine, drinking coffee, and reading whatever struck my fancy. Susan's face was beginning to blur. That's when I came across the brochure, the travel brochure on Tibet. I looked over the travel itinerary with a kind of delirious longing for the longest while. Then I ran my finger across the picture of the Potala, the great monastery palace of the Dalai Lamas, and decided to go. Mom didn't like the idea, but I think she knew I had to get away.

I had the best of the summer before me. Whatever I decided to do in September was another issue. I had time to decide. Mom could e-mail me with the details wherever I happened to be. Call me Ishmael. I just had to go, and go soon.

II

On the overseas flight I was able to sleep a bit. I started thinking about Susan somewhere over the Midwest, Kansas, I think. I tried not to, but it was no use. She was a part of my dreams even over California. I nodded off occasionally. Every so often I would awake with a start when my head nodded too violently to one side.

The flight seemed interminable despite half a dozen movies on the tiny screen in front of me. A kind of steady droning sound mingled at the back of my consciousness with spliced cuts of movies whose endings always eluded me as I drifted into fitful sleep. Finally we landed. I had a short stopover in Bangkok and then in a few hours I was in Kathmandu.

I was staying for a few days in Thamel, downtown, at the Kathmandu Guest House. I needed a few days to get over jet lag and make arrangements for Tibet. The whole place was incredibly funky with narrow twisted streets, and internet cafes, and street vendors selling everything from tiger balm to hashish. It seemed to me that there were quite a few attractive women around, backpackers mostly, from Europe and back home. Everything was so different.

Thamel was a wild scramble of streets, the offspring of a city planner gone mad. Perhaps that's why it was so charming in an off-beat kind of way. After I had checked into my lodgings at the Kath-mandu Guest House, I made my way to Durbar Square in the very heart of the city. Bicycle rickshaws were moving in both directions contending with cars, motorcycles, and pedestrians of every size and complexion. The rough, narrow streets were strewn with litter. The scent of incense and sun-cooked garbage filled the air. Two shabby-looking dogs were copulating in a doorway. As I walked I felt a sprinkling of something wet on the top of my head. Being a quick learner, after all, I'm a Yale man, I moved towards the far side of the street to avoid any further offerings from the second-story city dwell-ers. The tiny shops overflowed to the street, with masks, t-shirts, and sweaters hanging from the outer walls. I thought that if ever there were a tourist heaven, this would be it: ancient mysteries cheek-to-jowl with rampant commercialism and rose petals under your feet. Yale was never like this. A shrine to a god on every corner, and a hashish vendor to boot. What more could you ask for after conquering Everest, than the funky playground of Kathmandu.

Armed with a Guidebook, I did the tourist thing and set out to see a goddess if I could. I lowered my head under the low entranceway and stepped into the inner courtyard of Kumari, the living goddess, in Durbar Square. The wood carvings decorating the windows and overhangs of the building were superb. Pigeon droppings were every- where around me, staining wooden deities and brickwork alike. I was careful to keep a lookout for the pigeons, and avoid being caught directly under them. A small offering box stood in the low courtyard. An old man looked down upon me from a second-story window. A sign in English said that taking pictures of Kumari was forbidden. I dropped some rupee notes into the tiny slot on top of the box. The old man motioned for me to wait.

A few moments later a young girl, maybe ten, suddenly pre- sented herself at the window above me. She looked at me intensely, for just an instant, and was gone. A splash of gorgeous colour and a warm smile cast at me for a few seconds was all I could remember of her. Like a small and precious bird alighting on a branch and then gone. I felt so odd. It was not that there was any sort of physical attraction. She was way too young for that. It was the symbol of who she was that

struck me, whom she represented. She was a goddess, a living goddess, and that took my breath away.

Returning to the Guest House, I walked as if in a daze. The
streets, with their brightly decorated shrines, the smells of incense, the
overpowering stench from refuse, the gritty air itself, all of this melded
into a small universe, and I was ecstatic. Tears came to my eyes. I
suddenly knew that spiritual mysteries and the stinking filth of an open
sewer were there, at hand, and as close as they had always been. I
realized that you could make the choice to see whatever you wished to
see, and to see both at the same time if you wanted.

I stopped for a beer at one of the second-story terrace restaurants that are found everywhere in Thamel. From a table overlooking
the street I could see the people and the traffic coming together a short
distance below. I wondered if things were the same now in Nepal as
they were before, before the Crown Prince had run amuck in the
Palace. Somehow I didn't think so. A part of a country's soul can die
just as a person can die.

I sighed in relief at being here, here in this place so different
from Yale. I sipped at my beer and looked down upon a group of
backpackers striding through the street, laughing and going into a
small bakery for some ready-made sandwiches and a soft drink. I
ordered a light lunch of chicken chili and decided to spend the afternoon by walking up to Swayambhunath, the monkey temple, that I
could see from the fourth floor patio of the Guest House.

From atop the temple I could see much of the valley and the ring of mountains surrounding it. A polluted haze settled on everything, obscuring buildings, people, and plants. It seemed to me then that the world was getting smaller and smaller, and with every increase in speed, and in telecommunications, it also seemed to be getting grimier and grimier. At least, that's the way it felt to me. The beauty of the temple with its niched Buddhas, and above everything, the haunting eyes, the eyes of the compassionate Buddha, were like a promise, a promise from the past, and a promise to the future, but the gritty present was bleary and gray to me. I gazed towards Tibet and felt a surge of exhilaration that carried me through the afternoon. The next morning I made arrangements to take a bus tour to Tibet.

I thought the landscape would shake me enough to stop me thinking about Susan. Sometimes I caught myself mumbling in a whisper under my breath "Help me," just to get her out of my mind. I was half dreaming, half awake. I remembered a time in a Boston pub, near Fenway Park. I'd memorized a poem for her, from Yeats. I'd waited for the right moment, just when we were alone, and then raised my glass to her.

"Wine comes in at the mouth, and love comes in at the eye. That's all we shall know for truth, before we grow old and die. I lift the glass to my mouth, I look at you and I sigh."

Susan looked at me quizzically, then arched her eyebrows and shook her head. Whatever magic I thought the poem might have had was lost forever for me in the way she turned her head. But not a moment later she moved to the seat right next to mine and kissed me.

If I could be with her just one day a year, or once every two years, it would be enough I thought. All she had to do was say one word to me, to make that day a reality, maybe a French word. A word like a poet's name, a name like Rimbaud, that has always seemed to me to be like a burst of flame in darkness.

"Help me," I murmured to myself like a lovesick fool. I noticed my fingernails were bitten to the quick.

The bus journey to Lhasa was a wild mix of rugged mountain landscapes and sexual memories of Susan set against intriguing Buddhist temples, and the bright engaging faces of Tibetan peasants. There were plenty of Chinese troops in spots along the way. One Chinese officer spoke to our tour guide while the group was having lunch. Just after lunch, the tour guide gathered us all together and said that if anyone had mistakenly carried a picture of the Dalai Lama, that it should be handed in to him, now. Everything seemed really tense all of a sudden and quiet. No one had any pictures. The Chinese officer stood beside the tour guide and impassively surveyed the group. Then, abruptly, he turned and walked away.

I really hadn't paid much attention to the other tourists on the bus, or during the short tours. There were a few empty seats, and the seat next to me was vacant. The others on the tour were nice enough. I made the usual small talk over the meals we took together. Apart from me, the tour guide, and the Nepali driver, there were five others. Chloe and Astrid, a couple of tall English girls my age, athletic looking, with great smiles. An older man, Jack, in his fifties, always sported a Canadian flag on his clothing, or a pin. An American couple from Taos, New Mexico, Joycelyn and Michael, ancients like Jack, rounded out the group.

Joycelyn was a thin, cheerfully intense woman who was quietly authoritative, a little like my mother. I was wary around her. Michael reminded me of a revolutionary minute man, a real American type, lean, with chiseled features and laid-back competence. I liked him. At one of the rest stops they asked me to mind their digital camera and carry-on bag while they flew to the washrooms. They owned a bed and breakfast place, back in Taos, and needed a break they said. Like the rest of us, they were on a relatively inexpensive excursion to their own private version of Shangri-La.

An old man at one of the bus stops near a lake tugged at my sleeve and smiled at me. He was speaking Tibetan, so I just smiled back and nodded my head. He had wild, tousled hair and looked like an old, bedraggled lion. He spoke very quickly, but his speech was soft and gentle, a soothing flow of strange-sounding words, almost like a prayer. He placed a small, brown package in my hands and then grinned as big as a house. I turned away from him for a moment to get at some money to give him, but when I looked again, he was gone. I opened the package, and inside was an old, handwritten book of some kind, with some pages ripped out. It was in English and had been very carefully printed. I tucked it into my belt and returned to the bus.

That night I felt exhausted. The tour guide was cramming so much into the whirlwind tours that I just wanted some private space around me for a while. I fell into the cot of the weathered, flea-bitten hotel as if it were a five-star resort. I slept with my clothes on because it was so cold. But it felt exciting to have this strange night cloaked around me. I could hear voices in the outside corridor. Whether they were speaking Tibetan or Chinese, I couldn't tell. The last thing I remember before drifting off into sleep was hearing someone clearing their throat. I couldn't believe that anyone could have so much phlegm, or maybe a throat as a long as a giraffe's. After what seemed the longest time, the performance ended with a thundering, hawking expulsion.

Just before I fell into my customary deep sleep, my eyelids flickered once, twice, three times, then closed. I remember the images that flashed before me. The old, smiling, lion-headed man, his hair tousled and wild; the faces of Han Chinese, sweating and angry; a dark incense-filled room, and then emptiness, a void, followed by the noise and rough colors of a Tibetan drinking place; finally, a queue of beautiful women gently draping long, silken scarves around my neck. Each of the dream images could have lasted a fraction of a second or an hour, I don't know, but they were so immediate and compelling when I was experiencing them that I felt as if I was on a raft moving swiftly at night over the fast waters of a narrow river flanked by steep cliffs.

I think I woke up just once. The reason I'm not sure is because what happened can only happen in dreams. It had to be a dream. I mean, how else can you explain it. Very, very slowly, I levitated from the cot. Levitated: I mean that's what it was. I was about eight inches above the cot, lying horizontally, and then I began to feel myself moving headfirst up the wall behind me, rising ever so slowly and gently until my head touched the ceiling. I stopped then, for a moment, and then it began again, the slow, inexorable movement carrying me, until I was staring at the cot below me, thinking what a strange dream to have. Nothing in my body felt tense. Everything was comfortable and loose. I was warm. One part of me said that if this was really happening I was surely going to fall. That thought alarmed me, and these new doubts seemed to make me tense up. But even suspended from a ceiling, you can make decisions. I shook the fear off, eased back into feeling comfortable again, and then slowly descended, retracing the same route that had taken me up. I pulled the covers over my head once I was back on the bed. I slept well after that. The next morning I remembered it as one of those dreams that's so, so real, but can never be, because things like that don't happen in real life.

When I first saw it, I knew why a picture of the Potala was one of the few photographs Frank Lloyd Wright kept in his studio. The Potala is magnificent. Lhasa is a funky city, but there are parts of it that take your breath away. The Potala is one. Some of the market smells are another. I was happy just to look at it.

It was then that I saw the old man. He was the same man who had given me the journal, with tousled hair that was like a lion's mane. He was running, and I was surprised at his agility for an old man. He darted into one of the passageways of the Potala. Several Chinese troops were pursuing him and shouting loudly at each other. It was then that I was pushed roughly to one side as the Chinese troops followed him. I waited and watched for several minutes. The Chinese troops returned to the front of the Potala, but the old man was not with them.

That night I read the journal the old man had given me. Several pages were missing. I could see the jagged edges of the binder where they had been ripped out. The journal was very poetic. There were some penciled notations in the margin, but I couldn't quite make them out because of the poor lighting in my room.

After I finished reading, I tucked the journal into my backpack. It was a curious little journal, odd in its way, but somehow I liked it.

Reading poetry is the closest thing I can think of to getting into someone else's consciousness. You trace the same neural pathways in your brain as the poet's during the creation of the poem. In the poem you become one with the poet. If you commit it to memory, the synchronicity of identities is complete. At least that's the way I think about it.

I thought about the old man. No one had been able to tell me why he was being chased by the soldiers or who he was. Things just seemed to happen here, and who knows why.

I stared up at the ceiling and wondered. The paint was peeling in several spots and trembled erratically with the whirring movement of the ceiling fan. I focused on three cream-colored splotches of loose paint that curled in upon themselves and swayed in the turbulent air above the fan. My body was tired. The longer I looked up, the more it seemed that I could make out a human figure in the curling, loosened paint above me. A reclining woman was moving there with an abandon driven by the relentless rhythms of the noisy fan. I chuckled at what I was seeing: a naked woman in a few gyrating strips of flaking paint. I'd been away from home for too long. I kept looking at it and began to feel drowsy, but a little aroused too. Desire is an odd, improbable thing: a few thin, curling slivers of old paint fluttering above my head was enough to make me smile with delight and desire.

III

Pages from the Lost Journal of the Sixth Dalai Lama

As I come up from Shol to the Potala in the early morning light, I see him at the gate again. An old black dog, its face upon its paws, uptilted towards me. I stop and watch him quietly, the way one eye cocks up at me engagingly, subtly, taking it all in. I think he is too wise to bark. He knows where I have been. Imploringly, I look back at him, silently sending him my wish not to tell anyone that I left at dusk. I press my finger to my lips. I step around him, stopping for an instant to scratch him under his ear. His hind leg brushes against my arm as it digs into his belly. I hurry past him to my quarters high in the palace.

I stop once on the steep stairs to look at the moon in its fifteenth day, so bright and penetrating. I can feel it upon my face. I can almost see my love's smiling face within it. I am flooded with great power and love and tenderness. I ask myself if my feet are still on this earth, on this stone. The blue silk I am wearing is cool against my skin like a blessing. I feel like crying out that I am Dangzang Wangpo, the wild man, with many lovers down the valley in Shol and beyond. But here I must be quiet. Here my teachers are sleeping, and I must cover their silence with my own. The wine on my lips has no place here, here where I am Rigdzin Tsangyang Gyatso, honoured in the beloved line. I glide upwards on nimble toes. I write these lines in my journal. They are like grapes. I will take them one day and make songs of them, like wine from grapes.

I lie awake in my bed. I am restless with the thoughts of loving. The smile on my lips remembers the prayer flags I hoisted. The prayer flags brought her to me, and then her invitation brought me to her bed, this noble woman with the eyelashes like lassoes. I remember on the afternoon when I loved her how two turquoise bees buzzed above some hollyhocks in full blossom just outside the window. The sound of their dalliance mingled with our own, but by the early evening one of them was gone. There were no regrets. Lovers are not always together. There is no sense in crying over it. That would show a lack of understanding of fate.

I study hard. I focus on my studies and move within their orbit, but many times the face of a beloved will persist until only her face is left where the meditation began. My studies have always been successful, though there are some who do not understand my way and wish me gone. They do not stop. They never let me alone. They talk of mistakes, but the lineage is mine. I am clothed in great power, but I am vulnerable in that power. That is the nature of my being. I love this life, and I will sing and dance at the doors of creation as is my wont. The people know me. They know my virtue. The houses painted yellow in Shol attest to that understanding. My songs are their songs.

I lie awake, still restless. Will sleep take away this longing? I move and shift from one side to the other, my thoughts still racing. I see the face of my lost lover, the tall enchantress from Chungyal. So often have I seen her in my dreams, but never again in Chungyal or Lhasa or anywhere else. My longing finds her now only in my dreams. There must be a way to find her again. Some way. Yes, yes. I will ask a shaman to enter my dreams and bring her back to me. Then, I can meet her at the actual place my dream points to. Love is not always easy. It retreats into a dream to preserve its value. Not like a stone by a roadside, picked up from a heap, and then thrown.

In the morning, after my lessons, I joined my friends for arc-hery practice. The morning was cool and fresh, and the sun bright. My rings sparkled with life. We laughed at some of the wild shots that landed in the river, scaring a few ducks into mad flight. One of my arrows cut right through the target sticking into the ground on the far side. I shook my hair in triumph. When I retrieved it, I thought of the woman I had loved at the New Year's feast. My loving had followed her through the winter to the Spring's first green shoots.

I am so tired. I lie down alone in the deep grass by the river. Glowing pink clouds fill the sky. A crane flies overhead towards Lithang. This trouble of mine: it never stops. Desi Sangay never lets up. Like climbing a mountain in a dream. Just as I gain a foothold in the difficult, windswept rocks, the eagle begins its battering. My fingers ache with the effort to hang on. Desi Sangay and that crowd. Desi Sangay who preaches the way of a celibate monk and lives it not. I will not take the vows that would desecrate this office. I will advance in my own way. My songs are my own. I will sing them until the end. They are like my breathing.

I met my lover deep in the southern woods thinking we were completely alone, our private time and unknown to anyone. What a surprise to me then when I heard our secrets spilled in the public marketplace. The sweet songs of our forest tryst betrayed by loud parrots. Will they never stop talking? I cannot stop my loving. I do not sleep without a lover. I have never spent my seed alone.

Tonight at the tavern she smiled at everyone. Her face was shining and filled the tavern with joy. I watched her to see if she would look at me. When she did, I noticed she was sending her love from the unseen, subtle corners of her eyes. Those secrets carried me to her bed. I thought I had satisfied her until she raised her head and looked at me with a savage smile, her long hair tussled and wild against the bed sheets. It would be easier for me to tame a tiger with bits of bread and meat.

So many lovely women, like apples and peaches, ripe for the cherished tasting. Beautiful, mysterious beings. And at my back these prickly thorns. I've had enough of these thorns. I'll choose the fruit and leave the rest behind. I see no connection between the two, and so I know my choice. Walking in the market today I saw a parrot from the east and a peacock from Bengal, the one beside the other. I marveled at their coming together here in Lhasa. They've become companions here, destined friends forever.

My lover grows cold towards me despite all that I do to keep her love. But that too is natural. In the North I have seen a swan who fell in love with a lake, staying on that lake for as long as it could, until ice covered the surface. When the ice came, the swan flew away, naturally, without regrets.

I do not feel well today. It is like a little death. I have tried in-cantations to keep my beloved, but she is gone like the wild horses that escape over the hills. Lassoes and ropes may catch the horses, but not my wild love. Nothing can stop her, nothing can hold her, for she no longer loves me.

Whatever I write here and press into printed love songs will be ruined by rain. But what is deep within me, the love itself, the mystery that cannot be written, keeps inside, and it cannot be lost.

Without her love, I feel such desolation. Having known just her body's softness is not enough. I stop long and longer sketching these drawings in the sand to gauge vast distances across the sky. It's so odd to me that the stars and their influences can be gauged and assessed, but not her. I will never know her deepest desires for these are beyond my scope and powers.

Long ago I learned how to steady myself before lovemaking with a new beloved. Letting the desire run towards beauty without guidance is like a stallion trotting over slippery ice, some of it solidly frozen, and some of it not. The stallion's eagerness can take away the power of his hidden legs and he will buckle forward, scattered and spent.

IV

I was just about to drift off into sleep when I heard someone knocking at my door. I lay there for a moment wondering whether or not just to ignore it. But the knocking persisted. Finally I got up and went to the door which didn't have a peephole. I hesitated for a moment, still not decided. When I opened the door, I was met with two of the most welcoming smiles I have ever encountered. I guess I just stood there staring for too long because Chloe started shaking her head and Astrid giggled.

"Well, aren't you going to say hello and invite us in?"

I mumbled something incoherent, and then sat on a rickety wooden chair by the window. Chloe and Astrid sat on the bed because there was nowhere else to sit.

"What a day it's been. So many strange things happening, and some don't make any sense. Soldiers chasing an old man, and then the old man disappearing and then reappearing in different places. I mean how could he move so quickly, how could he be in so many different places at the same time? It just doesn't make sense. Why were they chasing him in the first place? It's all so strange."

As Chloe talked about what had happened, I couldn't help but wonder if it was the same old man who had given me the book and that I had seen too.

Finally, Chloe stopped talking and then glancing at Astrid, she looked at me again and asked, "Ben, do you mind terribly if we stay here tonight? So much has happened and we feel safe here, with you. Is that all right?"

"Sure, you two can have the bed, and I'll sleep in the chair. It's quite comfortable."

"No, that's not fair. We're the ones who are imposing," Chloe said. Astrid smiled and nodded seriously.

"You've got a double bed and that's room enough for the three of us. We're English, proper English from London, and we want to be fair. We just want to lay with you and get some sleep. Is that ok?"

In a few minutes I found myself sandwiched between two of the most attractive women I've ever met. I lay perfectly still on my stomach and tried not to move. They nestled on either side of me, and I breathed hard into my pillow. After the longest time, when I thought they were both asleep, I heard Astrid sigh and move closer to me. Chloe giggled and then it all began. It seemed as if only a moment or two had passed before the light of dawn streamed golden rays into the room.

I was the first to order breakfast in the small dining room. Invariably, breakfast consisted of a single boiled egg and some tea. Jocelyn and Michael joined me at my table. Jocelyn was smiling with a touch of mischief in her eyes.

"So, Ben, I see you're in fine fettle this morning. Sleep well?"

I nodded, sipping my tea, and looked across at Jocelyn's husband. Michael was totally focused on trying to repair a broken mechanism in his digital camera. He was using a table knife as a tool to move the mechanism back into place.

Jack entered the room and sat down at the table next to us. He was sporting two small Canadian flag pins on his shirt collar. The Tibetan waitress pointed at Jack's pins and then at herself. She did this several times. Jack, smiled weakly, and looked confused.

Chloe and Astrid came in and sat with Jack. There were only the two tables in the dining room.

Jocelyn turned her head slowly towards Chloe. "I was worried about you two. I knocked on your door around midnight when I hadn't heard anything, not even a single sound. But the tour guide said that everyone was accounted for."

Chloe cast a lightning-quick, withering glance at Jocelyn and said in clipped, chilled tones and measured words, "My mother lives in Belgravia, in London. She's there, this very moment, and sleeping soundly I fancy. I don't know of any other mother. I don't need any other mother. I won't have any other."

Jocelyn's face went ashen. "I was only concerned you know. I wasn't prying." Jocelyn looked to Michael for support. Michael was completely absorbed with the digital camera, oblivious to the conversation.

The waitress was gesticulating at Jack, pointing to his collar and then at her ear. Chloe watched and then said, "Jack, she wants your pins. She wants to use them as earrings."

"Well, I can give her one. But I didn't bring a lot. I've been saving them to give people who are especially kind or helpful. I never give two to anyone."

Astrid laughed uncontrollably for a moment and then caught herself. Chloe glanced at me, smiling with her eyes, and I smiled back.

Jocelyn reached into her bag and took out two US flag lapel pins and offered them to the rosy-cheeked waitress. The waitress declined them with a broad smile and looked back again at Jack.

Jack slowly removed one of the pins from his collar and gave it to her. She waited for the second pin, but Jack wasn't about to part with it. She stood there waiting, smiling. Jack focused intently on his boiled egg and began cracking its shell with a pure, focused concentration. The waitress stood a moment longer and then returned to the kitchen a little crestfallen.

A double silence hung in the air that was mercifully broken by the tour guide announcing our itinerary for the day.

V

When I returned home, mother had loads of mail for me. She had all kinds of news, but the news that interested me most was that Susan was engaged to a Frenchman. Oddly, the only emotion I felt when she told me was a kind of joy. I was happy for her. Mother suggested I call to congratulate her. I would have done that, but I needed to see her in person. I was curious about how I would feel then.

The first person I met when I arrived at Susan's place was her father, Thomas. He was standing with his hands on his hips looking at their renovated boathouse across a wide expanse of sloping, well manicured lawn. The large boathouse was actually a guest cottage replete with a sauna, a small library, and a well stocked wine closet.

"Ben, it's good to see you again. Welcome home. I heard you were in Tibet. How was it?"

I spoke to him for a while about Tibet, and then he looked again at the boathouse and said, "What color do you think I should paint it?"

"Something bright and cheerful, like Susan," I replied.

He looked at me sadly then, the way my mother used to look at me when Susan and I were considered together, as a possible couple, always ending in a sad dismissal of the thought.

"Susan's in the boathouse with Pierre. Why don't you go in and say hello?"

I didn't know quite what to expect when I opened the boat-house door. I hesitated for a minute, and then I was face to face with Pierre. He waited for me to say hello first. That was Pierre's way.

"Hello and congratulations Pierre. I'm happy for you and Susan."

"Merci."

Susan came rushing towards me and gave me a hug.

"I heard the good news Susan. I'm happy for you."

"Oh Ben, it's so good to see you again. You look different. Long hair, a blue silk shirt, and just look at all those rings! What have you been up to?"

I told her about the places I'd seen. Susan just smiled and nodded, really happy to see me, but Pierre didn't seem keen on what I had to say. He was looking intently at the tennis racket he was holding and fingering the strings.

"Pierre and I are off to play tennis and then we've committed ourselves to join in on a sailing regatta. Look Ben, why don't you stay here at the boathouse overnight, and we'll have a late breakfast together. What do you say? You can do some kayaking and check out Dad's wine cellar. Oh Ben, say you'll stay."

I just couldn't refuse Susan though I could tell Pierre wasn't that enthusiastic about it all. When they left I went out in the kayak and explored the shoreline of the lake for a few hours. It felt good to be exercising again.

Later, I made myself comfortable in the boathouse with an excellent bottle of chianti and watched some movies. The funny thing was I didn't feel bad about Susan getting married. It was just so good to see her again, and to know she felt good about seeing me. When the lights of the cottages across the lake started coming on, I went out to the deck with more wine, and thought about my adventures in Tibet and the lost journal of the Sixth Dalai Lama. If you have to spend an evening alone, some good wine, some poetic memories, and a great canopy of stars above, make all the difference in the world. I went to bed about two in the morning and fell asleep right away.

I don't know what kind of dreams you can have after drinking a couple of bottles of good wine, but it sure seemed to me that if desire and dreams meet sometimes, they had a magnificent collision in my boathouse bed. I dreamt that I felt movement in my bed, as if someone were getting in beside me, and when I groggily looked to see who it was, Susan was above me, atop me, her arms stretched out and just touching my shoulders on either side.

"Susan, is that you?"

"Shh. Not a sound. Just lie there. We've got some unfinished business."

Her hair was tickling my face, and then her lips were on mine and something seemed to ignite within me despite my fatigue. It was all a blur to me, and wonderful and mixed somehow, in some curious way, with the lost journal. I have to say that if some dreams carry our most heartfelt desires and impulses, that was the one for me.

The next morning, my left eye opened first and stayed open in wonder as I lay on my side. My right eye was closed like the trapdoor to a cellar. I was awake in bed, the boathouse bed, alone. So, it had been a dream. Strangely my mind felt clear and alert, and my body totally relaxed. It must have been very good wine without any chemical stabilizers. It was late, around eleven o'clock, so I hurried to the bathroom to shave and shower.

I was just applying the shaving foam to my face when I got the surprise of my life. There, displayed in the mirror, were three long scratch marks across my right shoulder. I couldn't believe it. With those three magnificent marks, my dream had become a reality, a baffling, blessed memory etched in skin, better than any tattoo. It was temporary, transitory, like a Tibetan sand mandala.

When I left the boathouse, I turned to look at the coat of bright yellow paint on the clapboard walls. Thomas had been hard at work. Everyone was still asleep at the house, so I left a note and drove home.

Mother had guessed that I'd stayed over, and she was a little miffed that I hadn't called. We talked about my plans for September. I didn't have any.

"So, what are you going to do until you have some plans?"

"A couple of friends of mine from London have invited me over. People I met in Nepal. I'm going to spend some time with them. We were talking about hiking in the Scottish highlands."

"Well, I'm glad to hear that. It's about time you had some male company."

CANADIAN CLUB

Devon Christie smiled as he listened to the enthusiastic ramblings of his countryman, Peter J. Powell. Devon had just arrived in Dhaka, Bangladesh, on a short-term consulting assignment, and had previously met P.J. a few years earlier. P.J. was a middle-aged, slightly paunchy, poultry expert from Calgary who had a real gift for mischief, one that you could see in the well-worn lines around his eyes, and the delicately ironic twist of a smile. With his patrician looks and engaging banter, he fancied himself a ladies' man, and seemed to relish playing the role, though he met with little actual success because of his own choosing. In reality, P.J. shied away from potential conquests that looked to be inevitable. He simply loved the chase, the flirtatiousness, the game.

"Devon, you have to realize that everyone who comes here must be a little weird, or off-beat in some way. Now, you have to admit, that's a given." P.J. enjoyed starting off an evening of drink and easy conversation with an unequivocal statement that demanded response.

"Why does it have to be a given?" Devon replied. "There are a lot of good people too... altruistic people, that don't strike me as being weird." It was so easy, Devon thought, to think about goodness within the confines of the Canadian Club, that expatriate oasis replete with beer at prices better than in Canada. Beyond that charmed perimeter outside of the Club's grounds lay a world of hardship and privation he could only guess at.

"Goodness can be obscene, Dev. Carried too far, goodness becomes a curse." P.J. was just about to get into one of his tirades about the damage missionary work had done, when a woman Devon had met at the project office came up to their table and invited Devon to a small party she was hosting. They chatted for a bit, and then Devon left for the solitude of the guest house where he was staying, a stone's throw away from the Club.

Devon liked his work. He felt it challenged him, and that it was useful. He liked what it brought out of him. At the end of a day, alone and pleasantly fatigued from the day's labours, he would enjoy one of the fine duty free Cuban cigars he had purchased in Dubai, usually a Montecristo, number four. He would smoke on the patio balcony of the Guest House as he watched the Bengali sunset over Gulshan, the sun redder and more vital than any he had ever seen. And, at about the same time he was enjoying his cigar, he would hear the prayers floating across the city, in different tones and cadences, just as the mosquitoes made their presence felt and forced his retreat inside. Everything was so strange and transitory in this place, but he loved the wayward beauty of it all.

What he hated were the crows: the carrion crows of Dhaka. They seemed to be everywhere. In the middle of the night, if he awoke, he would hear them, cawing and cawing and cawing, incessantly. The only other sounds he heard were the sharp yelps of the occasional dog being beaten, or the keen whistle of a security supervisor checking on the *chowkidar* at his night duty.

It was one of those uneventful social gatherings that are tepid and polite and devoid of anything like a spirited or intellectual discussion. A few drinks before dinner, an appetizer or two with piquant sauce, and some desultory comments on the *hartals*, the general strikes that shut down the city, and the current political mess. Devon did his best to stay with the mainstream in the conversations, endeavouring not to say anything that smacked of intellect, wit, or charm. The expat community was for the most part an inbred, sorry lot. Too many of them had been in Dhaka far too long, and those who were not disillusioned were cynical. They performed their largely ineffectual work, played tennis, socialized, drank, made love, and slept.

Devon was just about to make some specious apology to his hostess and make an early escape when he saw her arrive. The woman was magnificent. She took his very breath away. She was stunning and exotic, a dark-haired, dimpled beauty. Devon followed the hostess to the door. He smiled engagingly at the wonderful vision before him, and was introduced. *"Salaam aleikhem,"* Devon said, with a broad smile. But the beauty looked past him, just barely glancing at him, and quietly replying *"Aleikhem as-salaam."* She didn't really see him, the thin man in clothes a little too big for him, with a ruddy Anglo Saxon complexion. She was already looking beyond him to someone she knew. She smiled politely at Devon and was gone. Devon made his apologies to the hostess, a little wistfully because now he wanted to stay, but then left. It was the woman's beauty that had transfixed him. All of his ideas, feelings, and sentiments about beauty and femininity were corroborated in the woman's great personal beauty.

Devon's driver drove by the construction site, and Devon observed the mothers with their small children sitting on piles of brick rubble, shaded by sun-worn black umbrellas, busy at pounding the red bricks with ballpeen hammers that went into making the material needed for binding the mortar used in the building trade. Some of the children were no older than five or six. Young women carried baskets of brick pieces on their heads. It was heavy work, and they wore flip-flops. Bamboo scaffolding lashed together with rope sheathed the outside walls of the building they were working on. Their faces were tight and drained with the exertion. He considered ruefully that hardened criminals in Canada fared better than these poor souls.

Sometimes, on the drive to the downtown office, Devon would daydream and muse over the motorized rickshaws, the baby-taxis, as they were called. Brightly painted with folk art that jumped out at you, he marvelled over them. He imagined that some day a whimsical film director would create a Bangladeshi version of the Royal Canadian Mounted Police musical ride only with motorized rickshaws instead of horses. A lavish spectacle on a grand scale with thousands of rickshaws choreographed in perfect rhythm with startling visual symmetries and loops and circles and cloverleaf movements: a Bollywood fantasia with exotic Bengali beauties at the finale.

The traffic was chaotic, noisy, and noxious, but somehow things moved, and people travelled incrementally towards their destinations. It was a wide, wide world, bustling with energy and sound. Everywhere, on every street, thousands of people went about their business or lack of it. The beggars would try to catch your eye and showcase their deformities against the window glass. And the horns, always the horns, blaring sharply beside you, or a part of the general din in the background: the horns of Dhaka. Like the crows, always nearby, always on the periphery, but moving in inexorably.

Devon remembered a time during stop and go traffic when a bicycle rickshaw had bumped hard into the rear of his vehicle. There was the sound of plastic being crushed and broken. Rafiq immediately put the Land Rover into park and hurried out to survey the damage.

The Project Manager had always made it very clear that any damage to project vehicles would be charged against the driver's pay. Looking in the rear view mirror, I could see Rafiq speaking rapidly and quietly to the rickshaw driver who was clearly craven and apologetic. It was a certainty that the rickshaw driver could not afford to pay for the damage. Suddenly, Rafiq struck the man hard with his fist and returned. I asked him if everything was all right. He muttered something under his breath about a rear brake light on the right side being broken and drove on.

More than anything he loved to walk. He hadn't yet got a sense of the overall layout of the city. He knew Gulshan, the wealthy part of the city where he stayed, but couldn't yet determine how all of the other parts of the city fit together. He wondered if he ever would. What could he tell his friends about this place? Oddly, he didn't use e-mail for anything but business. The few postcards that he sent out of habit and obligation could never convey the riotous pulse of the place, the busyness verging on chaos, the odours that could bring a strong man to his knees. He smiled, wishing he could send cards with scratch and sniff patches on them.

A voice jolted him from his reverie. "*Bandhu*...you want woman? Two thousand taka. Nearby. You come?" The baby-taxi driver beside him craned his head out of the cab, motioning for him to come. Devon simply shook his head, and kept on walking. He noticed that the scene on the cab door was of a train crossing a bridge.

One of his friends, Bukowski, a management consultant from Toronto, worked with the Bangladesh Railway. He didn't see him often, maybe once a year, but he enjoyed the quirky sense of humour the man had, and his good stories. He had once asked Devon what he would do if he had one day in the year to do whatever he wished, whatever he desired, a day that all of his friends and family would support even if they didn't know what he would do on that day.

Devon couldn't think of anything at the time, but he had often thought about it since then. He wanted to experience something altogether different. It wasn't a woman. It wasn't any place as such. It was a simple wish, if you could call it a wish. He wondered what it would be like to spend a night in a *bustee*, a Bangladeshi slum, disguised and yet free enough to roam about the place as if he were a local. The idea had come to him one night while he had been smoking a fine Cuban cigar from his fifth floor patio balcony. Arriving late at night on a domestic flight from Chittagong, he had gone out to his balcony to watch the comings and goings.

There, five stories below him, he saw a man heading towards the Guesthouse from the Canadian Club nearby, a white-haired man with a thick mop of hair, a little tipsy and wobbly on his legs. Probably too much drink, Devon thought, as he watched him walking unsteadily across the poorly lit roadway until he disappeared for only a second in a pool of darkness just off the entrance to the Guesthouse.

And then he caught sight of the man walking again under the light, but something was different. The gait was the same, but the shock of white hair had transformed into a white turban, and the man now had a slight limp that made him wobble. He was a Bengali. Devon was surprised. There had been no time for someone new to enter the picture. Devon's perception had been wrong. It was something of a puzzle for him. He had been so sure it was one of the expats walking, a little drunk.

The next day he spoke to Khokan, one of the local drivers the Project used. Khokan was small, wiry, and a bit of a rogue, but always engaging. He was adept at adjusting the gas receipts for a little extra pocket money. Devon knew he did it, but the amount was so small that he didn't want it brought to the attention of the Project Manager. It would mean instant dismissal for Khokan. Devon knew he was just the man he needed for his *bustee* experience. After relating to Khokan what he wanted to do, Khokan looked at him incredulously. "Mr. Devon, no. Not good. Trouble, boss. No good to go there."

Devon stepped through the gateway, and suddenly he was in the *bustee*. Khokan was just in front of him, peering back occasionally, looking a little anxious. He was surprised at how good Devon's disguise was. He looked like a Dhaka man, wearing a *lunghi*, knotted at the waist. The colour of the skin application they had used on Devon, and the ragged clothes were just right. Devon followed him into the dingy shack. A crow swooping low just grazed his hair as he walked. The arrangement was simple: Khokan was to meet him at sunrise at the spot where they parted. Khokan thought he was a little mad, but Devon had always been generous to him.

As planned, Devon found a dark corner and curled up in it. He simply wanted to quietly observe things, to get a sense of what it felt like to be a part of it all, the *bustee*. Nothing more. Nearby, along the sidewalks and adjacent to a high brick wall, there were the squatters' huts, all of them put together with tin and sheets of plastic. Inside some of them he could see a rude wooden platform on which people slept.

Devon watched the comings and goings. So many people everywhere, moving, bustling about, talking. He simply wanted to observe, nothing more. A few children were crying nearby. An old woman sat on her haunches preparing a meal. The stench of a refuse dump behind the hut was overpowering at first, but in a few moments Devon had adjusted to it.

For hours through the night, Devon had stayed awake fighting his fatigue. He had not been able to sleep soundly for the previous three nights thinking about his venture into the slums.

From a small hole in the opposite corner of the ramshackle hut, Khokan could see that Devon truly looked like a sleeping Bengali. Khokan smiled as Mr. Devon dropped off into a deep-sea sleep.

Devon was dreaming. In the early morning light, Khokan observed Devon's eyelids moving rapidly and fluttering. Devon was dreaming that he was a Bengali man. The Bengali man suddenly woke up with a start, surveyed his surroundings, was reassured by the familiar, and then dropped back into his own strange dream. Devon awoke. He remembered his dream. In the first few seconds, he wondered if he was a Bengali man dreaming that he was Devon, or if he was Devon dreaming that he had been a Bengali man. There seemed to be a blur between the one and the other. For a millisecond there was no distinction.

Devon awoke. He was in a hut in a slum in downtown Dhaka. Khokan was there and smiling at him. He smiled back.

Devon took a very long, hot shower to remove the skin colour application Khokan had given him. The pigment washed off easily. Afterwards, he drank two pots of piping hot coffee with a piece of lightly buttered toast. He always wished the staff would butter the toast when it came out of the toaster rather than bringing the butter separately.

Must have been part of the British colonial legacy, he thought ruefully. Devon had always felt that the British had left much but taken more. A local man he had met while walking in Chittagong had told him that the British had dismantled and taken the house away, leaving only the floorboards behind. Rule Brittania.

At the Canadian Club that night, Devon met Bukowski. They smoked two Partagas Churchills and drank several Heineken beer. All of the regulars were there, but the two of them sat at a separate table by the pool. Bukowski asked Devon if he ever thought about the one special day when he could do whatever he wished.

Devon smiled, "I've thought about it, but I haven't come up with anything special yet."

P.J. Powell had reached the stage in his life where he didn't give a damn about what other people thought of him. Not a religious man and not needing to be loved by everyone, he spoke his mind, and in speaking his mind, he began to define himself, for himself. The small circle of expat Canadians who frequented the Club found him curious, and a little dangerous to their self-esteem. He had a first-rate mind, first-rate because he thought for himself, and didn't simply regurgitate the opinions he had read in the newspapers, papers which were always a few days old by the time they arrived at the Club from the Canadian Consulate Office. His comments were often barbed, spiked to elicit good, hard conversation or even debate, but most of the regulars feared him in the way a timid hockey forward fears a body check by some barbarian from the Northern Ontario bush. But he couldn't be avoided. He was there, implacable, like an unwanted gnome on a manicured, suburban lawn.

He ordered a double rum and coke and took it to a table just outside the tennis courts. A middle-aged woman with shapely legs was taking tennis lessons from the Club pro. She was having trouble with her serve. As he sipped his drink, P.J. noticed Devon and a fellow he hadn't seen before, entering the Club grounds. He smiled, and catching Devon's eye, he raised his glass in salute. Devon waved, and then the two men entered the Club to get drinks.

A moment later Devon introduced Steve Metcalfe, saying, "P.J. is our resident chicken expert. He's here to help the chickens grow bigger breasts."

Metcalfe stifled a chuckle and asked, "Are you having any success?"

P.J. shrugged, having often encountered comic sallies about his line of work. He placed a coaster over the mouth of his glass to keep the flies away. "It's all in the feed. If there's better feed, they'll be bigger breasts. But more to the point, gentlemen, why is there nowhere in this country where we can get a pint of draft Guinness. It's the closest thing to poetry in beer, and without it, I'm reduced to rum and coke. You have to remember that poetry is a national sport in this country. So why there should be no Guinness is a mystery to me."

Two of the regulars walked by their table and nodded in greeting. P.J. noticed that the woman on the court was missing more and more of the tennis balls that she tossed above her head, and was becoming a bit vexed.

Devon swallowed the last bit of Heineken in his glass and replied, "Have you forgotten that this is a Muslim country, and, by virtue of that fact, is as dry as a bone in the Sahara. We're lucky to have what we've got."

P.J. raised one of his patrician eyebrows in mock disbelief, and countered, "You know as well as I do Devon that there's a not so underground culture here where you can get a drink outside of the confines of the international clubs. That being so, and given the fine poetic traditions in this country, where is the Guinness?"

Metcalfe, a short, plump man with thinning blonde hair, waved a stubby finger in the air. "That's a non sequitur," he exclaimed as if he had just won a significant point in a debate.

"Yes, that is a non sequitur, I believe." P.J. observed the man closely and found himself smiling involuntarily at the extended finger of challenge. Metcalfe reminded him of a cuddly, overgrown cherub, wearing the trademark iron ring of the engineering fraternity.

"What, pray tell, is that Steve?" P.J. queried.

Metcalfe was flushed and a little embarrassed at having to ex-plain. "It's a term, a term that means it doesn't follow that just because there are poetic traditions in this country that there will be Guinness. It's a non sequitur. Beer doesn't have anything to do with poetry."

"Oh, doesn't it though," P.J. continued, "did you know that the late, great Al Purdy, one of our own great Canadian poets, said that if he were afloat on a boat on all of the beer that he had consumed, he couldn't see to the shore. Now that's the connection."

Metcalfe tried to say something, but nothing managed to come out but a few awkward stammerings.

Devon shook his head at P.J. who was grinning devilishly and asked, "You've been here all afternoon I presume?"

"No, not at all. I arrived a little before you did. I was reading a bit of Bangladeshi poetry this morning and felt the need for something to cap it. Since there's no Guinness, it had to be Captain Morgan, and the ubiquitous, cosmopolitan levelizer, coke."

"Well, well," Devon said, "I didn't realize you were into poetry. I thought women were at the top of the agenda."

P.J. smiled and leaned forward on the table, "Women, my dear friend are inseparable from poetry. Just as, I might add, that little iron ring on your finger is inseparable from your profession." Metcalfe nervously turned the ring on his finger, not knowing what to make of this strange chicken expert. He looked uncomfortable.

"But you were saying just a minute ago that beer and poetry were the connection to make," Devon said, enjoying the off-the-wall banter that was P.J.'s trademark conversational style.

"Devon, if the Vatican can promulgate the fantastic concept of a holy trinity, why can't I modestly suggest the secular trinity of poetry, women, and beer." P.J. sipped at his rum and coke, and then guffawed loudly in Metcalfe's direction. Metcalfe smiled weakly, his eyes searching for an escape route.

"Seriously Devon, if you subtract the beer from my argument, and take a look at Bangladeshi poetry, specifically the poetry of Jibanananda Das, you come across tributes to one Banalata Sen, the woman of his dreams and the object of his finest poems. Banalata Sen is the ideal woman."

Devon thought immediately of the beautiful woman he had seen at the party the week before. The name suited her, he thought to himself. Banalata Sen. He wondered who she was. She was certainly the closest thing to a living poem that he had ever seen. A lawn chair grated noisily across the patio flagstones breaking Devon's reverie. Metcalfe muttered something about saying hello to some fellows he had met on his bridge project, and was gone. P.J. toasted him with his glass and watched him slink slowly away to one of the far tables adjacent to the tennis courts. He looked askance at Devon with a mischievous smile.

"Hope I haven't offended the man Dev. He was so quiet- even for an engineer. Or maybe he doesn't enjoy talking about poetry."

"Could be," Devon replied, as he watched a woman take another wild swing at a ball she had tossed into the air. The late afternoon settled in around them. A waiter collected empty beer cans from the table beside theirs. Several crows were passing overhead, just beyond the high east wall of the Club. Three small children scampered about in the playground shouting in French and English.

Whenever he began to feel totally used up, drained from his work, and exhausted in spirit, he knew he needed to get away. Whenever the crowds seemed to be too much, the traffic too chaotic, the smells too offensive, he knew he needed to escape. Kathmandu was not much more than an hour's flying time away, but it was a different world, and a more joyous one somehow. He was going alone, although he sensed that P.J. wanted to come. P.J. had talked about going to Chitwan to see rhinos and perhaps even a tiger, but Devon simply wanted to be alone. He wanted to leave Dhaka behind him for a while. He wanted to see temples and to feel the excitement of Thamel, the tourist area of Kathmandu. He had no desire to go on a trek or to climb a mountain. That was too much like work. Some people, he mused, felt the need to be punished even on their holidays. So, they went trekking or climbing according to the scripted tour they had read about in the weekend papers, and talked endlessly to their friends about what a great experience it had been. That wasn't for him. He wanted the commercial flash of Thamel, and the grandeur of the Durbar Squares, the easy commingling of commerce, faith, and pollution that was the drawing card of the Kathmandu Valley.

Flying into Tribhuvan Airport, Devon always remembered a young engineer he had worked with years earlier. The man, ambitious and talented, had left his family in Bangkok for a short holiday while he returned to Kathmandu where they lived, and where he worked on a two year assignment. His return flight from Bangkok had crashed into the side of a mountain adjacent to the Airport, and he had perished, the bright promise of a gifted engineer extinguished forever. He remembered the man giving a lecture at their office with vivid slides of Kathmandu's streets and of the family enjoying an elephant safari at Chitwan National Park. It was that lecture that had piqued his curiosity about Nepal. The sad memory always gave Devon's landing at the airport a melancholy aspect.

Thamel was a wild hodgepodge of streets, the offspring of a city planner gone mad. Perhaps that's why it was so attractive in an off-beat kind of way. After Devon had checked into his lodgings at the Kathmandu Guest House, he made his way to Durbar Square in the very heart of the city. Bicycle rickshaws moving in both directions contended with cars, motorcycles, and pedestrians of every size and hue. The rough, narrow streets were strewn with refuse. The scent of incense and sun-cooked garbage filled the air. Two emaciated dogs were copulating in a doorway. Devon felt a sprinkling of something wet on the top of his head. He quickly moved towards the far side of the street to avoid any further offerings from the second-story city dwellers. The tiny shops overflowed to the street, with antiques, gurkha knives, and heavy sweaters hanging from the outer walls. Devon thought that if ever there was a tourist mecca, this would be it. Ancient mysteries spliced with rampant commercialism. A neighbour-hood shrine for a god on every corner. What more could you ask for after running rapids or scaling summits, than the funky playground of Kathmandu.

Kumari: the living goddess. Devon lowered his head under the low entranceway and stepped into the inner courtyard of the living goddess in Durbar Square. The wood carvings decorating the windows and overhangs of the building were ornate and weathered. Pigeon droppings were everywhere, staining wooden deities and brickwork equally. Devon was careful to keep a lookout for the pigeons, and avoid being caught directly under them. A small offering box stood at the entrance of the courtyard. An old man looked down upon him from a second-story window. A sign in English said that taking pictures of Kumari was forbidden. Devon dropped some rupee notes into the tiny slot on top of the box. The old man motioned for him to wait.

A few moments later a young girl, the Kumari, suddenly presented herself at the window above him. She looked at him briefly, for just an instant, and was gone. A splash of gorgeous colour and an indifferent gaze for a few seconds was all he could remember of her. Like a small and precious bird alighting on a branch and then gone. But Devon was awestruck by the experience. He felt a youthful innocence welling up inside him, something he hadn't felt in years. It was not that there was any kind of physical attraction for the pre-pubescent girl. It was the symbol of who she was, whom she represented. For Devon, she was the quintessential woman, the pure goddess, and he was moved.

Returning to the Guest House, he walked as if in a daze. The streets, with their brightly decorated shrines, the smells of incense, the overpowering stench from refuse, the gritty air itself, all of this commingled into a small universe, and he was ecstatic. Tears came to his eyes. He knew then, in one of life's sudden epiphanies, that spiritual mysteries and the stinking filth of an open sewer were there, at hand, equally accessible, and as close as they had always been. You could make the choice to see whatever you wished to see, and to see both at the same time was a revelation.

Devon stopped for a beer at one of the second-story terrace restaurants that were found everywhere in Thamel. From a table overlooking the street he could see the people and the traffic a short distance below. He sighed in relief at being here, here in this place so different from Dhaka. He thought about his little adventure in the slums with Khokan and wondered, a little sadly, what good it had been. Had he been anything but a slum tourist after all was said and done? A timid spectator of sorts.

What bothered him was that he needed to do something positive. He wanted desperately to find a way to do something more than to indulge in a curious kind of voyeurism. He sipped at his beer and looked down upon a group of young backpackers striding through the street, laughing and going into a small shop for some ready-made sandwiches and soft drinks. His own backpacking days were far behind him, but he could identify with them and a smile came to his lips in the fond and distant memories. He ordered a light lunch and decided to spend the afternoon by walking up to Swayambhunath, the famous monkey temple. It had beckoned from the fourth floor rooftop patio of the Guest House where he took his coffee in the early morning.

From the temple he could see much of the valley and the ring of mountains surrounding it. A polluted haze settled on everything, obscuring buildings, people, and plants. It seemed the world was getting smaller and smaller, and with every increase in speed, and in telecommunications, it also seemed to be getting grimier and grimier. At least, that's the way it felt to him. The beauty of the temple with its Buddhas set in niches, and above everything, the haunting eyes, the serene eyes of the compassionate Buddha, were like a promise, a promise from the past, and a promise to the future, but the gritty present was bleary, blasted, and gray.

Suddenly, he needed to pee. Here he was, at the top of the Monkey Temple, and he needed to pee, and pee at once. Devon shook his head. It was incredible to him that whenever he was in a bookstore, a museum, or a temple, he felt an overpowering need to urinate. It had been the same since he was a boy. He hastened down the steep stairs just below the temple. Young boys were using flattened plastic bottles to slide down short stretches of sloping concrete at either side of the stone stairway. He wished he had not had the beer earlier. He avoided people coming up the stairs by keeping one hand on the pipe railing. He was taking two stairs at a time now, and using all his powers of control. He gritted his teeth and carried on. When he reached the entrance gate with its huge prayer wheels to one side, he looked for a restaurant, for a shop of some kind, any kind.

A young man by the entrance gate came up to him, and asked, "You need tour guide... need ride to Thamel?"

Devon answered through his teeth, "No, I need to find a wash-room, a toilet. Do you know where I can find a toilet?"

The youth struggled with the words, and then said, "Yes, yes, you need pee-pee," he offered, wriggling his index finger, by way of showing he understood. Devon nodded grimly and followed him towards a side street. The boy stopped by a rickety tin gateway, off its hinges, and he went in, motioning for Devon to follow. Three, old, toothless women were in a backyard, sorting kindling. The boy spoke to them rapidly, pointing to Devon. One of the women pointed to a rough outhouse at one end of the yard. There were planks on the sodden ground that served as a pathway to the outhouse. The women began laughing uproariously while looking at Devon's pained face. Devon hurried to the outhouse. Inside, it was dark and very wet. He relieved himself while holding the ramshackle door shut with one arm behind him. He had to keep his head down to clear the low, uneven ceiling. He urinated above a filthy hole in the floor while balancing on two boards on either side of the hole. After what seemed a little eternity, he quickly returned through the yard and onto the street. The boy was smiling conspiratorially, and the women were hugely enjoy-ing themselves.

Devon left the boy with a few rupees and started walking down the sloping hill towards Thamel. An Italian tour group passed him, snapping pictures and talking animatedly as they made their way up the hill to the temple. He felt totally renewed and chuckled to himself at the state of the outhouse. It was without a doubt the worst of all the

Asian outhouses he had ever used. He had a new low benchmark to go by. Somehow, he wished he could forget the dozen or so decrepit outhouses he had used in over a decade of experience in Asia, but they were there, burned indelibly into his memory, never to be forgotten. The bittersweet joys of international travel in the new millenium.

The next few days were bright with short outings to nearby Patan and Bhaktipur. He met a middle-aged American couple from Los Angeles who toured with him. They spent their days visiting temples and shrines, and their evenings at different restaurants around Thamel, sampling the local Newari cuisine. The couple enjoyed shopping for chess sets, wool carpets, and silver anklets, enough anklets, Devon thought, to satisfy a brace of family and friends for several years to come. They were kind and considerate companions though, and Devon missed them when they left for Tibet. He desperately wanted to join them to see the sights in Lhasa, particularly the Potala, the monastery palace of the Dalai Lamas, but he had to return to Dhaka to complete his assignment. He left Kathmandu feeling refreshed and ready for his work.

P.J. Powell was about to visit Abdul Chowdhury, a man whom he respected and felt slightly diffident towards. Diffidence was an awkward emotion for P.J. to experience. He found it very odd, and somehow comforting, that he would feel an emotion such as diffidence. As he was shaving his throat and chin, he remembered the quiet way he had met Chowdhury.

P.J. had been at an exhibit of bicycle rickshaw art, the colourful folk art that covered the ubiquitous rickshaws of Dhaka. Chowdhury had been studying a piece that depicted the Tower of London. P.J., seeing his absorption in the artwork, commented that the British influence had at least inspired a portable kind of creativity. Chowdhury, amused by the insight, had remarked that the folk art on rickshaws was probably the only indigenous art that even the poorest sector of society could enjoy on a daily basis.

P.J. continued to shave his cheeks and the tender area he so often nicked just under his nose as he speculated on the future of the art form. He had begun to notice that more and more of the rickshaws tended to sport coloured photo layouts of recent Bangladeshi movie stars rather than the simpler, more artistic renderings of scenes and places. He showered and then dressed quickly and left for his appointment with Chowdhury.

On his way out of the Guest House, he was startled to see a huge black bull tethered in the vehicle waiting area just outside the reception office. The clerk told him that it was for the Muslim holy celebration a day away. It was a magnificent Indian bull with a huge hump. The creature was glossy black, and fat, and serene.

Chowdhury's home was very large and comfortably opulent, and there were books, books everywhere: on the side tables, on the window sills, and piled high on wooden chairs against the wall. His bookshelves, extending from floor to ceiling, were filled to capacity. He lived alone, P.J. had learned, his wife having died, and his only son living in England. He lived alone but enjoyed the company of a brace of friends from all walks of life. People were drawn to him by his great personal charm and warmth, his slightly distracted air, and his generosity. What struck P.J. was the refined, genteel elegance that Chowdhury exuded. He was a natural aristocrat but with an inviting, populist manner. There was an attractive intensity about the man, with his great mane of white hair, his golden complexion, and the long, delicate fingers that he used so expressively in conversation.

One of Chowdhury's house servants offered P.J. tea and some delicious-looking appetizers. As soon as he had finished, the house servant was there with more, but P.J. smiled and graciously declined.

There was a pause, a comfortable silence, as one of the servants announced that dinner was ready.

Soon they were called to an excellent meal of wonderfully tender beef and chicken dishes with rice and two kinds of dal. P.J. enjoyed the fine dinner, noticing how deftly Chowdhury ate with his right hand, Bangladeshi style. After dinner, they talked about rickshaw art, and about the place in the city, Bangsal Street, where they could be purchased. Their conversation ranged from art and the American writers they enjoyed, to the chaotic Dhaka traffic. They moved easily from topic to topic, enjoying the free play of ideas and opinions.

And then Chowdhury looked directly at P.J. and said, "So what do you think of my Bangladesh?"

P.J. could see the look of curious expectancy in his eyes. He didn't want to offend his new friend, but he knew too that he had passed the age when he could lie graciously with a half-smile on his lips.

P.J. put down his tea, "I've been coming here off and on for the last five years. It looks to me that things have gotten a lot better, but there's still a lot that remains to be done. Take the government and corruption. Corruption is too widespread. Too many public officials are looking for *baksheesh*, to supplement their incomes. I don't know how it can be done, really, but if that isn't made right, the big things aren't going to happen. Too many people are living too close to the edge, in city slums, and they need help. Your political parties, with the *hartals*, sometimes two or three a month, are holding back the good things that happen in a healthy economy, and that means suffering. Unless these nation-wide political strikes stop, real progress just isn't in the cards."

Chowdhury looked thoughtful and a little sad, his face down-cast. "Yes, yes, that is true. I'm afraid that even at the higher levels in the public service, it is a real problem. You see, it's a part of the aid mentality. Initiative in the public sector is a very tough issue. The wages are so low that many need to use their positions, to make them 'wet' as they say locally, to send off their children to the better schools here, and abroad, to universities in England, and America. Besides, we do not have pensions to soften our retirement as you do. A wet position, to be kind, is a sort of retirement savings plan. Consider that."

P.J. took a long sip of his tea, considering what he believed to be a specious argument about the need for "wet" positions. No wonder, he thought, that Bangladesh had been ranked as the most corrupt country in the world. He decided to change his tack. "I'm curious about the political situation here. I understand there are new political parties springing up with real popular support. Are these new parties strong enough to displace the two old contenders, the *begums*?"

Chowdhury took a long sip of his tea and smacked his lips with satisfaction. Powell could see him formulating his thinking, wanting to be precise and forthright. "In times to come Bangladesh will surely see a class of cultures and wills between the fundamentalists and the new democratic league. These are the new elements. The political contest is theirs. The old parties are dying away because of corruption, although it's a slow death to be sure.

I fear the fundamentalists. They are rabid and violent and extremely well organized. They are capable of anything.

The new democratic league, however, is something altogether new. Their leader, Iqbal Rahman, is a poet, a true poet, rare for a politician. If he can survive, then I think that we will see something very different in my country. You can, no doubt, guess my affiliation, but things are in such flux now, that I don't know what will happen. It is a most dangerous time."

Chowdhury paused for a moment, reflecting on what he had said, and then continued, "Things are changing. There's a new spirit in the game. What you say about corruption is true, but we have a new man in the country now. I believe we are entering a new, golden age."

P.J. smiled, his eyes bright. " Now that's the most interesting thing I've heard in a long time. Who is this new man?"

"I remember seeing Iqbal Rahman with the sun on his face at a political rally. Masses of people cheering wildly. His speech had resonated in their hearts. I know it did in mine. He knew it, and he felt it, I could tell. Across the city street, people were hanging from balconies and waving madly. Young women threw garlands of flowers at him. I could see there was something of great power that he was drawing from the crowd. The upturned, ecstatic faces were like ten thousand petals turned to face the sun. When he raised his arms, extending them in triumph, even his aides pressed closer to him, wanting to touch him. Everyone was standing and cheering. It was a great moment I tell you.

For a man like Iqbal Rahman, the reality of politics is like a game, a child's game of snakes and ladders. You can be feeling exhilarated as he was on that day, but you can also be disappointed and crushed just as easily the next day, or worse. Already he is receiving death threats. His new political party has swept through the country firing up the nation and attracting converts from the established parties. His impassioned speeches play on the instincts of a people ready for dramatic change. He believes in his destiny and he is ready for anything. What he cannot abide is for things to stay the same. Better death, you see, than the status quo. But the death threat is real, very real, and I am afraid for him.

The fundamentalists have even taken to throwing acid at their opponents. Yes, indeed, they've taken a page from spurned, would-be lovers and property grabbers."

"What do you mean?"

"Think about it. Even an improvised explosive device, the bomb by the side of the road, requires a certain amount of sophistication and training behind it, but sulphuric acid, battery acid, is readily available, as near as the closest vehicle. Cheap and convenient.

A suitor spurned by a woman obtains a vial of the stuff and throws it in the face of his humiliation. Or, someone covets a neighbour's property. He knows that the costs of plastic surgery, perhaps several surgeries, will often force victim families to sell their property.

You see, my friend, there are only two remedies, or partial remedies against an acid attack. The first is water, plain water, dousing the stricken part of the body with water just after it happens. The second is plastic surgery to correct, or try to correct the disfigurement. And now thugs, political thugs, use it as a cheap weapon to terrorize. Iqbal Rahman and his people are targets. They must be careful."

"That's unconscionable!"

Chaudhury chuckled grimly, "That's Bangladesh."

P.J. was just returning to the inside bar for a drink when he ran into the woman who had been so frustrated with her serve on the tennis court. He smiled warmly, and somewhat hopefully said,

"I hope that your serve is getting better." The woman looked at him quickly, her quick, sharp glance taking him in at one fell swoop. She liked the warm, smooth tones of his voice.

"I don't know about that," she said, "but I thought I'd better stop before my curses became louder."

P.J. thought she looked very compact and darkly attractive. There was a forcefulness about her that was almost daunting, but her allure was in her handsome features and sturdy frame. She had excellent legs. He introduced himself, and learned that her name was Lise Thibeault, a Vice-President from a private public sector reform consulting company operating out of Ottawa. He offered to buy her a drink, but she said that if he did, he would have to allow her to buy him one.

"Reciprocity," she said, "is a very Canadian thing."

Soon they were talking about their experiences overseas and some of the difficulties they were encountering in their work in Dhaka. By the time P.J. was enjoying his third drink with her, he was beginning to flirt with her, and she seemed hugely amused by him, enjoying the attention, and quietly trying to size him up.

"Do you play tennis? I'd like to have a game or two with you if you have some time on Friday."

P.J. laughed, "I'm sorry. I don't play, but I'd like to suggest a river cruise. My treat of course. You know, you really can't appreciate Bangladesh until you've seen it from its wonderful rivers."

Lise, her face flushed, raised her glass of red wine, and said, "There is absolutely nothing I would rather do, provided, of course, you have dinner with me when we return. And that is my treat."

Lise Thibeault sat next to P.J. on the upper deck of the cruise boat. A brightly striped blue and white awning overhead shielded them from the morning sun. There were only six other passengers aboard. The broad expanse of the river stretched before them offering vistas of life on the great waterways of the delta. Barges heavily laden with silt slowly made their way downstream, while sailboats plied alongside them under dun coloured sails.

Lise was impressed with this distinguished looking gentleman who was always ready with a quip or remark on just about anything. What intrigued her was that he hadn't flirted with her at all since they met early that morning. He seemed a bit shy and reserved towards her in the bright light of day. She smiled, wondering about him, and about whether or not she had been too forward in her approach. She was an aggressive woman who did not mince words, but she was also a woman of sensitivity and inventiveness.

P.J. felt a little awkward with this very self-assured woman. He found her incredibly attractive, especially when her eyes would light up to punctuate the point she was making. He was a little intimidated by her, by the manner in which she listened to him, with a slightly amused smile, as if he were a precocious child on a field trip. He began to experience the self-doubt that troubled him whenever he was truly attracted to a woman, whenever the flirtation that he so often indulged in seemed totally inadequate to the situation. She was being playful, and he felt so wooden, so inarticulate.

"P.J., I'm only here for three weeks. I want to make the most of my time here, and I think we can be friends, very good friends. Do you mind if we spend this time together?" She touched his hand as she spoke the last word.

P.J. was startled by her boldness. He admired the way she softened her voice as she spoke, giving him a hint of intimacy if he chose. "Of course, we can be together for this week, but it's so short a time. Are you coming back?"

"Yes," she answered, "but only for short two-week missions every few months. Can you live with that?" Her eyes teased him as she spoke.

"It's doable," P.J. said, making one of those instinctive, pivotal decisions that changes the course of a person's life, "if we can agree on one thing."

"And pray tell, what might that be, kind sir?"

"You'll stay with me at my house. I've rented a house in Gul-shan, beginning next month."

Lise smiled. "Don't you just love being older. We don't have to pretend. We can save time and just say what we want. A kind of time compression, isn't it?"

"Yes, my lady, so it is." P.J. spent the rest of the cruise in a state of contented delirium.

Once Devon had returned from Zia International Airport and unpacked, he went for a walk. He enjoyed walking the back streets of Gulshan in the early evening, just before the sun went down, and before the recorded prayers of the muezzins began. Many of the construction workers were still at work. He saw a man six stories up, perched high on bamboo scaffolding, putting some finishing touches on some mortar work. A man pouring tea in a roadside shop smiled, inviting him to stop. Devon returned the smile and declined, using the hand gesture he saved for these polite roadside encounters. He was always very careful not to eat or drink anything from the street. A few children ran by him, smiling, as they chased a small dog.

He noticed a few lights coming on in the wealthy residential area he was walking through. Adjacent to some of the luxurious homes, there were flimsy cardboard and tin shacks, mad, ramshackle arrangements, all the more noticeable because of the adjacent splen-dour of walled gardens and imposing patios. Looking into one of the open doorways of a group of shacks, he saw a woman squatting as she prepared a meal. The sharply spiced aromas were wonderful. He swallowed involuntarily. It seemed to him that he hardly used his nose back in Canada. Here, in this place, it was working to capacity every day.

As he walked through a narrow backstreet behind a mosque, he caught sight of a soft, golden light emanating from a single bulb hanging above a doorway. He walked towards it, drawn by it, attracted by the suffused and glowing beauty of the light.

He walked as if entranced, as if suddenly becalmed by a waking dream. He imagined that the lighted doorway was the entrance to a family of his own loved ones, a brace of kinsmen that waited in welcome, an elderly grandfather perhaps, a wife, children, and friends. The glowing, golden light was the light of welcome that beckoned him home. Home. He carried that shimmering fantasy with him as he walked by the well-lit doorway, and back to the Guest House, back to a world where dozens of shining lights paled to insignificance beside that single welcoming dream of home, a home that did not exist in any real world of his own.

The next morning, from his balcony on the fifth floor of the Guest House, Devon could see into the walled yard opposite him. Several coconut palms formed a perimeter just inside the low wall. There was a small garden, a few goats, and a simple house, with an outdoor kitchen. Several small children played with a stick and a bicycle rim, pushing the rim forward with the stick and keeping it moving around the yard. It could be a village house in the country, Devon thought. But what struck him was the colour of the front wall of the little house. He remembered the name of a colour: ochre. That name might describe it, he mused, but could the name convey the effect it had on him? It seemed such an ancient colour, with its variegated shades under the bright, early morning sun. The colour mellowed him, made him feel content and at ease with the world. He had never seen a colour like it in Canada. A bit of the paint was worn away, and revealed a slightly darker brown underneath. He felt so strange.

What was happening to him? Last night, the light in the doorway had seemed to him to be the entrance to a world of close relations and human warmth. And this morning, the colour of a wall, a sun-deepened light brown wall, touched him in a way no painting he had ever seen had. What was happening to him? He had just returned from a holiday to Nepal, feeling refreshed and rejuvenated. But something in his soul had opened to a lighted electric bulb in a doorway, and a sun-worn colour on a wall. Was he becoming sentimental and foolish from having spent too much time alone?

He went back to his work, reviewing a report he was working on. He wanted to push the feeling away, to get back to something clear and hard and logical like an engineering drawing or a spreadsheet where there were no confusing emotional tones.

That evening Devon was invited out to dinner. He looked for-ward to seeing the couple, the Coopers, and to eating some excellent roast beef. He smiled, thinking that the Coopers were the only expats he knew who not only had access to wonderful beef but to horseradish as well. Horseradish was a rarity. He had never seen horseradish for sale in any of the markets. But things were changing. Until a few years ago, potatoes were one of the more unusual vegetables to find in the markets, but now they were becoming very common thanks to an aid project that supported growing potatoes. He wondered about radishes.

A houseboy greeted him just outside the Cooper house as he left his vehicle. Devon instructed his driver to wait for him. As he entered their home, he instantly recognized the beautiful woman he had met at a party a few weeks earlier. She was sitting in their living room laughing at something Tom Cooper had said.

"Ah Devon, have you met Mina?"

Devon nodded, tongue-tied for an instant. "Yes, we did, at the party. The McCann party."

Mina looked at him smiling, and said, "Unfortunately, you left early. We hadn't a chance to talk at all." Devon was surprised that she remembered him. He marvelled at the bright fluid beauty of her face, the rose flush of her cheeks, the clear brow. She was beaming. It was all he could do to just pretend that this was simply a normal social occasion. He heard himself saying something, and then Tom Cooper responding. She was the most beautiful woman Devon had ever seen. Everything else was unimportant. Everything else seemed to recede.

Devon hardly noticed the roast beef. He ate perfunctorily. He chatted appropriately. He forgot about the horseradish burning his tongue. He looked at Mina in discreet glances, taking care not to simply stare at her too long. He felt like a schoolboy with a crush: full of innocence and hope.

At first it was Mina's eyelashes that captivated him, and then her raven hair, and then her dimpled smile, and then her perfect teeth. Everywhere he looked, she was perfection. He asked her about her work with an international aid agency. She answered in tones and cadences that numbed him, made him feel weak and warm and wistful. She seemed to be smiling at him with her eyes, and in truth, she was. She could see his distraction and was flattered, and a little surprised.

Devon looked at the wall clock in his room with its picture of the Guest House from its southern corner on the face of it. Toronto was eleven hours behind Dhaka time. By that reckoning he was living in the future. He loved that thought. He prepared himself a bath and chose a Montecristo number four to smoke while he bathed. He usually showered, but every couple of months he enjoyed a leisurely smoke in the bathtub. He opened the bathroom window, placed an ash tray on the ample sidearm of the tub, and lit up.

Time. Time in Canada seemed to him different than time in Bangladesh. Canadian time spilled into one day after another, endlessly, monotonously. But here, in this place, time was compressed, vital, intense. He would usually be on contract for three to six months at a time. But in that time, it seemed to him that he lived more, experienced more, felt more, than he ever did back home.

He watched the blue smoke curl up above him. In his work in Canada there was a stultifying sameness in his daily encounters, a deadening round of habit that made time extend meaninglessly from the present into the past, and this in spite of interesting work. Here, there was a richness to experience, a variety that confounded you at times, but one that never left you with a blank, dull look on your face staring at a wall. He remembered a phrase from some novel he had read: "the fascination of nugacity." That was what he remembered in time past, Toronto time. Time present and time future was Dhaka time: living time.

He wondered if it was because he was so lonely in Toronto. He had friends there and a few relatives that he rarely saw, but nevertheless, his experience in Toronto was essentially null. That was the word that summed up his experience there: null. In Dhaka, and in Asia, Devon was vital and sharp and thoughtful in an emotional kind of way that was a counterpoint to the hard logic of his engineering work. It surprised him, and delighted him. It made him feel extraordinary. He was careful to lightly tap the one inch of gray ash from his cigar to the ash tray.

That was the feeling that he cherished- of being extraordinary. In Dhaka he felt extraordinary. Nothing had really changed. He did the same work, engineering work of all kinds, to the best of his ability. But Bangladesh brought out something more, something enhanced. It was not really a question of work. It was more an experience of being. Here he felt different from the conventional, common self that he knew himself to be in Canada. Perhaps, he thought, it was the spirit of the place that did it.

The bathroom was quite smoke-filled after his hour-long soak, so he left the tub, dried himself off, and turned on the two ceiling fans in his bedroom. He propped up the pillows on his bed, flicked on the remote, and lay back. He watched the BBC news report barely paying attention. He thought about Mina. He thought about how hopeless it all was. She was probably about twenty-seven or twenty-eight, certainly no more. And Devon was a youngish forty-five, at least that's what he considered himself to be, and he wasn't far off. Most people thought he was in his mid thirties. He flicked to another channel. He smiled at seeing the Indian maiden being chased by her handsome suitor in some verdant valley below snow-capped mountains. He had seen the same scene in a hundred different Bollywood variations: the coy, young beauty singing her high-pitched melody while the smitten Romeo chases after her, through a field, around a tree, until finally, they embrace, diffusing ever so slightly, the highly charged sexual tension that constituted the real theme behind it all. He flicked through the channels again and again, mindlessly, not really registering anything on the television, until, bored and restless, he turned it off.

Devon was to meet Mina and her party at Savar, at the site of the fifty meter high memorial to the millions who died in the Bangladesh struggle for independence. Devon was surprised to see the size of the crowds there when he arrived. He made his way through the throngs of people enjoying the gardens and taking pictures of grassy platforms covering the graves of those slaughtered during the war.

He saw her standing near the base of the monument talking excitedly with her friends. She smiled brightly when she caught sight of him. She said something quietly to her friends, and they melted away from her, following discreetly, as Devon and Mina toured the gardens.

"Mina, you look wonderful, as always. I didn't expect these crowds."

"Oh yes, Savar is the heart of Bangladesh. Without their sacrifice, there would be nothing. My uncle, Iqbal Rahman, calls it 'the blood cradle' in his poetry."

"My friend, P.J., has spoken highly of him. He says he is the future of the country."

"Ah, I'm convinced of that, if he can stay safe. There are many who hate him and want to destroy him."

"A politician and a poet! Now, that's refreshing."

"Poetry is the soul of Bangladesh. Even here."

"What do you mean?"

"Did you know one of our liberation poets, Farhad Mazhar wrote a poem to a grenade?"

"Really?"

"Truly. It is quite wonderful. I will send you the poem. It is in a book of poems of our liberation war. Quite lovely, and tender really."

"War poems, tender?"

"You will see."

"I don't think I will ever understand the Bangladeshi soul."

"Why not? It is the same soul as yours but from under a different sun."

Devon looked at her closely, hearing the words she was saying but attending to something else within her, a pure stillness. He was entranced by her, by her beauty, by her innocence, by the fell certainty and confidence behind her words.

"You're staring."

"I'm sorry. I've never met anyone quite like you."

"I should hope not. I like to think of myself as one of a kind. Though I received a western education in America, and dress like a westerner, I am still a Bangladeshi woman, an individual Bangladeshi woman."

Devon took her hand in his and touched it to his lips. Mina withdrew it immediately. Her friends instantly appeared at her side. A group of young men stopped and stared.

"I'm sorry," Devon said.

Devon had just paid the bill for their dinner when he looked at Mina thoughtfully and said,

"Do you think if a thing is perfect, it can ever fail?"

"I don't understand you. Nothing is perfect."

"But the idea behind a thing can be perfect, and that's what makes it perfect."

"Nothing is perfect, ever."

"You are perfect."

"Devon, you're a silly, fond man, but charming."

Devon reached into the zippered pocket of his safari jacket and pulled out a gold chain.

"This is for you."

"It's beautiful. So fine and delicate. Help me put it on."

"There."

Mina reached over for a white jasmine blossom in the vase on their table and then touched Devon's cheek with it. "And this is for you."

"It's perfect. Thank you."

"No, it's not, but it's still for you."

The subtle scent of jasmine filled the air between them, and the days that followed were enchanting. Devon felt as if he were walking suspended three feet off the ground. Everything was brighter, bolder in outline, and somehow vitally connected to him. He began to notice the minute details of things as if they were magnified and open and accessible. Even a paperclip, he mused, held wonders for him.

As he stood on the flat rooftop of the Parbatipur Guest House, atop the third story, just outside the screened-in, tin-roofed patio, Devon was glad he had decided to come up for the weekend with P.J.

and the new woman in his life, Lise. She seemed a good sort, and obviously enjoyed P.J.'s company, always touching him, smiling or laughing in just the right way at each and every witticism that his friend came up with.

Devon loved the view from the roof. Straight ahead, towards the horizon, he could just make out the mountain ranges of Nepal. Towards the front of the Guest House, fronting the street, he could see far and clear to the huge railway buildings on the other side of the tracks.

Parbatipur was a railway town, named after a Hindu goddess, and brought into prominence by British railway men who had seen its potential as a northern center of operations. It was decidedly rural, and green, and sparsely populated for Bangladesh. To his right, just past the screened-in patio, he could see below to another roadway below him. There were some village houses beside a small pond. Two small children were playing with a white duck who was trying to escape their attentions. When they saw him on the roof, they started waving wildly and shouting in Bangla. Devon waved back and then went into the screened-in patio. The screened door closed behind him with a loud bang, just like a cottage door back home he thought. He sat in one of the red wicker chairs and became hidden to the children and the street below. He felt comfortable and relaxed, and free, totally free.

Devon put his legs up on a low wicker table just as P.J. and Lise entered the patio.

"Well Devon, I see you've gotten yourself into the right mode," P.J. said, a smile playing on his lips.

"You know, I'm glad you suggested I come up here with you. It's a real breath of fresh air after Dhaka. How about you Lise, what do you think about the place?"

Lise stood with her hands on her hips, surveying the Brueghel-like scenes on every side.

"I love it. I just love it. I wish we could stay longer than just a few days."

P.J. winked at Devon. "I think a few days is just enough. Any more would be too much. Right, Devon?"

"I suppose so," Devon answered, "but it works a charm on you, this place. I'd take a week if I could."

One of the caretakers came up to the screen door asking if any-one wanted a soft drink. No one cared for a refreshment, and so the caretaker, a Bangladeshi christian named Peter, left with a smile. The caretakers knew only a few words in English, but somehow communi-cation flowed readily enough: meals were served, laundry was done daily, and small errands were attended to. It was quite a life, Devon thought, depending on where you sat.

"I often think about the Brits," Devon began, "I mean look around... the solid buildings all around us were all built by them: the railway workshops, the residential areas for the managers, the station. Look at all of that red brick. And the colour, it reminds me of the map in my public school days back home. Do you remember, the British

Empire was that reddish-pink colour, and it took up a lot of good space on the world map."

P.J. stood up and took in the broad sweep of the landscape, the mass of the railway works, and the solid brick houses in little enclaves not too far distant from the railway station.

"You know Dev, I feel ambivalent about all this, what they left behind. It was good work, and you can be sure, the buildings would be in better shape if the Brits were still in them. Look at all the disrepair. Things are falling apart. But, I somehow think the attitude was all wrong. I mean they were imperialists." P.J. stood staring at a slow train moving to the south.

Lise chuckled, crossing her legs. Devon couldn't help but notice how shapely they were.

"You think they were any different with the French in Quebec?" she said. Devon looked at her, and he could hear the feistiness in her tone, the anger rising. There was something about her conversational style that waited for just such an opening.

"The English bastards did the same to us in Quebec, but no more. Now the game has turned."

P.J. sat back down, smiling carefully. "I don't want to talk about ancient history. Not here. I just wanted to remark that the Brits did a lot of good, but somehow, I don't think they were altruistic."

Lise looked at him with a sarcastic expression. "Altruistic? I think not. What about you Devon? Do you think they were working for the good of the country?"

Devon sighed, shaking his head. "They were empire builders. For the most part I think they were well-intentioned and hard workers. But they were here because they wanted to make a bundle of cash and go back home in style. They spent a lifetime here and then retired in England. The higher up they were, the more they took back with them. That's the nature of imperialists. They never intended to stay here."

Lise looked vindicated, smiling at P.J. "Well Devon, you speak well," she said, "I think the same way."

Devon leaned back in his chair and looked at his two friends. "You know," Devon continued, "Bangladesh is independent now, and the Brits have long gone. They left behind some very solid brick buildings. Did you see those Brit-built brick shit houses? Sure looked like they meant to stay. The British are gone. But things are the same in some ways. Look at us. We live better here than we do back in Canada, just like the Brits did in their time. We're at the top of the food chain in this aid-dependent country. We come here for little stints of work or for two or three years, and then we're gone, a bit richer, with fatter resumes because of the experience. It's much the same thing in a certain way. The British Raj is gone, but the big agencies have taken over the Raj's place. The trimmings are gone, the pomp and feathers and all that, but the people are still dirt poor. We're part of the retinue of the new international Raj."

"Now Dev," P.J. said, "you can't put that on us. There's a helluva lot of corruption and graft that is home-grown. Don't lay all of the crap on us. We're giving, not getting."

"But there are conditions, always conditions, on what we give, from a country to country level. I know it's well intentioned, don't get me wrong, but the donor benefits too you know. Our fees come from that aid. I'm not disagreeing with that. I like to eat too. But you have to admit we're getting as well as giving. That's what I mean when I say we're part of the new, international Raj."

"So what does that make me as a woman?" Lise asked.

Devon looked at her, somewhat puzzled at her remark, and smiled. "Nothing," he said, "nothing more than what you were before you came here: an intelligent, privileged woman, with great legs."

P.J. guffawed. Lise regarded Devon keenly and said, "Why Devon, I didn't think you noticed."

"I care about beauty in all of its forms and manifestations."

"Ah, a romantic," P.J. said, "after Keats. Didn't Keats say that beauty was truth and truth beauty, or something along those lines?" P.J. touched Lise's hand lightly.

"Sadly," Lise replied, "the only beauty that lasts is captured in art. In real life, beauty dies a slow and painful death."

"But the essence of beauty in real life never changes," Devon countered. "What I mean is that beauty issues from a timeless source. So, although, say, a beautiful woman might age, her soul is still beautiful, the spirit that informs the beauty."

"Tell that to my friends," Lise said. "They'd save a fortune on face lifts and spa treatments."

"Devon," P.J. said, "you're a rank idealist, more rank than ideal, I'm afraid. You can't tell me that you find octogenarians beautiful?"

"Why not? A different kind of beauty perhaps, but beauty nevertheless."

"But it's a decayed form of beauty which I don't find attractive in the least, particularly because it reminds me what's in store for me, namely decay and death." P.J. paused for a few seconds and then continued. "There may be a specious splendour in the colourful phosphorescence of decay, but you'll never convince me that that is beautiful."

Devon steepled his fingers together for a moment. "It's what's behind the beauty that gives rise to the beauty. Call it spirit or soul or whatever."

"That's a little too unreal for me," Lise said. "What about your beautiful friend, Mina? If she were to lose her beauty, as she and all living creatures must, would you, could you still find her beautiful?"

P.J. leaned forward, towards Devon, eager to hear what he had to say.

"I tell you," he replied, "it's her soul that I love. Certainly, she's beautiful, and that's what initially caught my attention, but beauty, true beauty, is more than that. It's far deeper that that."

"I think your argument is becoming tediously repetitious," P.J. said. "If she became obese, with dark patches of hair on her face and chest, what then?"

"It doesn't matter."

"Well, I think it does," he said emphatically.

"So do I," Lise said. "I wish it didn't matter, but it does, and that's the world we live in."

"In the end, it's about the essence of beauty. The outward form may change but the essence of beauty remains the same. I believe that."

"God bless you Devon," P.J. said. "That sounds like church dogma. The kind of earnest, idealistic claptrap that turns thinking brains into mush. You're up in the ether at thirty thousand feet while I'm here, right here, on the ground, or close to it at least, in Parbatipur, Bangladesh."

"It's a question of having faith in beauty."

"I'd sure as hell like to see you put to the test."

"I wouldn't," Lise said. "I hope he carries that kind of romantic idealism to the grave with him."

It was almost dark. Around them the sounds of early evening in a northern Bangladeshi railway town filtered through the screened patio, displacing for a few moments their memories, thoughts, and fancies. The laughter of children mingled with the sounds of bicycle rickshaws and barking dogs, and ducks splashing in the pond below. A lovely mellowness settled upon them, and they grew silent. The night covered them softly and easily, cloaking them like a distant, beneficent blessing from a Hindu goddess.

On the short flight back to Dhaka, Devon half listened to P.J.'s monologue on Bangladeshi politics and gazed out the small window at the rice fields and rivers and villages below. The low tones of P.J.'s monotonous voice lulled him into a curious reverie, a waking dream that beguiled him and held him a willing captive.

It was a dream he had once experienced while driving in Nova Scotia. It came back to him like a returned e-mail. At the time it seemed like a premonition, or a glimpse of some Canadian future. The dream infused him with the wonder of reverie commingled with an East Coast sunset. In the dream, he clearly saw a Canadian Prime Minister who was handsome, middle aged, stout, and of Bangladeshi background.

The Prime Minister moved slowly through the corridors, a smile playing across his lips, a response to some anecdote told to him by an aide. What was striking was the love and adulation on the faces of the people in the gallery he had just left. There had never before been anything like it in the country, and that thought was an aspect of the dream. It was odd, this dream sensation. Devon felt that he intuitively understood the feeling tone of the dream, and without knowing what had actually taken place, he was elated somehow and infused with good will.

Surrounding the Prime Minister was something like an aura, something decidedly tinged with grandeur. Yes, Devon thought, that was it. There was a feeling of a Lincoln walking about in the dream, a Canadian Lincoln, at long last, something achieved at great cost, but achieved nevertheless. Devon was suffused with a great tenderness and pride.

And then something had happened, something terrible. The colours of the dream were the colours of sunset. Pinks and golden browns were the dominant colours and hues. Devon lost himself for a while in the colours of the dream, in its sadness.

Suddenly, the reverie broke into fragments as the aircraft landed heavily and clumsily with a thud on the tarmac in Dhaka.

The next day Devon met Mina in the lobby of the Sonargaon Hotel. The observation that she was not wearing his necklace irritated him. They had coffee and a little cheese cake. Her face was warm and beautiful, the face of a woman in love. Suddenly he felt very old. Devon began to think that he was being foolish in seeing a future with this woman. People passed and smiled at her. Devon looked at her oddly, and she could see the trouble in his face.

"Devon, is something the matter? You're so distant suddenly. Has something happened?" Mina's face moved towards him in concern, her eyes bright in anticipation. In his pale blue eyes, she saw the asceticism of his love for her. There was a purity there, a burning white-blue flame in them, that was as intense as it was spiritual. She loved him for the qualities that she ascribed to him, and that she saw clearly and plainly in the high brow, the clear, ice-blue eyes, and the straight, angular nose.

"Nothing's wrong. I must be coming down with something."

Mina looked at him with a great and tender sadness, a sadness commingled with love. Devon had never had anyone look at him in that way before, and he never would again. After dessert, Devon excused himself and returned to his guest house.

Devon wanted to call Mina, but he didn't. He couldn't work in the evenings as he used to. He simply lay on his bed with the pillows propped up, and watched television in a desultory fashion, not really registering what he was viewing. He thought about Mina constantly. He knew she wanted him to call. She'd asked him to, the last time he'd seen her. But he couldn't. He was in a daze really. He didn't know if a relationship was what he wanted. It was all too late. Devon felt empty and wasted, as if he were recovering from a long illness.

He wished he could forget the expression on her face. Her tenderness haunted him. Perhaps, in some curious way, he thought, he was deliberately choosing his desire for solitude rather than love. He knew she was the only woman he had ever loved. There would be no other. Then why did he hesitate?

Why was he such a fool? Why was he so indecisive? She could have any man she wished. She was young and a beauty. She was a Benelata Sen, like the beauty P.J. had mentioned that had entranced a great Bangladeshi poet. She did not need him. He began to feel a profound sorrow, as if he experienced a death. He flicked off the television and went out to the balcony. A man was walking on the street below with a basket of chickens on his head. He looked up at

Devon and smiled. Devon tried to manage a smile but failed. The man continued on his way shouting, *"Mujir, mujir,"* until Devon could no longer see him.

P.J. hurried from his vehicle to the Guest House. As he crossed the parking area just off the reception office, he looked down at the dark red puddle at his feet. His brushed suede shoes and pant cuffs were splashed and stained. Looking to his left he saw two of the staff mopping up the area. He remembered the great black bull and the *Eid* celebration about to occur. Regardless, he thought, the shoes were ruined. He looked forward to his move to a house in a few days.

Just as Devon was enjoying the first taste of his Heineken, a barefoot beggar was making his way towards the gated compound of Iqbal Rahman's home, about a mile away from where Devon was sitting.

Devon was watching a tennis match and peeling the label from his bottle of beer as he sat in the screened-in section of the bar adjacent to the tennis courts. Evening was falling and the lights high atop the poles fencing in the grounds of the Club began to flicker on and gradually burn bright. The sound of a generator could be heard in the background. The patio area where Devon sat was not air conditioned, and though it was very warm and the air close, Devon found it agreeable, a counterpoint to the very cold beer he was drinking. He pulled the wet label away from the bottle in two strips. Then he crumpled each strip into a tiny ball and put them to one side. His habit was to place the balls into the empty bottle when he was finished with it. It was a kind of ritual that he was not even fully conscious of because he had been doing it for years.

A mile away at Iqbal Rahman's gate, a very unkempt man peered through the iron bars and waited. No one would suspect that anything was out of the ordinary if they had happened upon the scene. Beggars would often appear routinely at the gate and wait patiently for someone inside to notice them. Oftentimes, their patience would be rewarded with a bowl of rice and a bit of chicken.

Inside the compound a black Mercedes pulled up to the front door. The uniformed driver stepped out of the car and proceeded to open the rear passenger door, and then stood waiting for his passenger. In a moment the front door of the house opened and Mina gracefully exited with her uncle, Iqbal Rahman, following her into the front yard. He stepped aside to gather a sprig of jasmine from his front garden and gave it to Mina.

The unkempt man watching from behind the iron wrought gate could just see Iqbal Rahman smiling in the waning evening light. He also saw the female attendant wait for Mina to enter the vehicle first. They were moving very slowly, in no hurry to leave the warm ambience of the place.

A bright light was switched on above the driveway and the *chowkidar* stepped out of his hut to open the front gates. He said something in a preemptory manner to the unkempt beggar to step aside. The man moved instantly to one side and stood waiting.

When the car was halfway through the front gates, the beggar gestured pathetically, motioning to Mina to give him alms. Mina said something to the driver and the power window beside Mina came down. She reached into her purse for some small currency notes.

The beggar was very still, transfixed by her beauty and his singular purpose. She was about to pass the notes to the beggar when he reached beneath his tattered *gamsa* and pulled out a small vial. She was smiling and eagerly extending her arm beyond the window to give him the bills. He hesitated. Then she watched him unstop the lid of the vial and cast it directly at her face in a sharp, jerky motion.

For a moment it seemed to her that everything was moving in slow motion. At first the sensation felt as if someone had thrown a soft linen sheet over her. Seconds later, she felt excruciating pain.

The battery acid burned through the tender flesh of her left cheek, and then her left arm as she instinctively tried to fend off the attack. Seconds passed. Acid ripped its way through soft flesh, through clothing, and through a cream-colored jasmine blossom.

After an inordinate silence, there came a staccato of screams, shouts, and terrible, heart-rending cries. And then a flash of searing images and new sounds: the beggar shouting a curse and then running; the *chowkidar* raising his rifle; shots ringing out; the sharp, raucous cawing of crows.

Just as Devon was about to apply some marmalade to his toast, he saw Lise approaching his table. There was no one else taking breakfast.

"Devon, P.J. told me what happened to Mina. I'm so, so sorry. How is she doing now?"

Devon glanced away from Lise for a moment. "I haven't seen her. I've called several times, but she hasn't returned my calls. I don't think she wants to see anyone just yet."

Lise looked puzzled. "What do you mean? But you must insist. She needs you now more than ever. You must see her."

"I've tried. I can't break down the door."

"Have you gone to her home then?"

"No."

"But, why not? I don't understand you! This is incredible."

Devon turned away, shaking his head. He stood up from the breakfast table and made for his room.

"Christ, can't you be a man? She needs you. Go to her."

Devon walked away from her quickly, leaving Lise staring incredulously at his retreat.

"I want to see Mina. Please tell her I am here. My name is Devon Christie. I will not leave until I see her."

The *chowkidar* nodded, left his guard post, and walked up to an open side door where he spoke rapidly for a moment to someone hidden by the afternoon shadows inside, and then he returned.

"Please, come." The *chowkidar* opened the creaking gate and led Devon around the side of the house to a spacious walled garden. A woman dressed in a black *chador* stood with her back to Devon. The *chowkidar* nodded to Devon and returned to his post. Devon, standing eight paces away, recognized Mina's graceful form despite her dress.

"Mina, I am so sorry."

"Oh, Devon." She turned slowly to face him. Devon could see her eyes only behind the veil, the gold-brown irises as perfect as ever. Her hands moved away from her body in a gesture of abject helplessness.

Devon took a step towards her, faltered, and then stopped. He felt cold and remote, oddly unaffected by the great distress she was in. He could tell she had been weeping. She stood looking at him, and he felt she wanted him to hold her, to do something, anything, that would alleviate her pain. But he did nothing. He looked at her as if he were observing an actress on a stage, as if he were right there with her on the stage, but not a part of the drama. He was simply observing.

There was a beseeching, hopeful look in her eyes as she stood there waiting for him. Slowly, she raised her hand to her face and drew away the veil, observing him very intently as she did it.

Devon took a sharp intake of breath, not moving.

In his eyes Mina discerned the immensity of the divide, the abyss, between them. She caught, in that fraction of an instant, his look of utter horror, a horror that soared above her into the clear blue sky until it broke into shards of aversion and pity, and fell reflected in his eyes.

Devon glanced down for a second, breaking the connection, and then looked back again.

Mina waited for him until his eyes met hers.

Devon saw the imploring look in her eyes fade gently back, back upon itself into a shattering annihilation. He looked down and then back again, half afraid to see.

He watched her as she slowly veiled her face again, and then she turned away from him, forever. She heard the crunching sounds the soles of his shoes made against the graveled walkway, and she was not surprised at how quickly he made his way back to the front gate and elsewhere.

A week later, Mina planted a mango seedling in her father's garden. She had not slept at all. She planted it in the early morning before any of her family had risen. She was very intent as she worked. As she planted the seedling, she touched its roots, fanning them for good purchase in the soil. She watered the hole that she had dug in the soil before she set the seedling in. And then, very carefully, and beside the seedling, she placed the gold chain that Devon had given her. She had selected a bright spot in the garden, one where she knew its growth would be favourable. She patted the soil around it as tenderly as she would have touched a child, her own child. Anyone watching her from a neighbouring rooftop would not have thought it particularly unusual. But anyone who was kneeling beside her as she worked would have been upset to see the tears, as rich as liquid pearls, falling from her eyes. They would have been disheartened at the sobbing of such a beautiful woman who, if they but knew it, was planting the sorrow and the death of her love, for that was what she was doing in her mind. For her, in the truest light of her soul, she was giving up her love of Devon, and would never seek it again. But there would be life from her sorrow in this seedling. She stood up and returned to the house to clean her hands.

Khokan loaded Devon's luggage into the Land Rover and waited. Devon said that he needed to stop for a few minutes at the Canadian Club before going on to the airport. Khokan nodded sadly. He was going to miss Mr. Devon.

Devon hesitated nervously when he saw P.J. and Lise sitting adjacent to the tennis courts, their attention absorbed by a tennis match. He went inside to the bar and ordered a shot of Canadian whiskey. He said his goodbyes to a few of the regulars and the bartender, Babu, then threw back his whiskey, and went towards the tennis courts.

P.J. stood up and shook Devon's hand vigorously. "I'm going to miss you Dev. I'm sorry you're leaving, but Belize is just the ticket at this time of year I hear."

Lise looked at Devon flatly, stood up, and then walked inside to the bar. For an awkward moment, the only sounds they heard were the soft pops of tennis balls being hit back and forth across the courts.

"I'm sorry Devon. Lise is out of sorts these days."

"It's been great knowing you P.J. Hope we meet again."

"Me too. E-mail me when you get a chance. Keep in touch."

"I'll try."

Devon turned and walked across the grounds to meet Khokan in the outside parking lot, waiting there along with other drivers whose patrons were in the Club. He felt oddly empty, but free. Several crows cawed noisily from a rooftop. The close, humid evening enveloped him. He felt a bit sticky.

He stepped up and entered the rear passenger door of the vehicle as Khokan sprang to attention, having been dozing. The familiar sound of the power windows being rolled up as the air conditioner came on completely enclosed and separated Devon from the surrounding richness of the Bangladeshi night as they drove quickly from the place.

PAST REASON HUNTED

His trance deepened. Davis sat in the darkened room with his eyes closed. The image before him was hazy at first, and then slowly, incrementally, the outlines became clearly defined: three horsemen on the low rise of a hill. There was a feeling tone of imminent danger surrounding them. Davis wanted to bring the image closer. Steadily concentrating on the image, he breathed even more slowly and deeply than before. Now he could see their faces and the grim determination set in them. One of the horses reared and threw its head back, snorting. Davis wondered what the image meant, or if it held any meaning at all. His curiosity, the tight strain of it, broke his concentration, obscuring the image for several seconds until he drifted back, breathing easily again, into the trance.

Now he could see one of the horsemen dismounting and motioning to someone to come forward.

Behind the figure dismounting, from below the slope flanking the horses, Davis could just distinguish a hooded figure set apart from the rest. The man ventured forth a few steps and then stopped, leaned upon a staff, and peered directly ahead, in Davis's direction. Davis strained to see the man clearly, the image blurring as he did so. Trying too hard to capture the image seemed to have an adverse effect. He stopped straining and settled back into the cushioned seat, into a comfortable, relaxed state. Then, once he found the rhythm of his own deep breathing come back to him again, the image cleared, and his eyes began to focus on the scene before him. Just as he was about to discern the hooded man's features, a blinding flash of light shot through his consciousness knocking him down onto the floor. Nervously, he crawled to his feet, more puzzled than shaken by the event.

Davis was curious about the tribes that lived in the out worlds, as the areas around the domes were designated. Beyond the domed periphery of the urban sphere in which he lived, there was certainly not much to look at. Nothing, apparently, but scrub vegetation and sand dunes. Davis had met one of the outriders, the name for the men who patrolled the boundaries of the twenty-one domes and their interconnecting routes. The outrider, a man named Bach, was usually very loquacious after several drinks. He had told him of old, deserted towns amid blasted landscapes that dome-dwellers referred to as the null-lands. The reports of these null-lands were very sketchy for the exploration of them was not permitted because of the fear of radiation.

Bach was a hard-looking man, wiry and tough, an outrider whom Davis admired for the air of quiet dignity he carried with him. Davis had met him at the bar that they both frequented. Before they had met, Davis remembered watching Bach enter the bar, find a table near a corner, and then, alone, with his back to the wall, drink himself into a stupor. After a few hours of quiet imbibing, he would be all smiles, with an occasional leer at any attractive woman who happened by. Davis liked him. He knew Bach was an extremely lonely man who found it difficult to make the small talk necessary to normal social relations.

Before they had met, Davis had once requested of Bach a seat at Bach's table when the bar had been completely filled. Bach had simply nodded, not quite in his cups. Over the course of an evening, Davis found Bach to be an amiable, if somewhat cynical companion. Bach, recently divorced, was filled with seething passions that wanted some outlet. The divorce hadn't been his idea, and so there was an element of bitterness about him that he took great pains to conceal. Davis recognized it, and did what he could, when they met, to offset it. Davis, always fond of women, flattered and amused them even when he wasn't interested.

For Bach, observing Davis was a treat. Davis did everything Bach couldn't do with his easy banter and winning ways. Bach had to have several drinks in rapid succession before he could begin to socialize. And so, gradually, they became friends of a sort. Bach admired Davis for his social qualities, while Davis admired the tough outrider image, the loner who was willing to share with Davis something of the rugged life he lived.

"This last tour was a good one," Bach said. "Smelled smoke from a wood fire for the first time."

"Where?" Davis asked. "Who was out there?"

"Null people," Bach replied. "First sign of null life I've seen in years. The smoke came from an oasis about ten miles off interconnection twelve. I was beginning to think they'd all died out."

Bach took another long drink and then glanced up at the shapely woman entering the bar. He made a low whistle in appreciation, nudging Davis to look her way.

"Now there's a sight for a sailor's sore eyes," Bach said.

Davis smiled at the old earth analogy. Only one of the domes contained a large reservoir of water, and Davis remembered seeing a sailing regatta held there once. Various antiquarian events such as the regatta would be held just before an election to win public support for one or the other of the dome candidates.

When Davis turned around to see the woman, he was surprised at her height. She was just shy of six feet, and very attractive. Standing at the bar with one foot resting on the brass footrest, Davis couldn't help but admire her. Wearing a tan-coloured snakeskin pantsuit that emphasized every curve of her body, she had every man in the room enthralled.

"She certainly has a proud bearing," Davis said. "I've never seen her here before."

"She must be new to this Dome," Bach said.

"And not too soon either," Davis replied in a low voice. Bach slowly sipped his drink while Davis sauntered up to the bar. The scent of the woman's perfume clouded his mind for a moment, as he stood beside her and ordered a drink.

He tried desperately to think of something appropriate to say to her. Finally his mind cleared, and he smiled.

"Boa?" he asked, smiling and gesturing at her snakeskin suit.

"I'm sorry," she said, puzzled by the remark. She looked at him in a cool, detached way.

"I'm curious about your skin, I mean, the clothes you're wearing. Please don't get the wrong idea. I'm into fashion and I thought the design and make of it might be worth taking a closer look at."

Davis found her cool demeanour very appealing, and he observed the amused look playing about her eyes. Her nose was a little too large for her face, but he liked the incongruity.

"That's a rather novel approach," she said.

"What I really wanted to say, but I knew I shouldn't, was that I'm experiencing an emotion, and I wanted to ask you about it."

"Go ahead," she said smiling with amused curiosity.

"Maybe you can tell me why it is that when I meet certain women my heart begins to beat a little faster, and I suddenly begin to feel warm all over," he said.

"Corny, but cute," she said. "Cute".

"My name is Martin Davis, but everyone calls me Davis."

"I'm Rachel," she said.

"Rachel?" Davis queried, hoping for a last name.

"Just Rachel," she replied.

"Would you care to sit down with me and talk a bit?" Davis asked.

"I'm waiting for someone," she said.

"Now that's something I've heard before."

"I'll bet you have," Rachel said. She was smiling broadly now and thoroughly enjoying the attention but trying unsuccessfully to conceal it.

"Couldn't you wait for your friend with me?"

"No, I don't think that's such a good idea."

Her eyes suddenly moved over Davis's shoulder to look at someone who was motioning to her to join him.

"There's my friend. Bye-bye. I hope you always keep friendly to strangers."

"Wait, please wait," Davis said, following her for a moment.

"Oh, by the way," she said, just looking over her shoulder, "it's faux lizard, not boa."

Davis chuckled as he watched her walk away, her shapely legs delighting him with every step. Davis expected Bach would be amused by the scenario that had enfolded before him, but one glance at Bach's look of dark apprehension told him otherwise.

"Your new acquaintance keeps bad company, Davis, my boy."

Davis followed Bach's gaze over to the table where Rachel was sitting. A good-looking man dressed in the blue officer's uniform of the League Defence Militia was talking intently to her.

"That's Devlin. He's in charge of special trooper operations," Bach said.

"What do they do?" Davis asked.

"It's a commando wing of the militia that actively seeks out and kills any null personnel they encounter along the boundary regions surrounding the domes. Trouble is, as I've told you before, there's very little sign of life in the boundary lands, let alone what they call 'null personnel,' so they make raids on areas that are technically off limits to militia and outriders alike."

Davis looked at Bach in disbelief. "Are you on the level?"

Bach nodded slowly. His disgust was apparent as he continued to look at Devlin. The rest of the evening went as so many had at the Phoenix Bar, but every now and then Davis would look over Bach's shoulder and catch Rachel's eye. She would smile back at him.

Davis believed that life outside the domes wasn't pleasant, a radioactive wasteland with little more than unfortunate mutants struggling to keep alive. At least that's what he'd been told life was like out there, a grim and savage place in a hostile environment. But he also knew that his own life was lacking something, not in any physiological sense. All of his material needs were satisfied. He ate well, lived in a comfortable apartment, made love on weekends when the opportunity arose, but there was something missing.

For one thing, he had nothing to do. Like most dome citizens, he didn't have to work for a living. He received his bi-monthly stipend from the League Authority and was left to his own resources. Although the League had organized countless clubs and associations, Davis preferred his own rather desultory approach to finding areas of interest. Any of the really meaningful work was in the hands of a cadre of League specialists. No more than a score of individuals were required to effectively operate and maintain his Dome from a practical standpoint. And the same was true of the other domes. Life, for most, had become very comfortable. Davis pinched the flab around his waist and sighed in disgust. He had everything a citizen could want and more.

He decided to walk over to the Phoenix, thinking Bach might be there. Davis was bored, and Bach, at least, would have something to say. Davis hated being in this mood, but every now and then it descended upon him and he couldn't avoid it. He wondered why there weren't others who felt as he did. Maybe there were, but he certainly hadn't talked to them about it. Everyone seemed so content. That's what irked him. The placidity of people. In the past when he had felt like this, he simply thought it was time to meet a new woman. But now he knew that it was different from that. It wasn't a woman that he needed. It was something within himself. But what? He desperately needed a change. He thought about Bach. He wondered if he could convince Bach to take him on one of his assignments. No one would have to know. It could all be done secretly.

As Davis walked towards the Phoenix, he looked up at the high central tower of the Dome. He remembered when his father had first taken him there. He couldn't have been more than thirteen years old. The tower trip had been a reward for placing first in his class. The tower was the highest point within the dome structure. Davis savoured the memory of the event. He remembered how he had felt.

From the top of the tower he could see the null lands in the far distance, the very edges of the world where the null-creatures lived. He could also see the intricate network of transportation systems between the smaller domes that lay to the Northeast. It was only with a special telescope that he could see traces of green in the far distance, a green that was brighter and more vivid than any he had ever seen in the gardens within the Dome. He wondered if the other domes in the League held brighter greens than his own. He had promised himself that he would find out someday. He looked above at the great transparent covering atop the Dome. From the Tower, he had an unobstructed view of the vast expanses of desert that surrounded the Dome. Only here and there could he see a patch of green that was magic to a young boy's eyes. The day with his father was wonderful. It was a whirlwind tour of sights and exhibits and sounds and laughter. His father bought him a miniature replica of the Tower and watched his son's beaming face as the boy held it tightly with both hands.

In his dreams the boy sometimes flew beyond his Dome and further, past the other urban sphere domes of the League. He would fly high above the sands that surrounded the life he lived within the transparent enclosures of the Dome. He would fly nearer and nearer to a great green oasis while all the while a feeling of mingled apprehension, excitement, and wonder grew within him. And then he would be over an oasis and there he could see water, turquoise-coloured water, and the sun bleached orange-red remains of ancient buildings.

This was his great adventure, and there was terror in it. The null creatures lived there. At least that's what he had been told by his father and his tutors at the learning centers. He had never actually seen pictures of any null creatures in his youth. They were a mystery to him then. And so in his dreams he could only see shadowy figures scurrying far below him through verdant shrubs and towering palms.

When Davis reached the Phoenix, he learned that Bach hadn't been there that evening. He decided on impulse to visit the Tower. Making his way to the nearest tube shuttle, he quickened his pace and mentally noted that he'd have to walk more often if he wanted to lose a few pounds and feel better.

Within an hour he was at the top of the Tower. There were sightseers about, and he noticed a team of scientists in a section reserved for taking readings of radioactive contamination levels. They were very officious in manner and went about their duties with the kind of self-importance that Davis had always found offensive to the extreme.

Everyone knew that life outside of the domes was terminal. Why, he thought, there should be this never-ending record-taking of contamination levels outside of the domes he could not fathom. His education had led him to believe that there was only death outside of the domes. An individual might live a few days, perhaps even weeks, but ultimately, there was only death, horrible death, beyond the privileged confines of the domes, the inter-connectors between the domes, and the shuttles. Beyond these enclosed realities, there was nothing. Nothing. The null people were not to be considered. They were the contaminated, the afflicted, the deformed. The League spokesmen referred to them as null creatures as if to underscore the difference between them and the people of the domes.

Davis marvelled at the fact that it had taken him by surprise when he had learned that there were indeed actual people out there in the null lands and not the bogey men of his childhood fears. He was shocked at how closely the null people, when the League finally released three dimensional visuals of them, resembled dome people. They were indistinguishable, it seemed to him, the one from the other.

As he looked below, at the great contained space of the Dome, he remembered his father's pride in its architecture, and in its accomplishments. So much ancient history he thought, but a history that shaped the very Tower he walked upon. Far below he could see the tube shuttles ferrying people about.

High above him, just outside the Dome, an outrider was moving his hovercraft in a wide arc along the periphery of the Dome checking for any faults in the transparent covering. Initially Davis thought it might be Bach, but then Davis remembered Bach was off-duty. How he envied Bach. For Davis, Bach was the epitome of the man's man: quiet, strong, and compassionate. Davis had come to know Bach well over the brief time they had known each other. He had learned of Bach's unhappy marriage, of his great love for a woman that became a casualty of his prolonged absences from home. Bach hadn't really expected her to leave. There had been arguments, tears, silences. Still, Bach had thought that they could work it out somehow. They didn't, and she left. All of it followed the simple logic of broken relationships.

As Davis walked away from the Tower, he felt very isolated. He wanted so much to experience something true in his life, something charged with meaning and vital, and yet there was nothing, nothing that he could feel would move him past his feeling of nullity. What he could feel was the great emptiness of the space within the Dome, an emptiness that encapsulated his own. He continued to walk, without seeing, without registering any impressions at all. Abruptly, something came home to him. He remembered his trance, the trance that had left him dazed and wondering on his living-room floor. Something very real had touched him then.

He stopped walking and stood rooted where he was. He was remembering the episode not in a logical, fixed way, but all at once... a million neurons racing through his consciousness in pathways never traced before. Something deep, deep within him was attending to what he had experienced.

The trance had left its mark on him. He remembered: the riders, the hooded man. What did it mean? Why hadn't he been able to see the hooded man's face? It was all so strange.

What had begun as a lark, a curious game to amuse and attract women, had become something other, something he half feared. His study of old-earth hypnosis was proving more fascinating than he could have dreamt.

The trance seemed to connect him with another reality. Initially, he had used his skill in inducing trance to intrigue women, but gradually, his interest grew deeper than the sheer novelty of it. He began to find the practice of self-hypnosis extremely absorbing.

He studied everything he could find on the subject. Very early in his study he had been amazed at the way he could induce self-hypnosis. By concentrating on small movements in his fingers, by encouraging the movements, by suggesting them, subtly, little by little, he found that he could make his arm rise from the chair as if lifted by some force other than his own. And now he stood, his very confusion a creative flux. He wasn't aware of time as he stood there. He was completely absorbed and immersed in the memory of a trance state. Suddenly, he was jostled from behind by someone hurrying to board a shuttle, and his reverie was broken.

"Watch out, you idiot! You're in the way."

Around him, dozens of his fellow citizens swarmed to board the shuttle. He moved quickly, wondering for a fleeting second about the loss of civility in the Dome.

Bach was still dressed in his outrider fatigues when he sat in front of the flashback monitor in the living-room of his apartment. Just back from a tour of duty, he felt it imperative to put things down while they were still fresh in his mind. He wanted to provide a truth record of what had happened on this latest tour. He knew that the outrider crew he had made the journey with could deny everything he said, so he very carefully proceeded to document the incident. The flashback monitor was connected to the EVA, the Experience Verification Analyzer, a very sophisticated apparatus that reported on the precise details of every remembered event with uncanny accuracy. Bach placed the EVA headset over his head and then positioned himself carefully in front of the camera. He pressed the flashback remote and then the recording began. His face was drawn and colourless. He spoke very carefully so as to register every nuance of the experience. A blue light flickered on the voice monitor each time he spoke.

"This is Outrider Matthew Bach... #421 771 130. Special Report submitted to the Investigations Branch of the Outrider Service. This concerns Mission #62, an unauthorized flight over the Delta Islands, deep over null territory. I am using the EVA to corroborate my report. The Outrider team was conducting a routine security patrol along the base perimeter of a mini-dome supply base when movement registered on the aircraft scanner. Initially, it was thought to be a mutant rodent herd of approximately sixty. Although the sighting was technically out of bounds, the general consensus was to hunt the rodents for sport.

Five of us were equipped with individual flying units and hand-held lasers. We left the aircraft and set out. I did not know one of the team, Trooper Krvo, who had been seconded to our group from the League Defence Force, as part of a broad career development initiative. He was a stranger to me. But the others, Blake, Forbes, and Dunn, were all dome outriders like myself. This was one of those rare occasions when we traveled together. I assumed there was to be some extensive maintenance work.

Krvo insisted on leading the hunt. With each of us in a single flying unit, we were over the original sighting in a few moments. It was early morning, and there was a light mist over the low scrub islands of the Delta.''

As Bach spoke, the blue verifying flickers of light danced across the EVA monitor. There was an absolute calm about his expression as he reported on the events.

"Krvo sighted what he communicated to us as a small animal herd. He broke formation and flew approximately twenty feet above ground level. From above, we could see the bursts from his laser as they hit the ground. I recollect there was an odd pitch to his voice that alarmed me. He was extremely excited. When the rest of us flew lower to join him, it became very difficult to see anything because of the clouds of dust thrown up by the laser hits. I could readily observe life movement on my monitor, but I refrained from firing until my actual visibility was clear. Blake, Forbes and Dunn were flying in a low sweep formation directly behind Krvo. I was flying in the rear slot. I can remember feeling something was not right, not correct. I communicated my intent to the others to cease firing and investigate. Everyone complied except Krvo. He continued firing at whatever moved.

When he finally stopped, and the dust cleared, I couldn't believe what lay around us. There weren't any animals. There were the dead bodies of fifty null-people by my count. The special lasers we used are designed to destroy the nervous systems of mammals. All of them had been hit, and there were no survivors. Krvo did not appear surprised that null-people had been killed, and that they were not animals as we had thought. He appeared greatly amused at my concern. The others were shocked at what had occurred. They had never seen null-people before the incident. When I asked Krvo if he had known that he was firing at null-people, he merely replied that he had not known at first, but when he recognized them as nulls, he did not think anything of it. He reported to me that it had become common practice in other militia sectors to seek and terminate nulls. Being convinced that this could not be the case, I decided to report in full upon my return and request a full investigation into the matter. This report of the Delta incident is registered on the EVA monitor. End of special report from Outrider Bach."

Bach felt relieved. He knew the investigation team would be thorough and deliver a sound judgement against Krvo. It couldn't be otherwise, Bach thought. Krvo was very dangerous and unbalanced. What alarmed Bach were the comments Krvo had made about the killing of null-people in other sectors. Bach had heard nothing of this before then, and yet what reason would Krvo have to lie about it. Krvo had actually laughed at Bach when Bach had called him aside to tell him that he would be submitting a report. Bach saw in his eyes that the man was amused at Bach's concern over the dead null-people, the "nulls" as Krvo called them.

M arta wept convulsively as she thought again of the massacre. Sitting on the floor with her legs drawn close to her chest, she rocked back and forth in grief. Two of her brothers had been among those slaughtered near the Delta. They had been gathering shells for the festival of the Elders. There was something so unreal about it all to her. They had left her laughing and full of eager anticipation for their adventure. And now there was nothing left of them, of their loud boyish charms, of any part of their being, it was gone. There was nothing now but the dull and barren pain of her grief, and the confusion of it all.

She lay on the kitchen floor in one of the homes in the outer village. She wished to be alone in her grief. It was here in the empty rooms of the deserted village that she felt some comfort. It was a shelter that enclosed her pain. Far below her, in the subterranean world of her people, life was carrying on as before. As if her brothers hadn't died. As if they were still alive. It was all so strange to her. The aching pain she felt, the memories of them, the horrible realization of the way they had died. It was all so incomprehensible.

From below the floor where she lay, Marta heard the muffled sound of someone calling her name. She rose slowly to her feet and she pushed the carpet away from the trap door. Lifting it, she could see far below to the tiny cloaked figure motioning to her. The great cavernous walls of the underground city were well lit, and she could discern that it was Dirk calling to her.

"Marta, Marta... come down."

She looked at him, and wearily, she waved. She felt grateful to him for caring. He had been trying to console her, and she appreciated his friendship. She slowly made her way down to him, descending the circular stairway in measured steps as she went.

Dirk was struck by the elegance of her movement as she came down the stairway. He wanted so much to be able to comfort her.

"Marta... I only just heard. I am very, very sorry. I am truly sorry. Can I do anything to help you?"

Dirk's compassion had softened the hard, lean features of his face. He was a slightly built man, but extremely powerful. The Delta massacre had confirmed his growing suspicions about an organized group of killers from the dome worlds. There had been a number of people killed in what had seemed to be unrelated incidents, but Dirk sensed a common hand in all of the killings. He had related his fears to the Elders, the council of senior representatives from the towns and cities of the colonies. They had heard him, but no action was taken. They could not see his point of view. The killings, they said, were unfortunate but unrelated. But now, with the massacre, Dirk's fears had been justified. Dirk knew that now he would have a better hearing when he spoke.

"Dirk," Marta said softly in a tired voice, "they were so young. I don't understand why. It doesn't make any sense. I try to understand, and I can't. I just can't."

Dirk held her as she sobbed against his chest. One part of his mind was actively planning, forming a strategy, to gain support for his growing band of warriors. He caressed her very gently and spoke to her about her brothers, helping her search out fond memories that brought up a smile of joy through her tears. There was a small garden off to one side of the great corridor where Dirk had brought her once before. Now, he again guided her to the same spot where she had so much enjoyed seeing an enormous hibiscus blossom.

Marta sat quietly by the same pool as before, wondering at the change between then and now, at how her grief moved with her, with her hand as she drew it through the water, still and cool. The feel of the water was so odd to her. It was a curious sensation to her, and one that distracted her from her grief for a moment. She passed her hand back and forth in the water until it was the only sensation that she was conscious of. Dirk watched her closely, wishing there was something more he could do to console her. Suddenly, Marta looked up at him and took his hand in hers. She looked at him and he saw the trust and comfort in her moist eyes. Dirk felt a surge of joy, and then he remembered the massacre. Looking away from Marta, his jaw clenched hard and a silent fury came into his eyes.

The huge underground caverns were made up of a series of interconnecting tunnels and corridors and great halls. The largest of the caverns served as the meeting place. Its floors were of polished marble, and there were places where intricately carved benches made of precious wood arose from the marble floors. In the very center of the cavern hall was a spring, and it was there, around its bubbling waters, that the Elders sat and held council.

The Elders presided over all aspects of life in the colonies, as the tightly knit communities of the null people were called. It was this trusted group of nine who set the policies that were followed by all of the colonies. Before any major decision was made, the council of nine Elders would meet, and in open assembly they would hear any colonist who wished to speak. Every colonist had the right to be heard, regardless of being elected or not. However, it was the responsibility of the colonist to be well-organized and to the point in their speech to the assembly.

Dirk felt a tremor of excitement as he walked into the great cavern that was the meeting place of the Elders. The huge assembly hall had always impressed him. It was here that he had heard some of the greatest speeches of his life- and some of the worst. He smiled at the memory of one terrible orator, so poorly organized and rambling in his speech that he was cut short by thunderous applause. It had begun with a few handclaps by some disenchanted listener and then it had escalated into roaring, tumultuous applause. The man had left the podium puzzled and dazed by it all. The applause did not subside until the unfortunate man had left the assembly hall. After that event few dared to address the assembly gathered in the hall unless they were very well prepared. No one wanted their speech interrupted by such an avalanche of applause.

Dirk strode to the very center of the cavern where he could sit beside the bubbling spring. There he sat quietly and thought about Marta's grief, the massacre, the Elders. Would he be able to persuade them now? Would they see a common thread in the killings? He pondered these questions, and he knew that if action were not taken soon there would be more killings, perhaps on a much greater scale. Dirk wanted to be clear and focused in his mind at the next assembly before the Elders. He knew, as surely as he felt the cool waters of the spring with his hand that he needed to be convincing when he spoke before the assembly. Otherwise, there would not be enough time to prepare to fight the terrorists.

The next assembly of the Elders was a fortnight away. He knew that his arguments for armed retaliation must be lucid and well-organized. Dirk's eyes focused on the bubbling fountain as he meditated on everything that might turn the balance in his favour. The

Elders had always sought peace above all other considerations. It was the way of the colonies. But now, after the massacre at the Delta, they must see the urgency for a new policy.

The attacks had probably come from the great dome worlds, beyond the boundaries of the colonies. Little was known about these worlds, but there had never been any trouble. As long as Dirk could remember, and before his father could remember, and his father's father could remember, there had never been an incident. There was no history of war with the dome worlds, none. There was peace in the great separation of land and distance and time that kept them apart.

The water cooled his hand and settled his mind. He harboured no doubts as to what he must do. Already, several young men had approached him with offers of support, and they had told him that others would follow as well. He mused over the situation and knew that he must have the support of the Elders. Behind him, he heard the sounds of someone walking towards him. He sprang to his feet and turned to see who it was. The elderly, cloaked man in front of him was Mayerling, one of the most respected and honoured of the Elders. He was smiling.

"You move quickly Dirk!"

"Mayerling, have you heard of the massacre?"

Mayerling's face darkened. "Yes. It is all so senseless. One killing after another, and now so many. I had hoped it would not come to this."

"To this!" Dirk exclaimed. "And what of the next? Every few weeks some of our people are found dead. There is no reason for it. None. We have done nothing to deserve these murders."

Mayerling sighed deeply. "Yes, you are right."

"Well surely then," Dirk continued, "the council can see that we must take action and fight against whoever it is that is doing this thing."

"That is one course to take, to be sure. There are others," Mayerling replied.

"Others? What do you mean... others? Surely now, the council will move to stop them... whoever it is!" Dirk stood dumbfounded. He couldn't believe that Mayerling could not see the course of action the colonies must take.

Mayerling sat down and placed his hand in the water.

"Dirk, if you will allow me to digress from our discussion for a moment. Imagine a group of warriors about to face an invading force. The warriors, braced and ready, decide to resist with the less proven, less experienced among them in the first ranks. The best warriors are kept in reserve. Their strategy, you see, is to save their best for the last. In ever-increasing circles of power the warriors wait, encouraging the ones that go before. The very last circle is made up of those without weapons of any kind. And yet they are the most formidable of all. Their fear is not of the invaders. Their sorrow is for those who have gone before them, and on their lips is an ancient chant... 'Storm rises when the tiger roars, clouds gather when the dragon soars.' In the final circle, the warriors wait."

"You talk in circles," Dirk said impatiently. "This is a time for action, not your useless stories. Mayerling, I need your support when I speak before the assembly. I'm pleading with you. Help me!"

Mayerling moved his hand into the water; he was smiling gently all the while. Mayerling looked at Dirk and said, "You can count on the circles."

"You foolish old man. Enough talk," Dirk said. He was utterly disgusted at Mayerling's response to his concern. Dirk left the great hall in a silent rage, barely noticing a few passers-by who entered as he departed.

B ach walked unsteadily as he left the Phoenix. Too many drinks had left him a little less careful than he might have been. But the massacre was too much. The incident was so fresh in his mind. He wanted an easier diffused reality, and the alcohol gave him that, at least for a while. Staggering down the dimly-lit pathway, he remembered Davis. He wished Davis had been at the bar. He needed to talk to him about the massacre. Davis would have been able to provide him with an objective viewpoint. That's what he needed most, objectivity. What a curious word: objectivity. The world got curiouser and curiouser. He laughed at the play of words in his drunken consciousness.

Just then, he heard something and looked up. Two men were approaching him. They weren't talking. Bach's mind sharpened. They were walking more slowly than they should have been, Bach thought. He braced himself. Curious, how slowly they're coming towards me, he thought. And then the pattern broke. One of the figures darted directly towards him, at him. Bach lurched sideways escaping the first blow. The second man kicked high, from his hip, at Bach's chest. Bach deflected the blow, his quickened senses now responding to the attack. The next blow hit him hard against the side of his neck. And then a second and a third blow, crashing into the top of his head. Bach even managed to grab one of his attacker's ankles, twisting it sharply and hearing an odd crunching sound as he did so. He swung around to face the other, but his reactions were too slow. The sudden impact of a kick to his groin stunned him. And then, a storm of calculated, precise kicks brought him down. He didn't remember any of the blows that struck him after he had fallen.

When he regained consciousness, bleary-eyed, hurt, and nauseated with the taste of blood in his mouth, he knew that professionals had been at him. He spat out the blood and walked unsteadily towards the nearest shuttle.

Davis sat comfortably in the special chair he used for his trances. His small apartment was sparely furnished, but filled with souvenirs and small items that had caught his fancy at one time or another. Bach had said that Davis had a packrat mentality. Davis adjusted his position in the chair. In a moment he was relaxed and concentrating on observing any minute finger movements in his hand. Another moment and he saw a slight twitch in the index finger of his right hand. He followed that movement, building on it, suggesting that it twitch again. Seconds passed, and then his fingers spread apart and his entire right hand jerked up about two inches. He wasn't making it happen; he was allowing it to happen.

He was simply following the movements, and taking the time, the time that was necessary, to encourage the involuntary movements. He was fully relaxed and fully aware. He watched his hand and arm move upwards very, very slowly, one step at a time. Once his hand was at eye level, his wrist turned, and the hand began to move towards him, and at that point his eyes closed.

What happened next always amazed him no matter how often it occurred. In a series of autonomous, stepwise movements, the hand approached his face, his arm bending at the elbow to accommodate the movement. It was magnetic, inevitable, the hand slowly gliding towards his face. He was so relaxed, so involved in the very move-ments of it all, that he couldn't have stopped the process even if he had wished. He knew he had tapped into something deep within himself when that happened.

And then suddenly a finger touched his lips, and he went even deeper, deeper into trance: so relaxed, so still. The hand settled, descending to his lap.

With that, he inhaled deeply and then waited for the images. Moments passed. Davis could see nothing in his trance, He had expected to see an image, something clear and focused, perhaps even the hooded man and the riders that he had seen before in trance. But there was nothing. He relaxed even more, following the rhythm of his breathing, moving deeper and deeper into the quiet, still place he had come to experience in his trances. He was only barely aware that his head had begun nodding forward, involuntarily. Within the complete comfort of the trance, his body was signalling its receptiveness. It was all so effortless, so easy. He drifted away from conscious thought, from expecting anything to happen. He was so comfortable. Nothing needed to happen.

And then, almost inaudible at first, he heard the sound of muffled laughter, easy laughter. It grew until it was as if the laughter were in the very room he was sitting in. Rich, full-bodied laughter, laughter rolling in great curves and circles around him. It was so soothing to hear it. It brought such great joy to him, just to be there, surrounded by the laughter: deep, full-throated belly-laughter.

Then, abruptly, the laughter stopped. There was absolutely no sound. Davis was startled at the suddenness of the halt. There had been so much generous laughter, and then nothing, nothing but silence.

Davis slowly came out of the trance. Gradually, his eyes focused on the familiar patterns, the table under the mirror, the miniature replica of the Tower, the empty food trays he hadn't returned to the kitchen. He was utterly confounded by the laughter he had heard in the trance. He had expected an image, and instead there had been sound, the sound of laughter. Something odd was happening.

About a dozen of the colonists were working the soil with handmade tools. As they worked, they sang a song of renewal, an ancient song of the earth lifting its bosom to the sun. They took great joy in singing the song, for it was a song that for generations had only been sung in the underground colonies. It was only a scant twenty years earlier that the first colonists had left the safety of the underground and ventured above, on the earth again, after decades below the surface.

Their work was rhythmic, slow, and sustained by regular, even arm strokes. There was beauty in the way the men moved, and the way their voices carried high into the spring skies above them. Their song lifted their spirits and made the hard work of loosening the soil a joyous thing. The men were invigorated and vital. In a few weeks seeds would be sown, and the cycles of germination, growth and abundance would begin. A small bird flew above them, and one of the men stopped his work to look at it. He was delighted at the way the bird arched high into the clear blue skies and then fell, gliding to the earth below.

T he sensitive instruments aboard the patrol craft registered the slight blips of sound and movement in precise orange dots. The pilot and co-pilot grinned with anticipation as they began a slow circling motion that gradually reduced the circumference of the circle they were making high above the nulls. The hum of the air-motors was low, almost inaudible.

Franco was the first to hear the low drone of the patrol craft's engine. He stopped his work and stood quite still, trying to make out the sound more clearly. He was puzzled. The sound was so ominous to him on an instinctive level, and yet he didn't know why it should be so. He and the others working beside him hadn't yet heard of the attacks on the colonists who lived near the delta lands far to the east. The young lad, Peter-boy, first noticed that something was the matter when he chanced to look over at Franco. Franco was so intent, so concentrated.

Peter-boy signalled the others to stop work. The big man, Tanner, felt a premonition of dread. His gnarled hands gripped his hoe tightly. His face tightened.

In the patrol craft, the pilot moved deftly, manipulating the controls. Then he fired a burst of fire bombs in rapid succession. Within seconds the null group was surrounded by a circle of fire.

The pilot navigated his craft in hover-position directly above the nulls. The ring of fire was about a hundred yards distant from the nulls, a deliberate calculation by the pilot. The pilot turned to the co-pilot and invited him to join in on what he called a game of fire-clean.

There were three new troopers in the small passenger section of the patrol craft. They were very excited about what was happening and hoped they'd have a chance to fire a few rounds at the nulls themselves. For the longest moment everything was suspended, frozen. The patrol craft continued to hover above the null group. The perimeter of fire raged around the colonists, too far away to pose any immediate danger. Franco looked quickly at the men around him. The shock of the situation they were in was passing. Now, they were waiting for something to happen.

The co-pilot asked permission to move closer for a better look at the nulls. The craft descended to about thirty feet above the ground. Now the co-pilot could see their faces clearly. He reached into his pocket, flipped a dome coin and called it. He won the toss. The first hit was his. He looked below to the group of standing men, and then past Tanner and Peter-boy to a short, husky man. He waited until their eyes met and then activated one of the small weapons controlled by him from his side of the craft.

The man, aware that he was being singled out and targeted, looked across to Franco, smiled awkwardly for an instant, and then exploded when the impact of the blast hit him. Franco winced, and then gathering all of his strength, he flung his hoe in wild desperation at the white metallic underside of the patrol craft. There was a sharp cracking sound when it hit. His hoe had scraped the hull, just piercing it before it fell back to the ground below.

The co-pilot laughed at the futile gesture. Then, he moved to sight Franco with his weapon. The pilot, however, nudged him aside and claimed Franco as his kill. Franco could see the pilot adjusting his sights. Franco spat in defiance. Suddenly, he caught sight of something. There was just a trace of smoke escaping from the hull of the aircraft where he had struck it with his hoe.

A tense moment passed. Franco could see both the pilot and co-pilot manipulating their controls frantically. The aircraft was alternately losing altitude and then regaining it- in fits and starts.

The men around Franco began to cheer. Big Tanner knelt beside the smoking, shattered remains of his friend, still in shock from the unprovoked attack.

The patrol craft was losing power quickly now, with smoke billowing out of the pierced hull. The perimeter of fire was dying down. And then, with an odd, jerking movement, the aircraft spun around, fell sharply, and struck the ground still under some power.

For the longest moment there was a curious, stunning silence. Franco quickly motioned to the men to surround the aircraft. They did so cautiously, taking great care to look out for any sudden movement from the downed ship. Once they were positioned, Peter-boy threw a clod of earth at the windshield just below the cockpit. Big Tanner looked again at the lifeless corpse that had been his friend. He felt a wave of rage pass through his body. He had never felt anything like it before.

Suddenly the side door of the ship was manually flung open from the inside. Smoke poured out of the opening. Three of the troopers clambered out, each of them coughing hoarsely from the smoke. They were unarmed. The pilot and co-pilot followed them. Both were armed with light laser pistols. They motioned to the nulls to stand back, threatening them with the pistols. None of the troopers could see clearly, their eyes smarting from the sting of the smoke.

Big Tanner looked closely at Franco for some sign. Peter-boy had climbed atop the downed aircraft, above the troopers and was unseen. He saw Franco nod decisively at Big Tanner, giving the signal. Peter-boy leapt high into the air, gauging his leap so that he could land squarely on the co-pilot below him. Simultaneously, Big Tanner went for the pilot. Peter-boy landed hard on the co-pilot breaking the man's shoulder bone in the process. Franco dove to the ground as he saw the pilot level his laser pistol at him. The blast missed him but caught Luka, one of the men nearest him, in the stomach. Simultaneously, Big Tanner was at the pilot, smashing hard at the pilot's helmet, trying to get at him. Desperately, the troopers raised their hands in surrender. It was too late for surrender, and they knew it.

The colonists fell upon them furiously, striking at the blue uniforms with their hoes, striking at their helmets, striking everywhere, striking mercilessly. When it was over, a profound silence , a grim silence, enveloped them all. No one spoke. The spring air seemed surreal and shattered by what had taken place. Only a few wisps of smoke from the fire remained in the air.

Franco saw to it that the two colonists who had been killed were buried according to custom. The troopers and the pilots were then dragged to a far part of the fire perimeter that was still smouldering.

For some reason Franco thought to have their uniforms, boots and helmets removed. The aircraft itself he had camouflaged with shrubbery. Big Tanner had wanted to destroy it, but Franco knew somewhere in himself that it would be useful somehow. The bodies of the troopers were unceremoniously tossed onto the fire that had been revived. No one spoke. Slowly, they made preparations for the return home.

Franco felt curiously still within himself, oddly relaxed, an emotion he had never felt before, at least not like this. He knew the Elders would be shocked and disheartened by what had taken place. He also knew that he and all of his friends could easily have been killed. The troopers had meant to kill them all, of that he was certain. Two of his friends were dead. And there was absolutely no reason for it, no reason at all. Strangely, the sky was clear blue again, as if nothing had happened. So odd, Franco thought, so odd.

Dirk watched the youth as he trained. He climbed the hanging ropes so easily, moving from one to another almost effortlessly. The youth was in perfect control of his body. He climbed to the top of the platform where the ropes had been secured. Once there, he shouted encouragement to his friends below, three of them straining to reach the spot where he stood. Dirk marvelled at Jak's power and grace. He was a gifted athlete. Jak let out a wild cry when he saw his friend Dirk watching them all from below. He motioned to Dirk to climb up and join them. Dirk chuckled, taking up the challenge. He was in good shape and looked forward to the exercise. As he climbed, Jak admired Dirk's power, his forearms moving like pistons as he climbed.

In a moment Dirk stood beside Jak. They embraced, and then, as they always did, they closely appraised each other physically.

"You're still fit," Jak said.

Dirk chuckled, enjoying the emphasis on physical conditioning. He countered. "And I see you're looking much better than when I saw you last. Five pounds lighter, at least!"

Jak roared in delight.

Dirk knew that Jak was tough and resilient, like himself. Men like Jak were needed if the colonies were to survive. Dirk had a premonition of disaster to come.

He knew deep within himself that these sporadic attacks were just the beginning. He looked up at the vaulted ceiling of this part of the great underground complex and noticed that some of the light was flickering weakly. Dismissing it from his mind, he turned to Jak.

"Jak, about the Delta massacre. I don't think it's going to stop there. I'm afraid it's going to get a lot worse. The Elders don't seem to be prepared for it. Together we could organize a force to fight them, for I fear they'll attack in greater numbers soon. I need your help Jak.

Unless we're prepared, it could be disastrous for all of the colonies. Can I count on you?"

Jak turned away from him. He was deeply troubled by what he was about to say for he knew how it would affect Dirk.

"Dirk... I know what you want to do. I want to help you, but I cannot follow if the Elders have not given their consent. I'm sorry but they must decide."

Dirk was shaken at his words. "Jak- surely you know what is happening. There's something more to all of this than a few isolated incidents. There's a pattern here. I don't claim to know why, but I know that we must be ready to respond. If we don't... ."

Jak shook his head sadly. "Dirk, I cannot, no, I will not go against the Elders. It is the way of the colonies. Unless the Elders agree with what you are planning to do, I will not be with you."

"Jak, I can't believe what you're saying. The Elders have great wisdom, but this is something they know nothing about. They know nothing about war."

"But we're not at war," Jak answered.

Dirk looked at Jak in disbelief.

"What does it take to convince you? Another massacre?"

Jak was wounded by Dirk's words. He looked away, trying to think of something to say. And then very quietly, very deliberately, Dirk said, "Jak, are you afraid?"

"I am no coward, you know that!" Jak snapped back.

"Well then, help me," Dirk implored.

"Not without consent. Not without the Elders' approval. I will not join you without their approval. That's final."

Dirk looked at his old friend with a combination of shock and disgust. He could see the resolve in Jak's face, and he knew that Jak was fixed in his opinion. Dirk turned away from him abruptly, grabbed one of the climbing ropes nearest him and descended rapidly to the floor of the gymnasium below. Jak smashed his fist against a canvas bag filled with coiled rope. His instincts were with Dirk, but his first allegiance was to the Elders and the colonies.

D avis was in trance. Sitting in what he called his trance chair, he felt very comfortable and a little strange. He no longer used his crystal or any of the props that he once needed to induce trances. With practice, he had become proficient in the kind of relaxed concentration that was necessary in developing a trance. It had only taken him a moment or two to completely relax, and now, with his eyes closed, he discovered that his head was nodding gently, back and forth, without the least effort on his part. The sensation of the movement, so steady, so relaxing, prepared the way for the image that was beginning to form.

The image beneath his closed eyelids was that of an old man. The old man was in a seated posture about fifty feet off the ground. He was sitting in mid-air without a chair and simply looking ahead. Davis did not find the image bizarre or incongruous in any way. He could accept the validity of this image in his trance. In trance, as he was beginning to realize, anything could happen. It was a strange but comfortable experience.

Davis began to look intently at the image. There was a great and open space surrounding the old man. The way the old man was sitting, his posture, reminded Davis of the way in which ancient earth kings had been depicted. It was as if the old man was sitting on a full throne, with his legs bent and slightly apart. It wasn't a static image. There was a feel of brisk wind in it, and life moving unseen in the landscape below and beyond the old man.

Suddenly, Davis began to hear the sound of laughter, the same kind of laughter he had heard before in trance. The old man was laughing. It was he, Davis thought, it was this same old man that he had heard laughing before. But then, there hadn't been an image. There had been only the sound of laughter. Now it connected. As soon as he remembered this and thought about it consciously, the image began to fade and the laughter grew fainter and fainter. Soon it was gone, all of it.

Davis roused himself from the trance. He felt rested and alert. He walked over to the window that looked out to the shuttle tube installation below. He could see people moving quickly to find seats. As he mindlessly observed these movements, he thought about the old man, his laughter, and the way he had been sitting in mid-air. It was all so intriguing.

The child was playing in the sand. Over and over again he delighted in the sensation of the warm, white grains of sand passing through his fingers. He was totally absorbed in the experience of it. Sitting, he turned and looked over at one of the men standing about fifteen feet away and he held up a handful of the sand, offering it to the man, in play. The man smiled broadly at the three year old. He looked across at the other two men indicating he was going to join the boy. They nodded almost imperceptibly, and continued to keep watch. These southern colonists had heard of the Delta massacre and the other attacks and they were extremely vigilant, even here, so far removed from the northern Delta colonies.

And the child, this special child, was in their charge. It was a great honour for them that they had been chosen by the Elders for this service. They kept a watchful lookout around them, and beyond to the broad, flat expanses of sand ahead of them, the wide, dazzling white beach, and the vast horizon of sea and sky. These men were the child's guardians, and they would die before any harm came to the child.

The child gave the man, Petar, a tiny handful of sand. Petar smiled, murmured his thanks, and pointed to a high-flying seagull above their heads. The child was ecstatic at seeing the bird. He ran towards the beach following the seagull with Petar and the others close behind. And then, stopping, the child listened intently to the sounds and cries the seagull was making.

Petar attempted to shade the child with a small, white parasol, but the child would run ahead to be free from any obstruction between him and the bird. The other men smiled openly at seeing Petar's massive hulk bending, stooping, and following the child in fits and starts with a tiny parasol clutched in his hand.

The child began to imitate the seagull, with arms outstretched and running in wide circles simulating a flight. He uttered sharp, piercing cries into the sea air that carried high into the skies above. A moment passed. The seagull descended to the beach and emitted a few barely audible sounds in the child's direction. Petar could hear the child gurgling in the back of his throat with delight. He answered the bird with a single medium-pitched note.

Petar and the others watched as the bird came directly to the child and nestled in the sand at his feet. The child stroked the bird several times and then gently nudged the bird towards Petar.

Petar looked in disbelief as the bird approached him. Petar stroked it, and then watched as the bird turned away and then flew off again. The three men looked at each other in wonder, and then again at the child. The child looked up at them and smiled, his eyes squinting from the bright sun behind them.

D avis heard a knock at his door. He was too tired for company and wanted to ignore it, hoping whoever it was would go away. The knocking persisted. He lay in bed for what seemed the longest time, trying to be oblivious to the patient, persistent knocking. Finally, he decided, more out of curiosity than obligation, to see who the mystery knocker might be. He threw on his bathrobe and went to the door. He was actually very startled to see who it was. Startled and delighted.

"Rachel! Why, hello."

"Hi Davis. I haven't seen you at the Phoenix for a while so I thought I'd pay you a visit. The bartender, Bryce is his name I think, gave me your address. Hope you don't mind me dropping by like this but I got lonely."

"No, no, not at all. Come in...please come in."

Rachel was wearing a tight-fitting black dress and Davis thought she looked positively voluptuous. For a while they chatted about trivial things until she reached over and touched his lips with her finger, tracing the outline of them with her finger.

"Davis, I came here because I want to make love with you." Rachel smiled broadly, waiting for his reaction.

"Well, that's wonderful," he said awkwardly, a little taken aback by her frankness and at the same time wishing he had said something a little less vacuous.

"Rachel... it's been on my mind too, but I didn't know how to... how to broach the subject."

"Well now we've broached it, silly boy. To broach or not to broach, that's the question. No more talk about broaching. Where's your bedroom?"

"Over there," Davis said, his mind a little befuddled with desire. He led her to his bedroom, eager, excited, and exuberant over the prospect before him.

As soon as they entered the bedroom Rachel sat on the bed waiting for Davis to make the first move. Davis gently pushed her back on the bed and began kissing her. She giggled. He moved his fingers through her silky black curls and then buried his face in her hair. The smell of her hair was wonderful to him. Rachel pressed her hands against Davis's chest and then sighed deeply. And then she remembered the game she had brought with her. Davis discarded his bathrobe while Rachel went for her handbag.

"Wait," she said. "I've got something for us to try out." She removed a small transparent tube filled with tiny, coloured pellets from her bag. On the side of the tube there was a cylinder with a ring attached to it. She pulled the ring, and then with her eyes flashing, she said, "Find me if you can!"

Immediately, Davis heard the sound of contained pressure being released and then a riot of coloured shapes of all kinds and sizes began to fill the bedroom. They were rubbery-firm to the touch and yet elastic. He tried to reach through the ballooning shapes to where he thought she was, but found only still other shapes that yielded to his touch, giving way before it, and yet impeding his movement.

Davis began laughing, enjoying the sudden delight of the colours and the game. As he probed and pushed his way through the elastic shapes, he could hear the peculiar sounds the shapes made as they were pressed against each other. Low, sighing sounds, almost moans, that were all the more suggestive and indicative of the kind of game that was being played.

And then Davis lunged at a shape that looked deliciously familiar. He grasped Rachel, his arms around her waist. She laughed, murmuring something about him taking so long to find her. The coloured shapes jostled against them with every movement they made. Davis simply held her for a moment savouring the experience. And then slowly, extricating herself from the delicious tangle of arms and legs, Rachel moved away and stood, drawing Davis along with her until both of them stood on the floor displacing the rubbery shapes around them. The shapes all around them continued to bump against them, and together, they receded into the abundant night.

Bach knocked loudly on Davis's door. He knew Davis was ripe for adventure, that he was tired of his sedentary existence, and wanted a change. But Bach wasn't quite sure if Davis really meant it, or more to the point, if he had the stomach for what he had in mind. Maybe, he thought, Davis was one of those quietly desperate souls who every now and again cries over a drink or two about how boring his life is, but does absolutely nothing about it. Bach was surprised at the alacrity with which Davis answered the door. He had only knocked once or twice before Davis opened the door. Davis seemed a little surprised that it was Bach.

"Oh, it's you," Davis said, with a touch of disappointment. "C'mon in."

"Well, don't act so delighted. Expecting someone else maybe?"

"No, no," Davis said, barely glancing at Bach. And then it registered. He looked Bach full in the face. Davis could scarcely believe what he saw.

"What the hell happened to you?" Bach's face was terribly bruised and still puffy from the beating he had taken.

"Ran into a shuttle," Bach said. Davis studied his friend's face. Bach's nose was broken and there was a deep, ugly cut under his left eye.

"How many stitches did that take?" Davis asked, pointing at the cut.

"Only sixteen," Bach said, looking away from Davis and surveying the apartment. Davis could see Bach's eyes scanning the place, registering the placement of furniture and the pick of things that Davis surrounded himself with. He liked it, admiring Davis's taste, though he mused that it could have been a lot tidier.

"Enough about that for now. How would you like to go on an all-expense paid trip to the null lands?" Davis was surprised at Bach's offer.

"You better believe I do," Davis answered with undisguised enthusiasm.

Bach looked at Davis closely, studying him, wanting to be sure. It was a dangerous mission, and he didn't want Davis to regret it.

"It won't be a holiday. But I can tell you, you won't be bored. My plan is to cruise over the null lands and check things out. Interested?"

"Sure am," Davis said excitedly. "But how can I get security clearance? I mean, what you'll be doing is official business, isn't it?"

"Not exactly," Bach said. "A lot of things have been happening lately, all of them unofficial it seems to me, and I want to find out how things really are... maybe things have really gotten out of hand."

Bach related to Davis what had transpired on his last mission, and then he told him about the beating. He told him about all of it so Davis could back out if he had any second thoughts about going to the null lands. Davis, so accustomed to not listening closely to anyone, listened with rapt attention to every word that Bach uttered. Davis was beginning to feel more alive than he had felt in a long, long time. First Rachel had arrived on his doorstep, and now Bach, with the promise of adventure. Things were changing in his life, and he was eager for it. He couldn't help but smile as Bach went on about what he knew of the mysterious null lands.

D avis peered through the scanner and followed the changing colours of the filaments of light that paralleled the contours of the terrain below. He found it all exhilarating. There was a true sense of adventure in accompanying Bach on the mission. For Davis, it almost seemed too good to be true. But here he was, with Bach, and on a mission.

There were moments when he felt a bit inadequate in being Bach's companion, but his confidence in himself was growing from the trust that Bach had in him. He wondered how he could have ever felt so complacent about life, so indifferent to the wider, larger, brighter world beyond the domes. And here he was, scanning a landscape he had never seen before.

Somehow he could feel the presence of the null people in the lands below their aircraft. Bach examined the monitor closely. Davis was looking out of one of the side porthole windows, gazing at the distant line of the horizon, completely oblivious of Bach's intent scrutiny of the topography below. Bach was on to something, and he knew it. There was something unusual that was being picked up by the scanner. A break in the pattern had caught his attention. The scanner's depth perception monitor revealed some very fine contour lines just below a long ridge of surface vegetation. It indicated a radical shift in elevation that didn't seem to be in keeping with surface patterns.

Bach motioned to Davis that he was going in for a closer look. Davis nodded, delighted to be part of an adventure, something as real and exciting as the night with Rachel. There was a change taking place within him, an experience of life as being something luscious and rich and infinitely desirable. Even the strangeness of his recent trances was a part of that experience. He began to watch what Bach was doing closely. Bach made another pass over the scrub land, pushing the scanning device to its limit. In a few seconds it was displayed before him. The monitor described a huge subterranean cavern with adjoining tunnels and extensive walkways crisscrossing large open spaces. Tiny bits of radiant light revealed the presence of life forms, the null people.

"Bach, there's life down there... look at all that movement. There's life down there!"

"Davis, my boy, the past is prologue. Let's go down for a closer look."

Bach descended and manoeuvred the craft into the small pocket-like depression of a sand dune beside some bushes. Bach surveyed the area with a small hand-held sensor, looking for any irregularities, any breaks in the surface patterns. The sensor could detect below-the-surface incongruities as well. Its miniature screen picked up a rectangular shape amid some of the bushes. Bach asked Davis to investigate.

Davis scrambled among the bushes, pushing the branches aside and kicking at the sand with his boots. Very soon he uncovered a small trap door just beneath the sand covering. He dropped to his knees and began searching with his hands across the top of the trapdoor. Once he had found the handle, he gave it a great pull, and suddenly, sand flew from the top of the trapdoor as it sprang open. Bach noticed the hinges were lubricated. Both Bach and Davis looked inside the opening. A ladder was attached at the lip of the opening and it descended about twenty feet to a platform area.

"Let's check it out," Bach whispered. Davis proceeded to go down first. He was a little nervous, but excited. The metal rungs of the ladder were rough, as if they had been fabricated from something that had been designed for a different function originally. Davis noticed the sunlight streaming in from above suddenly going out as Bach slammed the trap door shut. Davis hesitated for an instant, his grip tightening on the rung, and then slowly, carefully, he continued on.

Once on the platform they peered over the end of it into what seemed a great, open dark space. It took a moment or two for their eyes to grow accustomed to the darkness. They stood there in silence at the brink of a great chasm, an unknown place that drew them down, deeper into the mystery of it.

Bach walked carefully around the edge of the platform. Davis followed, observing Bach closely, looking for patterns to follow. Davis was out of his element. Bach was the key to Davis's survival here, and Davis knew it. But he was learning fast, and Bach admired the way he picked up on things quickly. He was about to say something encouraging to Davis when all of a sudden there was a whooshing sound and a splash of brilliant light, a circular ball of white light, immediately in front of them. They covered their eyes and turned away from the shocking, dazzling brilliance of it.

Both of them stood rooted to the spot, not knowing what kind of threat the white light posed. The light hovered at about waist height and moved very slowly to within three feet of them. Its luminosity lit up the platform area on which they stood, but beyond the circle of light the darkness seemed almost palpable.

Bach stepped slowly to one side and the light too moved in a parallel reaction, a correspondence, to his own movement. Then he moved towards it, stepping boldly directly in front of it. As he did this, the light moved away from him. Davis stepped towards the light, and it reacted to his movement in the same measured way it had done with Bach's movements. They discovered that with every movement they made, there was a reciprocal movement on the light's part. It was all quite strange to them.

And then they heard the same whooshing sound they had heard earlier as the light just as suddenly disappeared.

"What the hell was that?" Davis asked in a whisper.

"I don't know," Bach answered, "but I'm pretty sure it's some kind of monitoring device. We'd better get out of here. Something's up."

"I'm with you," Davis said, anxious to be out into the open again. Bach led the way as they made their way up the ladder.

Bach was just about to reach for the trap door as a metal plate automatically slid above him, locking into place, and preventing him from reaching the small handle on the underside of the trap door.

"Dammit, we're trapped," Bach said. He pounded at the metal plate above his head with the heel of his hand, but nothing seemed to dislodge it. They descended again to the platform and waited. It wasn't long before they heard sounds coming from beneath the platform.

Bach looked at Davis and smiled weakly. Davis was beginning to feel a little sick. He tried to smile back at Bach but could not.

Three men clambered up onto the platform. They were followed by four others. They quickly surrounded Bach and Davis. Without saying a word, one of the men, a tall, sombre-looking fellow, approached Bach and removed his sensor. He held it up and examined it briefly.

The platform was illuminated by a curious kind of light that seemed to emanate from a medallion-shaped object that each of the men wore on their chests. Davis swallowed hard and fought back his fear as the same man gently placed a small, yellow dot on his throat. He did the same to Bach. And then he placed one of the adhesive dots on his own throat.

Bach looked across at Davis. "I think it's some sort of language translation device. They want to talk to us," Bach said. Davis said nothing. The sombre-looking man simply nodded and then motioned to Bach and Davis to follow him. No one spoke.

D evlin had hoped that Bach would stay clear of him. Early in his career he had known Bach, and he knew that Bach could have easily attained a high position within the Defence Force had he been able to submit to arbitrary measures. Bach had a streak of the pure renegade in him and a temperament that didn't endear him to those in authority. That fact had effectively prevented him from becoming anything other than an outrider. One of the minions, Devlin mused, nothing more than a maintenance man on the periphery of things.

Because of his political connections, Devlin had managed to intercept Bach's EVA report of the Delta massacre. Devlin knew that Bach would eventually discover his interception, and that Bach would submit still another report. That was Bach.

And so, Devlin had him beaten. Devlin knew that the beating wouldn't deter Bach, but he wanted to send a signal to him that would be easy to understand. And now, Devlin had learned, Bach, and a civilian companion had left the Dome and had headed for the out worlds, or perhaps even the null-lands. Devlin wondered if they would meet some of his elite troopers. He smiled grimly at the thought. He had given orders to Krvo to have Bach killed in any operation outside of the domes and their inter-connections. He didn't need this "little irritation," as he referred to Bach among his inner circle. He had known Bach would give him trouble sooner or later. So be it. He would deal with it.

As he sat in his study, Devlin scanned the visuals on the monitor from his last mission. They were good, he thought, very good. He brought some of the images closer, so close he could see the terror in the faces of the nulls. It stimulated and excited him. Using his stylus, he intensified certain portions of the visuals. He was ecstatic. On some of them he could see the very moment when the lasers had struck, the very millisecond of death. He loved the technology spread before him. He focused on one particularly attractive null girl. Her mouth was slightly open, and her eyes showed the pure terror of a victim knowing that death was imminent. Devlin focused on the eyes, magnifying them; she was extraordinarily beautiful. And then again he focused on her mouth. What a beauty, he thought. What a pity she was gone. Devlin laughed at his sensually motivated compassion. Abruptly, he flicked the monitor off, stood up, and began pacing the room.

He stopped in front of a large framed photograph of himself taken at the end of a successful military exercise. He began to study himself carefully. The reddish-brown hair was receding above the pale complexion. The face was good, he thought, despite the pallor. The jaw-line was strong, the nose distinctively aquiline, the features decidedly handsome. But the eyes, the eyes were unique. At first glance, there was an apathetic quality to them, but on closer inspection there was something else, something unmistakably cold in them, and with the coldness, confidence. The smile was extremely engaging, he thought, the result of long practice. His eyes, however, were not compromised by the smile. They were cold and unrelenting in their gaze.

It was almost puzzling to him, that the figure in front of him was himself, that this man was Devlin, and no other. He turned away from the photograph, anxious and agitated. Devlin reached for a button on the panel in front of him and called Tara. He wanted a release, an outlet for his anxiety. There was no answer. Devlin lay back on the sofa and mused.

Devlin had risen quickly through the ranks of the League Defence Force. He was a natural, a leader who was single-minded in his devotion to duty and to detail. He was capable and solid. The only failing that was perceived and noted by his superiors in their personnel evaluations was an over-zealousness with respect to patrols of the outlands and the null territories.

The outlands or out-worlds, as they were sometimes called, were those adjacent lands bordering on the dome urbanspheres and their inter-connections. He was known to have disobeyed a commander on at least one occasion in order to pilot a flight that made an in-depth survey of null territory. Although his mission had failed to detect any signs of covert military operations as he had hoped, he did return with evidence of an intricate network of what appeared to be underground warrens. This discovery had generated some interest and speculation in the rationale behind the tunnels, but it was not considered to be a threat to the League in any way. It was dismissed as some sort of primitive shelter that the nulls had constructed against surface contaminant dangers. The mild interest it had sparked prompted the disciplinary action against Devlin to be dropped, but little else had come of it.

Devlin looked up through his skylight and above it through the heavy transparent plate of the Dome. He watched the grey scudding clouds move high above the Dome and then away. He longed to be out there, far out there in the null lands, searching for nulls. Searching for them and destroying them. It wasn't hate he felt for them. It was loathing. A loathing, that was irrational and absurd. He had even tried to analyze it, the loathing he felt for the nulls. And what he had come up with was so simplistic that it irked him to even consider it.

There were memories from his childhood. He could remember the nightmare spectres of deformed creatures oozing with their open sores, creatures crying out in pain, creatures who had wanted to embrace him. He could remember crying out in the night , trying to fend them off wildly, frantically, with every ounce of his strength, until his mother had broken their empty threat with her embrace and sympathetic sounds, calming him with her reassurances that the nulls were far beyond the Dome walls, far beyond the safe enclosure of the Dome.

He could remember these experiences vividly, but these childish fears were not the reason, could not be the reason for why he felt the way he did. Devlin couldn't have explained why he was so adamant in his loathing of the nulls. He simply wanted to exterminate them. Eradicate them. Wipe them out, pure and simple. In some obscure way he knew he feared them. He believed passionately that they posed a threat, however minimal, to the League way of life. He would do everything in his power to protect the domes, and the nulls constituted for him the one predominant threat from the outside.

He would be pre-emptive in his approach to the null threat. He would seek them out, search for them and destroy them in their own lands. And he would give no quarter. Neither would he expect any. That was one curious part of his character. Once he had set his objectives, he would meet them, regardless of the opposition.

Wherever he had applied his considerable energies and talents, he had always been fully committed. And now, despite the setbacks he had encountered, he resolved to redouble his efforts to convince highly placed League officials of the null threat. It had become an obsession. He believed that in times to come he would be remembered for the decisive actions he had taken against the nulls.

But whatever the result, whether exonerated in future times to come or not, it mattered little to Devlin. His loathing of the nulls was part of his character, his very being. He had been given the authority to form the special trooper brigades to patrol the outlands, but he had not been authorized to venture further afield into the null lands.

Despite this, he would send special missions into the null lands to do what damage he could, until he could eventually muster the greater support that would enable him to send a massive military force to deal with the nulls once and for all.

Devlin's plan was methodical. He would continue to send out small contingents of elite troopers. They would obtain whatever intelligence they could, and perhaps even incite nulls to counterattack. Destroying them had been so easy so far. Too easy. He wondered if they had the will to fight back. He found them so disgusting. He wished he could exploit something about them that would enable him to gather the needed League support. He knew so little about them. But he would know more, much more. Thinking about the nulls helped to relax him. They were creatures without hope. He would see to it that they would be without a future as well.

"Who or what is this Infanta?" Devlin cried.

Two of Devlin's officers had just told him of a child, a special child, from the null lands to the far south. They looked at each other in surprise, puzzled at the effect the news had on him, and curious over the strange tone of dread they heard in his voice. The officers wished they hadn't mentioned the Infanta. After all, they were only relating the dying words of a null creature, nothing more. They had only mentioned the incident because Devlin had insisted on more and more detail, until they had had nothing more to add to their briefing. A pathetic-looking null creature had said with his dying breath, "The Infanta, the Infanta, will come and cleanse the world!"

For Devlin, the news had focussed his deepest fears. The words suggested that the nulls had created a symbol, a personage that could give a form and a shape to their resistance. It was a dangerous symbol. So far, it had all been little more than a deadly game, this extermination of nulls. There had been no evidence of any organization, or belief system behind the random groups of nulls his men had encountered.

Initially, Devlin had thought that null hunting could be a kind of military sport useful in keeping his troops in good form while solving a problem at the same time, the problem of the very existence of null groups. But this new twist suggested to him that it would not be as easy as he had thought. The Infanta. Why did the word have such a menacing ring to it? Devlin hardly knew where he was.

He looked at his two officers. He looked around the spacious office that was his, the gleaming desk, the floor to ceiling windows, and then out to the large square below where throngs of people were walking about. Everything felt so odd, so different. Why did this word intrude on his consciousness the way it did? It was only a word. Infanta. The word reverberated in his mind. Not even looking towards them, he dismissed his officers with a curt gesture. The Infanta. He felt off balance, out of sorts. He sat in the large, ornate chair his troops had given him. He tried desperately to control his thoughts. Infanta. The word haunted him. Why?

P etar and the child walked along the wide expanse of beach. The other guardians were watchful, standing several yards away, amused by the manner in which Petar went out of his way to entertain the child. Petar picked up two large clumps of sea grape that had been washed ashore. He set one of them atop his head and held the other, simulating a bushy beard, across his face. The child laughed heartily. Petar's face shone.

The child found another clump of sea grape and imitated Petar. And then he threw it up against the sky, watching it fall a few feet away. He did this again and again, delighting in the game. Behind them the delicate, windswept pines set the backdrop to their play.

The guardians, signalling Petar, headed towards the pines, to the place where the opening to the great caverns was concealed. Petar hoisted the child atop his shoulders, and the child rested his chin upon his head.

Petar waded through the shallow waters leading to the caverns. There were great openings and sink holes in the cavern roof, here and there, allowing light to penetrate and spill in dazzling profusion where they walked. The child could see the sandy bottom at Petar's feet, no more than a foot below the turquoise waters. He turned his head to see the other guardians following behind. He waved to them with one arm while with the other he pressed tightly around Petar's forehead for support. They moved into the caves and sudden shade.

The child extended his arm to touch one of the several sculptured rock columns that rose from the bottom to the ceiling of the caves. There was a grandeur, a splendidness to the stone columns that marked the place as sacred to the southern colonies. The men were quiet, reverential, as they walked. The child squealed in delight as his hand brushed against the smooth carved face of their summer god. Petar stopped while the child shifted his weight atop Petar's massive shoulders in order to trace with his tiny fingers the features of the beloved god.

Beneath the expansive, smiling countenance of the carved god, the inscription read, "Laugh master, like a summer god." All of the guardians stood in awe as the child laughed heartily while brushing the palm of his hand back and forth against the wide cheek of the god. Petar felt a lump in his throat at the great honour he had received in being called to protect this marvellous child who seemed to transform their common daily experience into something rich and surcharged with meaning.

After a moment the group moved on past the caves into dazzling sunlight again. They were walking across a short stretch of beach which ran to another series of caverns. The child could see the breakers crashing against the coral reefs about a thousand yards south of the beach. The morning air was cool against their skin.

The Elders of the southern colonies were all of them women. The council of thirteen kept in close contact with the other colonies far to the north. Communication between the colonies, as one of the matriarchs was fond of saying, was flighty.

Messages to and from the colonies were carried by the birds of paradise, as the specially trained carrier birds were called. Their patterned chirping and cooing sounds were a code known only to the Elders of the colonies. It had been the Delta birds that had informed the Elders of the southern colonies of the attacks on the northern colonists. This news had alarmed them greatly because of the danger it posed to all, but now, particularly, to the child, to the Infanta. Even before they had received the news, there had been premonitions among the Elders of a massive force moving against them. It was then that the Elders had decided to select the guardians to protect and defend the child if necessary. He was only just beginning to know his powers. Under the guidance of the three matriarchs from the inner circle of the Elders, he would be able, one day, to fully harness the abundant energy at his fingertips. They knew it would take time, and time was what was needed most. The child's education and personal development was essential to the long-term well-being of the colonies.

The child's parents had been killed two years earlier after a hurricane had wrought havoc on the small island they had been exploring for potential habitation by the colonists. Their mission had been to determine how feasible it would be to cleanse the island of residual contaminants. They had perished in the mission. Fortunately, the child had been left with his grandmother, and his survival was now recognized as a great blessing among the southern colonies.

D evlin waited. He had been thinking about Tara for most of the day. He wanted her most when he had to wait, and she knew it. She knew it by the way his voice sounded when he asked for her, the pauses between words, the throaty way he spoke, the urgency behind whatever it was he had to say. Devlin poured himself a drink and savoured the anticipation of her coming. It had been two weeks since he had last seen her. He looked out upon the domed city, enjoying the night lights that spread a fine, lustrous sheen over the buildings and shuttle-ways. He sipped at the drink, a fiery sensation invading his mouth with the exquisite subtleness of its flavour. He noticed several of the lights dimming for just an instant, and he wondered if it meant power cutbacks. He made a mental note to check into the matter.

Then he heard someone knocking: three short raps. Devlin walked to the door very slowly, enjoying the feeling of his desire, his anticipation, his longing for Tara. He opened the door and was startled by her costume.

Tara's appearance at the door was a mild shock to Devlin. He tried not to reveal any surprise, but she saw the slight twitch around his mouth and the momentary trace of a smile that left him unguarded for a fleeting moment. She smiled in triumph. Devlin motioned to her to come in with one of his quick perfunctory gestures. She didn't appreciate the gesture; she found it demeaning somehow, and she resented it. But as he turned and moved towards the floor to ceiling window, she felt a surge of desire move through her. She watched him closely as he stood leaning over the upper, open section of the glass. The way he stood touched something in her.

Tara especially relished the time between them before they had had any physical contact. It made her almost think that she could walk away from him and be free of him without touching him. That she could be satisfied with just his company, his presence. But she knew it couldn't last. Each successive time she saw him made it harder for her to leave him for good.

Devlin turned to her. "You certainly know the way to a man's heart, my lady." Tara responded with a full warm smile, her cheeks flushing with the pleasure of hearing the word. It was the closest Devlin came to expressing any tenderness he felt towards her.

Devlin's eyes moved over her now, taking in the black velvet hood and body wrap that she was covered in from head to toe. Only her eyes were clearly visible. Her mouth and nose were covered by a piece of black gauze. He felt a hollow longing in the pit of his stomach. He moved towards her suddenly, meaning to touch her. She moved away quickly, as lithe as a cat.

"You're magnificent," he said.

She laughed, delighting in the game.

Tara stopped and looked at him. Her mouth went soft and sad. She reached up and held his face. She knew he was unfaithful to her. She knew some of his women. And she knew he would forget her the moment after he possessed her. But she cared for him. She loved him. It didn't matter to her who he had been with, or what he did when she was close to him like this. In this moment they were inseparable: the concentrated moment before consummation. It was all she had: the desire in his eyes, the feeling at the back of her throat, the weakness in her thighs.

Devlin caressed the nape of her neck. It was intoxicating for her. He picked her up, cradling her in his arms. Slowly, he carried her to his bedroom, the "bubble", he called it. The bedroom was the only room in the penthouse apartment that cantilevered out over the streets of the city, forty stories below.

From the inside of his bedroom, the view of the domed city was spectacular. On a clear day even the outline of Dome Fifty-Eight could be seen in the far distance. But on this night they could see only to the lights that illuminated the streets below, and there was little else that was visible. It didn't matter to them. Only the charmed circle of the bedroom that contained them was what mattered.

Devlin placed Tara very carefully in the center of his bed and touched her cheek lightly. He began caressing her then, passing his hand against the black velvet length of her body garment, wanting this moment of complete control, savouring it as a choice delicacy of the moment.

She pushed him roughly, shoving him backwards, knocking him from the bed. The strength of her surprised him. He was on the floor. Below him, through the transparent, high-density plastic floor, he could see the tiny, flickering lights of the city. Looking up, he saw Tara's face, aroused, aggressive. Suddenly, abruptly, he turned quiet and apart from her.

"Enough... stop," he said. Suddenly, he felt out of sorts, not in control.

"What, love?" questioned Tara.

"I said to stop! I've had enough."

"What's the matter? Did I do something wrong?"

"No, it's nothing. I've, just had enough, that's all."

Devlin left the bedroom, agitated. He poured himself another drink and sat in the great chair. Very quietly, Tara entered the living room. She was wearing one of his robes. She placed her arms over his shoulders and began gently kissing the back of his neck. She was apprehensive. Devlin pushed her away roughly. He stood up without even glancing in her direction and walked briskly to his office closing the door sharply behind him.

M ost of the troopers were asleep when the alarms sounded. On either side of the long dark corridor Devlin's troops sprang to their feet, dressing hurriedly, wondering what it meant. There wasn't even time for speculative conversation before they heard the words "night raid" blaring over the voice interlink. A tense excitement filled the air. Teams of men raced for their aircraft. The precision with which everything was done marked them as the elite guard they were. Devlin's own personal crew had already fired the engines on his silver-gray Striker, the fastest airship in the fleet.

The sound of the engines was deafening. Devlin's ship was already hovering above the departure platform. The roof of the hangar was slowly sliding open, revealing an immense full moon. Devlin's co-pilot, Dawkins, looked a little ragged from the abrupt call to arms after a heavy night of drinking. His hands trembled nervously at the control panel. The inside of his mouth felt terribly dry, and his head was pounding from the roar of the engines. He glanced at Devlin, recognized the emotional state he was in, and knew at once that this was going to be a night to remember. Devlin looked agitated and angry. Dawkins swallowed hard, momentarily forgetting his hangover.

Within moments the fleet was flying in V-formation just a mere twenty feet off the ground. The Domes were already far behind them. Ahead Devlin could see a pool of light spreading beneath the moon. He felt a wave of nausea pass through his body.

Devlin led his fleet over the shining moonlit surface of the Great Lake. He smiled at the grim speculation of what lay beneath the surface of the contaminated lake. What grotesque leviathans, he mused, moved through the murky depths of its polluted waters. Some day, he thought, he would turn his attention to ridding the Great Lake of its monstrosities. But first he must deal with the nulls. He must destroy them utterly, so completely that they could never pose a threat to the dome worlds. That was his mission, his trust. He would exterminate them all. The deformity was in them, in their very existence. It didn't matter to him that they resembled the dome inhabitants in their outward form. Appearances were like the surface of the Great Lake on this moonlit night- so fair and serene on the surface with creatures from hell below. Devlin caught a glimpse of some movement below the surface of the waters. When he looked closer, he could see nothing but a bit of foam that was already disappearing.

Devlin activated all of the scanners in his ship. His body was tight, and he could barely conceal his frustration and anger. He wanted more than anything to vent what he was feeling. He glanced at Dawkins. He could see the pores and blemishes on Dawkins's face. It nauseated him. He looked away in disgust. For the longest time nothing was sighted. The fleet cruised over the null lands without the scanners registering even a small blip on the screens. Devlin gazed involuntarily at the moon and then back to the screen again. He jumped when he noticed a tiny yellow blip that signalled null movement. He zeroed in on the target. A null was walking along the bank of a small creek. He seemed so out of place against the bleak landscape.

He was taking a stroll in the middle of nowhere. Devlin's mouth twitched into a wry smile. He could hear Dawkins breathing heavily.

Devlin pressed a command button ordering the fleet to stand by, in hover formation, while he prepared to investigate the situation. Devlin's ship landed a few yards in front of the man. The man appeared to be very curious about the landing. Without the slightest hesitation or fear, he walked up to the ship and peered in through the starboard porthole. A moment passed.

Devlin opened the cabin door and approached the man. From their hover position the troopers could clearly see all that was happening: Devlin and the man standing close to each other in the full moonlight. The man lifted a hand in greeting. Devlin simply stood there looking down at the man, who was several inches shorter. The man said something to Devlin and smiled. Devlin's eyes raked over the man, noting the loose tunic and baggy trousers.

Devlin felt a little giddy with excitement as he looked into the man's eyes. He noticed the man's expression changing from open friendliness to something altogether different. A look of fear was in it now, but the fear was mingled with the man's curiosity about what was going to happen next, almost as if he were a spectator watching someone else. The man swallowed. He groped desperately in his pocket for something he wanted to show Devlin. Devlin smiled at the man's discomfort, and then for the benefit of his troopers, he signalled the fleet's lights to be directed upon himself and the man.

The man offered Devlin a small, round, yellow dot, a miniature device of some kind. He gestured to Devlin that the dot be placed upon Devlin's neck, just under his chin. Devlin pushed the man's hand brusquely aside. The tiny yellow dot fell down into the creek. The man watched it falling, feeling hopeless. He turned away from Devlin and pointed at the moon. He was trying even more desperately to make contact with Devlin. He pointed to it repeatedly, seemingly oblivious to the bright glare of the lights from the aircraft above him. Devlin seemed amused by the man's wild gesticulations. He was trying to say something to Devlin.

Finally the man pulled a piece of paper from his tunic and offered it to Devlin. Devlin smiled, took the piece of paper from the man and stuffed it into one of the pockets in his uniform. The man looked weak and demoralized with fear, his mouth slightly open. Devlin felt a strange triumph in being able to elicit such fear. He also felt disgust. The man's hopelessness disgusted him. A quiet charged space enveloped the pair. Everything was incredibly still and bright and quiet under the glare of the lights from the fleet.

Devlin reached down and drew something out from the top of his boot. In an instant he whipped a very thin wire cord around the man's neck, jerked it suddenly, and with great force dragged the man to the ground. The man flailed his arms wildly, trying to insert his fingers inside the wire cord. He was tearing away at his own throat, desperate for air. Devlin strained and tightened his hold on the man. Several seconds passed like small eternities. The man became still.

Devlin stood up and lifted his boot high above the man's neck and stomped down hard upon it with all of his force. And then, very deftly, he retrieved the cord from around the man's broken neck and quickly strode back to his ship. He was breathing hard when he took his seat and ordered Dawkins to lift off.

Devlin's ears were ringing. He could hear Dawkins laughing. He looked at him. Dawkins's mouth was open as he laughed. Devlin could see the entire inside of Dawkins's mouth. The man's tongue revolted him. Devlin could see everything so clearly. Dawkins's pockmarked face, the loathsome pores of his skin, the attempt at a beard to conceal the devastation of his skin.

Devlin pierced Dawkins with a look that made Dawkins tremble. Dawkins turned away, focusing intently on the controls. He could feel Devlin's agitation within the confines of the cockpit. He busied himself until he could no longer feel Devlin's eyes upon him. Dawkins crouched over the controls, his skin pale and clammy under the crisp, blue uniform. The fleet followed them closely as they sped over the null lands.

Devlin examined the piece of paper the null had given him. It was written in a script he could not understand. He would have it translated by one of the language specialists at the Dome. He began to wonder about the small yellow dot the null had offered him. It struck him then that it might have been a device for communication. He wished he had taken it with him. It could have proven useful. He pushed the scanners to the limit hoping to find a group of nulls somewhere, anywhere. He needed more of an outlet for his frustration, for the deep anger that was tearing away at him. He could find nothing. He needed to think, to think clearly about a greater strategy that he could use in his null campaign.

Devlin reviewed in his mind the necessary actions he would have to take to escalate his campaign of terror against the nulls. He knew that he must gain far greater support from the Central Dome Committee. That would be difficult, he thought, since there were no apparent hostilities on the null front. They would permit Devlin's limited forays into null territory as a defensive measure, nothing more. Indeed, some influential members of the Committee had commented on his "overzealousness," as they put it, in the null arena.

He only wished the nulls had something of value to warrant a full-scale invasion of all of their lands. Was there anything of value in their worlds? Surely, there must be something. He knew that the Central Committee would have to be soundly convinced. It was a certainty that he would be reprimanded severely if news leaked of his missions into null territory for the express purpose of liquidating nulls. He wanted a purpose. He needed to find a reason for massive strikes, a motive that would appeal to Dome interests.

Marta had heard of the two captives who were being questioned. In her soul, she hated them. She wanted them to pay for what they had done to her brothers. But she needed to know why. Why were her brothers killed? Why were they doing such terrible things to her people? Why? Her grief was still raw and reeling from what had happened. She had called on Dirk to enlist his aid in getting to see them. She knew it wouldn't be easy. The Elders had called an emergency meeting, ostensibly to give the people an answer to their fears, to find some direction out of the tumult that they were presently in.

Dirk was exercising vigorously when she met him at the athletic center. He was in good form. She found him performing reverse-grip chin-ups with an abandon that startled her. Dirk would swing up and high and then down again, in great driving thrusts. He did it again and again, concentrated in his power. When he caught sight of Marta he dropped lightly to the ground and smiled brightly at her. His face was flushed and focused from his exertion. She laughed heartily at the sight of him.

"Dirk, if you keep that up, you'll be able to fly one day."

Dirk chuckled hoarsely. "You know Marta, it's the closest thing to real flying that I've ever done." Dirk watched as her face contorted in pain with the fresh memory of her brothers. He knew that she was suffering.

"Dirk... will you help me get to see the ones who've been captured? I need to see them. I want to know why they have killed my brothers."

Dirk grimaced. "I don't think we'll be able to get near them. Things have happened. Some of our people killed a group of them who came on a killing spree. The Elders have forbidden any more bloodshed. The two men have been hidden away. We wouldn't be able to get near them. But I do know where they are."

"Dirk, please help me. I can't do it without you. I need your help."

D avis pondered his fate. Here he was in the null lands, hundreds of miles from the nearest dome, a prisoner in a place that he did not know. He knew that he had no business being where he was. How could he tell his captors that his only motive was curiosity? How could he tell them that he was impelled by a sense of adventure that he needed in his life, a life that was boring and without joy, except for the odd tryst now and then.

He looked over at Bach who was sleeping on a rough cot. Davis wondered how Bach could sleep at a time like this. It would be easy for him to blame Bach for his predicament, so easy. His tales about the outrider life had been so alluring. He knew though that it was himself who was to blame. Life in the Dome may have been stagnant at times, but it was certainly safer than this. He sighed again, and noticed that Bach had begun snoring. Davis turned away and tried to sleep.

Suddenly there was a tremendous crashing sound as the door to the cell was torn off its hinges. Three men armed with crude tools barged into the room and abruptly stopped, and stood watching them. The men were quiet for what seemed the longest time. For Bach and

Davis the silence was very intimidating. There was a heaviness in the air, an ominous feeling that filled the charged spaces between the men. The feeling of dread was palpable.

Davis was terrified, and he began to tremble uncontrollably. Bach was experiencing something he'd felt only once before in his life. Everything, for him, seemed to be happening in slow motion. He had suddenly clicked into an acute awareness of the events and minute actions around him. It enabled him to think and move with the greatest alacrity. The sudden fell danger of their situation had prompted this strange, instinctive reaction. He touched the yellow dot on his throat wanting to be sure it was still there.

Bach noticed a slight movement in the finger grip of one of the men brandishing weapons. It was a very small movement, barely caught in the periphery of his vision, but enough to register in Bach's consciousness. Bach forestalled any further movement by shouting at the man.

"There's something you know that you don't know you know, and as soon as you know what it is that you don't know you know, you'll be able to leave us alone until you hear differently." Bach's voice went very low and with great emphasis on the words at the end of his statement. Davis, still in a state of shock, looked as puzzled and confused as the other men about him.

Bach levelled his gaze at the man and said, "All we want is a fair hearing. We have done nothing against you."

One of the men in front, a short, muscular man with a grizzled, hard look to him, gazed intently at Bach and said, "Men dressed such as you attacked a group of us and meant to kill us. Yes, dressed such as you are. Those are the same uniforms that brought death."

Bach met his gaze with an even, calm look and answered, "They were dressed like us, but they were not us. The colour and markings on the uniform would be different, I am sure. We have come to help."

The man was impressed with Bach's fearlessness, but even more by the simple, matter of fact way in which he spoke. Bach then related to the men what he and Davis knew about Devlin and the death squads. He spoke in a slow, measured way, all the while carefully observing the effect of his words on his listeners. And indeed, they were listening. The hard, cold cast of their eyes was changing. They were becoming relaxed, open, but very slowly. Davis marvelled at the change that was happening in front of him- from one of the most intimidating situations he had ever been in, to one of quiet understanding, an attentive encounter between men after desperate circumstances.

As Bach spoke, a rather small, odd-looking man slowly approached the gathering. Bach noticed him immediately. Just behind him two figures were hastening towards them.

Marta and Dirk were trying to make out what was happening. Dirk recognized the man Franco and a few of his followers. They were the colonists he had heard about who had survived an attack, and had accounted themselves well. They were brave men who had killed in self-defence. Dirk hoped to talk to the leader of the group, Franco. He needed men like him, to join him and organize against the killers. Before he could say a word, three Elders joined them.

O ne of the Elders smiled gently at Bach and nodded. Davis watched as the Elder turned to the man called Franco, touched him lightly on the shoulder and spoke a few words to him, very softly. The effect this had on the man was startling. Suddenly, he looked distraught. The Elder turned and spoke in low, hushed tones to the other men with Franco, and then abruptly, the group of them left.

Dirk stood back and watched. He marvelled at the ways of the Elders. These gentle, old men who appeared to hold such power over warriors. He respected them and their leadership, but they had not been able to prevent the massacres. Despite all of their quiet power, they were still unable to stop the killings. This disturbed him, for he knew how the colonists honoured them. Unless he could convince the Elders to act, he knew his efforts to rally a fighting force would be doomed. Dirk looked closely at the captives. They didn't look evil, or even threatening. He found it curious that there was nothing in the outward appearance of a person that could definitively mark that person as evil.

Marta was speaking to one of the captives. The Elder was listening to her. She was very upset. She was talking of the massacre at the Delta. She asked why, knowing within herself that there could be no satisfactory answer. Nothing said could compensate for the deaths of her brothers. Suddenly, she spat at Bach and was just about to strike him when the Elder stopped her.

"Enough," he said, in a quiet, soothing tone. "You do not know if these men are the same men who have done these things. Why do you do this? You and the others are determined to vent your hate, but you have not even taken the time to learn about these men. Are you so certain they are the killers? Let it go child. Let it go now."

Davis studied the woman's face. There was such sorrow and hurt marked across her face.

Bach simply looked at her, feeling sympathy for her. He was struck by her great beauty and was moved by the woman's emotional outburst. She was a very handsome woman with strong, handsome features and full chestnut-coloured hair. A few strands of it, moistened by her tears, stuck to her cheek. She was sobbing now, the anguish and grief over the death of her brothers brought home to her again by the sight of the uniformed strangers.

The image of her standing there, so vulnerable, so grief-stricken, touched him to the quick. Bach had never encountered a woman who had had such an effect on him. The man accompanying her, a tall, lean, powerful-looking fellow, was attempting to console her. He was not having much luck. Dirk threw a fierce look at Bach when he saw Bach looking at Marta. Bach met his gaze directly. Both men were strong in their resolve, not put off easily. Dirk drew Marta away from the group. Bach watched them as they left, wondering if he would ever see the woman again.

Davis looked about him, a little confused by it all: the sudden intrusion, the distraught young woman, the curious old man who seemed to have had a calming influence on everyone. It was all so strange. A scant week ago he had been in his apartment anticipating a night of drinking and carousing at a trendy bar. But now, here he was, not only in the null lands, but a captive deep within the confines of a subterranean world. He sighed. What was he doing here? What had possessed him to join Bach? He was out of his element. But, he reflected, that kind of thinking would lead nowhere.

He looked around his cell. All of the objects within the cell were so clear, so distinct in outline, and yet there was no artificial light. It was a kind of natural light, but where was the source? Where was it coming from? This quality of light deep underground was remarkable. His mind raced and reeled with questions. The nulls were considered primitives by Dome standards and yet everything that he had seen showed evidence of a very sophisticated civilization. How could this be? Even the walls of the cell in which he sat were made of some substance that was definitely man-made. It was incredibly fine material that he would have sworn was woven.

After the incident Bach and Davis were taken to another, larger room where there would be no chance of intrusion. The Elders were fearful that tempers might flare if there were any more killings. They were often visited by one or another of the Elders. The Elders would ask softly probing questions, curious questions about the domes and the life that was lived there. They were gentle, quiet, soft-spoken men except for the one called Anton, a plump little man who laughed a lot and seemed immensely pleased with everything around him. Whenever he laughed there was always a look of astonishment on his face as if any event, even the most trivial, was a discovery of some kind.

He took a real liking to both Bach and Davis from the start. At every opportunity he would talk with them and inform them about the world of the colonists. He told them about the first days, when, in the time of his ancestors, the great shafts and tunnels had been dug to protect the colonists and create a world beneath a world. He showed them the Great Hall, with its marble floors and polished furniture, furniture made of still living trees. Bach and Davis marvelled at how such a world could have been engineered. There was nothing in the domes that could match it. The Great Hall alone was the size of an enclosed sports stadium with an elaborate system of venting and air conditioning controls. But there was still no evidence of the light source. Neither Bach nor Davis could detect any trace of an artificial lighting system, and yet there was soft, radiant light everywhere.

Anton explained how the original colonists, fearful of the high residual levels of radiation in the air, had gone underground. There, in individual colonies, they had built towns and cities deep within the earth. On the surface of their world though, they erected modest dwellings that were replicas of villages left behind. There was a curious kind of nostalgia in this, a yearning for the life left behind. Ghost towns connected by underground shafts that brought colonists to the surface for short periods of time. Then, in the passage of time, when the radiation levels were lower, colonists could once again see the blue sky and feel the warmth of the sun against their skins, but not for too long. The very winds that caressed their bodies brought contamination and death. And so they went below to a world they had fashioned out of their desperation, their dreams, and their fervent hopes.

And there, they dreamed of the way it was, and eventually, their children dreamt their fathers' dreams, and imagined the way it might have been. Still, there was always this yearning to be on the surface with the wind, the sea, and the moving sky. Whenever the radiation levels were low enough, there would be a pilgrimage back to the surface, to one of the ghost villages that dotted the landscape above the great underground colonies.

Recent developments had been very encouraging. Air filtration techniques had begun to cleanse the air of the radioactive contaminants, but the colonists were still decades away, in the best prognosis, from enjoying the kind of environment that their ancestors had taken for granted. Despite the negative forecast, there was a new excitement circulating in the colonies. A small group of colonists had even begun some experimental agricultural work on the surface, and they had spoken rapturously about the time they had spent toiling and cultivating the soil using antiquated tools from the underground museums.

But even that bubble of hope had burst when Franco and his team had been attacked by the troopers. As Anton spoke of these things, a tired, sad look came into his eyes. He couldn't understand. There was no reason for the killings.

He looked at Davis intently for a moment and then smiled. "You have come to us without weapons and without hate. But why have you come?"

Davis listened to Anton closely and noted the sadness of the tone in his voice. "We have come," Davis answered, "because of what's happened. We know that some of our troopers are murdering your people. We wanted to see for ourselves if this situation, these killings, were unprovoked. We want to do what we can to stop the killings."

Anton's face darkened. "We have done nothing. We keep to ourselves, quite apart from your domes. We have observed your dome dwellings and have kept well clear of them. Since the old, troubled days of war, we have kept apart. After that time of nuclear blasts and counterblasts, the people that survived chose either to live in the domes or in underground colonies. During that time, in the first of our days, our leaders led their people to what you have called the null lands. The world was a desolate place. Everything was devastated. Death was in the air. The early colonists would have died from the radiation but for the vision of the first of our Elders. They led the colonists to caverns, dark, dank places at first, but in time, the caverns became our home, and we began to thrive. So you see, we have survived one disaster after another. We have created victories out of our losses; we have fashioned new worlds out of the earth. It has been a great time for the colonies. But now the killings... the old sorrows are visited again upon the colonists. It would be a great thing if you can help us stop this senseless killing."

Davis was deeply impressed with Anton's words. He would do anything in his power to help the colonists. For the first time in his life he had found something bigger than himself and his little circumscribed world. It wasn't a mere adventure now, a little episode to talk about in the Phoenix over a few drinks. This was a life and death issue, and he could help.

The child was playing near the entrance to the grotto. He was scooping up the coral sand with his hands, delighted by the feel and movement of it through his fingers. Behind him there were several tree trunks that rose from about two feet of warm tropical water to support a stone roof. Lattice-like stone walls carried the weight of the roof as well.

The child looked at his guardians, his eyes suddenly excited and bright. He scampered into the shallow waters of the grotto. The child revelled in games of hide and seek. Hiding behind one of the columns, he made a face at Petar, and then stuck his tongue out at the other guardians. Petar pretended to be shocked and slowly approached the child with his arms outstretched as if he were a huge monster. The child squealed with raptures of delight as he feigned terror and eluded Petar by splashing his way to another column. Petar and the other guardians smiled at the child, this special child whom the Elders called the Infanta. All of them loved him. This wonderful child with his dark eyes, curly brown hair, and his one dimpled cheek.

The protectors were very proud to have been chosen as guardians. They were hard, carefully selected men who would protect the Infanta with every fibre of their being. They knew this was their role, and yet the Infanta made it seem so pleasant, so joyful. Here they were hovering about him with feigned menace and tender smiles. He would have been like any other child but for the gift.

The Elders had discovered his uncanny ability to heal with his touch. Once, during an open council session of the Elders, the child had noticed an older boy who was lame. The Infanta had approached the boy who was a friendly, heavy-set lad and had said to him, "Hurt? Hurt?" The boy had smiled while the Infanta had passed his hand lightly along the boy's crippled leg. The boy, amused at first, listened attentively to the strange, almost inaudible sounds the Infanta was making. The boy felt a tingling in his leg, a numb feeling that became something else, something responsive and strong. He shouted with joy and kissed the Infanta. The Infanta smiled. The Elders who had witnessed the act looked at each other and nodded appreciatively. It was a gift, they agreed, but a gift that must be nurtured and developed for the good of the Infanta and for the good of the colonies.

Petar smiled, watching the child play in the sand. It was a splendid day, clear and bright and fresh. Petar could see the sunlight spilling through the latticed stone walls creating a sun-dappled effect on the shallow waters beneath the stone roof. The smooth tree trunks supporting the roof resembled the brown bodies of ancient warriors standing at attention. Petar had come to love the child deeply. But he was growing ever more fearful of dangers that might befall the child. There were reports, reports from the northern colonies, disturbing messages of unprovoked attacks on colonists, of a massacre. Petar knew of the great domed worlds far to the north, and he felt instinctively that the danger lay there.

Marta was wandering alone through the Gardens when she recognized the man she had wanted to attack at the cell. He was looking intently at the floating lily pads, obviously intrigued at some aspect of the plants. Since their last encounter she had learned that the two men were not the killers she had thought them to be. There were even rumours that they had come to help and offer what services they could. Very tentatively she approached Bach. In a circuitous manner she came closer and closer to him. She was curious about him. Totally absorbed in his observations, he didn't notice her until she was almost upon him.

Suddenly Bach turned, and saw her. They were both startled. Marta moved to leave, but she saw the look of concern in Bach's face. She hesitated.

"Please," Bach said, "don't leave. Please. I'd like to talk to you."

Marta looked at the strong, lean face of the man, the features softened by the gentle hazel eyes and the warm sympathetic tone in his voice.

"Yes, yes," she said softly. "But before you say anything, I want to apologize to you. I'm sorry. I know now that I was wrong. It wasn't you. You weren't responsible for the killings, and I was rash... no, I was stupid. I'm sorry... believe me, I'm sorry."

Bach could plainly see the anguish in her eyes. Her face revealed so much. Her brothers' death and the sorrow of it ran deep in her soul. And now, together with all of this, this new feeling of embarrassment made her feel awkward and timid. She looked away from Bach.

"I understand. I want you to know that I am very sorry for what has happened. I know who is responsible, and my reason for being here is to stop the massacres if I can."

Marta touched him softly on his forearm, knowing that his compassion was real. Bach was grateful for her touch. No one had touched him in such a gentle, caring way in a long, long time. Once again he saw the great beauty that she was, and smiled. She hesitated briefly and then returned his smile.

They were together in a huge underground garden. The lush beauty of the place was breathtaking. Ferns, vines, and tropical trees festooned with blossoms of every colour and hue surrounded them.

They walked through the well tended garden pathways and began to talk quietly about themselves. A few hours passed like minutes. Quietly, softly, an understanding grew between them that was as rich and lush and as full of promise as the thousands of buds that were everywhere around them.

They walked along the meandering paths, through the heavy, verdant foliage, each exquisitely aware of the other, each hesitant to speak and break the comfortable enchantment that they created together. Every now and then Bach was puzzled over the innocence of the emotions he was feeling.

Marta pointed to a cleft in some rocks ahead of them, just behind some flowering hibiscus bushes. She asked Bach if he'd like to see the Pink Coral Cavern. Bach nodded his assent. Just to be with her was an exquisite experience for him. He followed her through the opening in the rocks, and once inside the cavern he saw a sight he had never beheld before.

There were people everywhere enjoying themselves amidst steady streams of pink steam and vapours issuing from openings on the cavern floor. It was so incongruous to Bach, seeing the cloudlike gushing formations, so pink and fluffy, emanating from the rock underfoot. There was exuberance in the air, something festive and delightful, and altogether wonderful for Bach.

Children were playing hide-and-seek, shrieking with laughter and delight, leaping and running through the pink, pearly clouds at their feet. Bach looked across at Marta and smiled broadly. He couldn't remember ever having felt so good. It was a joyous feeling, and he could see it reflected in Marta's face. Marta took his hand in hers, and with the very slightest squeeze, she communicated her tenderness towards him. The rest of the day passed in such a wonderfully idyllic manner, amidst the colours and forms and sounds of laughter, that it marked a threshold in their relationship, a special place and a beginning for the two of them.

Bach looked again at Marta. He had never felt this way about any woman. It was as if he were walking two feet off the ground. The world was charged with meaning. Everything was brighter, bigger, better. She pressed his hand tightly as they walked. She wanted to share the garden with him. She too felt a growing tenderness developing with this man, a tenderness edged with excitement and wonder. It seemed to her at times that she ought not to feel this way. There were sharp moments in which she experienced the horrible realization that her brothers were dead, forever gone.

How could she feel this way, so joyful and exuberant, after what had happened to them? They had as much right to life as she did. They should be here in this garden, walking and laughing and living.

Bach could see the sudden sadness in her eyes, and he wanted to distract her. "Marta, what is that creature, there... do you see it?"

Bach pointed to a curly-tailed lizard darting across their path.

Marta laughed. She touched his arm, explaining to Bach how difficult it had been initially to habituate lizards, imported from the southern colonies, to the underground worlds. It was only when the energy of neutrinos had been developed and harnessed to light the underground colonies that more and more surface creatures were able to make the transition. The great holocaust, she explained, together with the environmental degradation on the surface, simply posed too great a threat to the overall quality of life there for all creatures.

The dome worlds, Bach reflected, had preserved the human quality of life within dome structures, but not a single non-human creature was permitted to exist within dome territory. On several of his duty tours he had seen large mutant rodents and other strange creatures that he didn't have names for, but that he had wondered about.

Marta was eager to show him everything. It was her world, and she wanted to share it with him. She even bit her lip wondering if he might stay here in the colonies. She was giddy with excitement at the thought.

Bach smiled at this charming, handsome woman whom he had had the immense good fortune to meet. Suddenly, she turned to point something out to him and found her face close to his, almost touching. He could feel her breath close to him, intoxicating him with her presence. His lips found hers, and she felt her knees go weak and she leaned against him, against his strong thighs for support.

In the delicious, delightful weeks that followed, the love between them blossomed and grew. Davis was glad of it. Bach was being transformed before his very eyes. He followed Marta everywhere, enraptured by her, smiling at everyone. Whenever he grew serious, thinking about the past, reflecting on his failed marriage, she would sense it immediately, and tease and poke at him lightly until he would leave the past behind with its bitterness and regret and lost possibilities. Soon the past ceased to have a hold on him, and its spoiled memories were lost in the rich, bright details of his present experience, the living moment with his Marta.

Davis was happy for him. Seeing them together made him think of Rachel, and the remembrance of that one encounter in his apartment was like a powerful drug to him. He wondered if he would see her again. Davis walked across the polished marble floors of the Great Hall and looked at the great expanse of contained space. It was amazing. High above him he could see dancing neutrinos of light rendering everything that they fell upon with a sun-bright brilliance. As he walked he could hear the sound his footsteps made against the marble. There was no one else but himself in the Hall, and so he felt he had an opportunity to examine things more closely.

The great podium was massive, and as Davis moved his fingertips over a part of it, he marvelled at the smoothness of the structure that was similar to the petrified wood he had once seen in one of the dome museums. The podium was very solid at its base and then arched out in an elegant fashion high above Davis's head. He remembered Anton telling him that it was here that the Elders addressed the colonists on matters of importance.

Davis looked over the lip of the great podium and on to the marbled floor beneath him. There was a majesty and sweep to the design of the place. He could imagine the Elders meeting here to address large audiences, moving them with the power and passion of great oratory.

He closed his eyes and began to breathe deeply, trying to envision a vast assembly of people, there, in the great space below him. For the longest moment he continued to concentrate, relaxing all the while, until be felt his head nodding slightly, ever so slightly and involuntarily. Suddenly there was a phrase in his consciousness, words that urged him to speak, impelled him to articulate his thought. Slowly, he felt his mouth open slightly, and the muscle of his tongue began to move.

"Around every circle, a larger circle can he drawn." He repeated the words again and again and then began to concentrate on his breathing.

Davis felt a great wave of comfort swell up under his concentration. He was utterly relaxed and attentive to his trance experience. As his eyelids slowly lifted, he saw a figure moving across the marbled floor below. There was an ease and grace in the movements that Davis thought was wonderfully quick and elegant at the same time. As the figure came closer, Davis discovered that it was an old man, his lively movements a contrast to the wizened, lined face that was radiant with joy. There was a blurred edge to what Davis was seeing, a haziness around the periphery of his vision. He was conscious of it, but he wasn't distracted by it.

The old man's face, suffused with a glowing gentleness and a quiet mirth, looked up at Davis from below the platform on which

Davis stood. The old man winked at him. And then Davis saw him engage in a series of physical movements of great beauty, elegance, and precision. There was an absorbed attention that marked even the smallest finger movements of the elderly gentleman. As Davis watched, he felt surges of joy that paralleled the majesty of the old man's movements across the marble. He was dancing a marvelous dance.

Davis was totally absorbed in following the slow, practiced motions of the man. Around everything he saw, there was a hazy perimeter, as in a dream. Davis began to feel a growing sense of elation. He was experiencing something of a profound nature as he stood there observing the figure against the marbled backdrop. He was happier than he had been in a very long time. For the next several moments he enjoyed the individual spectacle in front of him. When it was over, he watched the small, slim figure walk slowly away, receding further and further into the distance. Just once he saw the man turn and wave at him. The man was smiling broadly.

Davis sensed something just behind him. Anton touched Davis's elbow. Davis turned slowly, his head and neck moving in short, step-like movements, to see who it was. Anton's congenial smile drew him out of the rapt concentration of his trance. Anton's eyes were curious, speculative.

"What did you see?" Anton asked. Davis was coming out of the trance. He was happy to see Anton.

"The strangest thing," Davis replied, "an old man, dancing... but the dance... it was unlike any I have ever seen. It was very slow and very beautiful. The old man was lithe and quick, and he moved incredibly gracefully. Each of his steps, each gesture, was fluid and easy. It was like a dream, Anton, and I feel so relaxed now. There was something about the man and his dance that had me so absorbed that I forgot where I was." Davis fell silent remembering the event. He stood motionless, staring at the marbled floor.

"What did he look like?" Anton asked.

"Small, slim. He was very fit looking, but he looked very old. He was so elegant and confident in the way he moved. He waved at me, Anton, just as he was leaving. It was something I never expected to see... the dance I mean... I remember every detail, everything."

"Good! Good!" exclaimed Anton. "You have seen something most special Davis, most special. You have seen the dance of Chi, one of our finest and most beloved founding fathers. No one living has seen the dance, and there were no records kept of the exquisitely fine and lively steps of the master. You say you remember everything. Can that be true? If it is true, you have been given a very special vision, a vision into the past that can prove a legacy to us here and now. Oh Davis, this is a most remarkable thing! You see it was only after Chi was long dead that people remembered the joy the dance brought... the performance of it... to all who saw it. Chi simply danced. He never insisted that people adopt it. Of all of the Elders of that great period none is remembered so fondly as Chi for what he gave us so graciously, and for what we have lost."

Davis looked thoughtfully at Anton.

"Anton, do you mean that this vision that I have had is important?"

"Oh yes, yes," replied Anton. "You have tapped into something here in the Great Hall. Something magnificent. A resonance of a past performance by Chi. A moment that only you have accessed. You have told me that the dance was a joyful thing to experience. We had lost that till now. Only you can link us up to that event. It is a thing of great beauty. Many have speculated on what Chi's gestures and movements meant without actually seeing them. Some have tried to duplicate the dance from what scant records exist but with little success. We know only that Chi's dance gave joy to those who looked upon it, an actual physical experience of joy... of that we know. You are a very special man Davis, very special." Anton embraced Davis and then asked him to describe his vision again, going over everything in minute detail.

Dirk entered the great marble hall. He walked resolutely toward the kneeling figure, and he stopped a few paces behind the man. The Elder, Mayerling, turned and smiled, rising to greet him.

"You have asked to see me Dirk." Dirk was impressed with the Elder's poise.

"Yes, I wish to know why you said to Jak that you wanted to help prepare a defence group. I had thought you were against any military preparations."

"I was," he said, "but I have had some unsettling visions lately, and now I know I must move in a way that is linked with yours."

Dirk was eager for the support the Elder could give him in building a force. He knew that Jak and many others would join willingly with this news.

The Elder smiled, "Dirk... I wish to take an active role in the training of the warriors, a very active role."

Dirk was a bit perplexed. "Forgive me my bluntness, but apart from your influence and your support as an Elder, how can you help us with the actual training?"

"Ah, you are sceptical of my abilities in that quarter. I thought you might be. We spoke once before... about circles, do you remember? I know you were annoyed at the imagery I was using. But we cannot defend ourselves against a greater force without the right kind of training. Come, I will show you what I mean."

For the next several weeks Mayerling revealed to Dirk the subtle, perfected motions of a master warrior. Mayerling spoke very little. He was very attentive, however, to the warriors that Dirk had assembled, watching their every move. Both Davis and Bach were impressed with the colonist warriors that Dirk had assembled. He had a special group of about fifty that he set apart from the rest. They were a high-spirited lot, boisterous and proud. Bach could see they were restless and eager for action. Dirk was able to contain them, but just barely.

Davis noticed that one of the Elders, Mayerling, spent a lot of time observing the men, attending to what they were saying, and smiling over their incessant chatter. Davis learned that Mayerling would be training the men along with Dirk. Mayerling was a very quiet man who was held in high regard by the colonists. He was short and wiry, with a square chin and a bright, intelligent look about him.

Mayerling asked Dirk to sit while he spent some time with the men. He walked up to one of the biggest men, and he tossed a short staff to him. Mayerling motioned to the man to attack him. The man resisted. Mayerling, after all, was an Elder and barely reached the shoulder height of the man he challenged. Dirk nodded to the big man to go ahead. Davis looked at Bach in disbelief. The Elder would be seriously injured if not killed. The big man charged at Mayerling letting out a fearsome cry as he lunged at the still, poised body of the Elder. Mayerling leapt aside at the last instant, whirled around, and kicked high at the man's stomach. Big Tanner fell to the ground, grasping for breath. Mayerling had moved so quickly that Davis could scarcely believe his own eyes. Bach smiled in appreciation. This was an Elder of high spirit, and he mused, high kicks as well.

"Noise and movement," Mayerling said, as he helped the big man to his feet. "These give you away…let's try again." Mayerling pointed to a couple of lean, muscular men and Dirk gave them a signal to go after Mayerling. Each of the men advanced slowly, from opposite sides of the Elder. And then, abruptly, they rushed towards him. Mayerling stood motionless, waiting. At the last possible moment, he leapt to one side as the two men collided. Before they could get to their feet Mayerling was upon them, numbing each of them with a finger thrust just under the jawline. Stunned and shaken, they joined the others.

"Leave noise and movement behind. Seek the pivot points in yourself and others. That is all for today. Just one thing... don't talk so much." Mayerling smiled kindly at them all. He inhaled very deeply and then exhaled audibly. Taking up his cloak, he left the hall quickly, just stopping long enough to say a few words to Dirk.

On the tenth day of their training with Mayerling, Dirk asked if they were ready. "Not yet... they're pushing too hard, still relying too much on noise and movement. Not yet." After another ten days, Dirk asked again.

"Much the same," Mayerling answered. "All flash and sound. Nothing true."

Another ten days passed. "Well?" Dirk queried.

"They're not comfortable yet. Too much spirit and ferocity in their engagements."

On the fortieth day, the question was asked still again. "I believe they're as ready as we can hope. Look. Do you see any loudness or swaggering? They have found the stillness of their pivot points. They're comfortable in it. Any enemy would be too terrified to face them as they are."

Mayerling looked around the hall, content.

D evlin awoke abruptly. He felt lousy. His eyes were puffy, and he felt a great weariness around them, He tried to forget the feeling in his stomach. It had been a good night. We pay for our pleasures, he thought, as he recalled the night with Tara. He remembered what she had said to him. It was almost like a refrain in his mind. He kept on hearing it again and again.

"You tell me that you love me. You tell me that you care. But you don't really love me. You don't really care."

In the throes of their passion she had stopped herself, stopped him, had held his face with her hands in the darkness for a moment, and had said that to him. She had said it flatly, in a matter of fact manner, but there seemed to him to be such an element of sadness in it that it touched him and had him confused in the instant she said it. But immediately after she had spoken, she resumed where she had left off, and their passion seemed to ignite, to explode into such exquisite sensations that it took their very breaths away.

When he thought about it, that night was the highest peak in their relationship. Tara had rocked him as she had never rocked him before. He had never known her to have such raw power, raw force. When the last surges of their lust was spent, they fell back against the bed, sated with their encounter, dampened by their desires, and laughing, laughing that such an incredible experience could have actually happened, and happened to them.

A day earlier Devlin had sent off the note he had been given by the null he had killed. More out of curiosity than anything else, he had sent it off to be deciphered by the Special Services group under his command. A messenger had just arrived in his office with the news.

"Sir, it's an odd piece. It doesn't seem to make much sense. The language was easy enough to decipher; however, the message is poetic in nature. And that makes it difficult to establish a clear meaning. It's ambiguous, something about a magical child, an infant in some place, an island, we think, far to the south."

Devlin grew agitated. His face went ashen, and his voice trembled as he spoke, "I want you to find out where this place might be, given what we know about the null areas to the south. Give it... special priority," Devlin said almost in a whisper.

"I want to have this child brought before me ... at any cost. Do you understand me?"

The messenger nodded quickly, feeling the intensity of Devlin's eyes upon him. It made him feel uneasy. He saluted and left, leaving the translated piece with Devlin.

Devlin thought back to the man he had killed. He remembered how the man had been trying to speak to him, the fumbling desperation of a man who knew he was in grave danger. How Devlin wished he had let the man communicate to him. He remembered the man offering him a tiny yellow dot. He wondered if it might have been some sort of communication device. What was the man doing there alone, in the middle of nowhere? Writing poetry under a full moon? How absurd Devlin thought.

D avis had never before felt such excitement, He was learning about the world of the null people, and there was great ad-venture in it. Their feats of engineering below the ground were even more impressive than those above-ground structures of the dome worlds that he knew so well. He was even discovering that there were certain areas where engineering left off and something altogether different began.

Anton had explained to Davis how all of their energy needs were met. Neutrinos, the quintessential energy source, had been harnessed to provide the underground colonies with all of their heat-ing, cooling, and lighting needs. With his own eyes, Davis had seen Anton manipulate the energy of the neutrinos in a playful, imaginative way. There was nothing to compare it with. There were no reference points. Bach too could not understand it. Both he and Davis had discussed it, and puzzled over it to the limits of their understanding. And then they had fallen silent over the mystery of it. Anton was keenly amused at their confusion. He found it immensely amusing that they found it so hard to accept something they could not rationally explain.

Davis marvelled at the wide range of work and recreational ac-tivities among the colonists. There seemed to be a general spirit of contentment in the air as people went about their work. Whether a person was sweeping a floor or painting a wall mural, there was a keen absorption in the activity at hand, in the "living moment of it," as Anton had described it.

Davis was curious about it all. He was curious about the life direction the null people had taken, a direction so different from the dome way. He caught himself. They were the null people no longer. He knew them now as colonists, as people like himself. Null. The very word had such negative connotations. As nulls they were hated and hunted. As colonists, as friends, Davis wanted to be at one with them. He wondered why they hadn't effectively countered the threat that Devlin and his troopers posed to their way of life, to their very existence. Judging from what he had already seen of their world, they seemed capable and organized enough to fight back, to defend themselves, and perhaps even beat Devlin's forces at their own game. He speculated on this for a time, and then he noticed Anton motioning to him to join him in the Great Hall.

Anton was alone in the Great Hall looking at the light source high above them. Davis watched him. He was so concentrated, so absorbed in the rich brilliance of the light that Davis thought he had forgotten about summoning him. Anton turned to Davis and invited him with an upwards hand gesture to watch what was about to happen. Davis looked up for a moment, but nothing changed. Anton was smiling as if he had made a fantastic joke. Bach had joined them wondering what they were up to. And then the light dance began, very slowly at first, and then gaining in power and velocity, gathering what seemed to be a momentum of its own.

Anton could see the wonder in Davis's eyes. High above them, the light source, the myriad neutrinos of light were moving in great swinging patterns from one end of the Hall to the other. Anton delighted in the dazzling display of light movement he was creating. Every now and then amid the splendid changing patterns, Anton would look to see the astonished wonder in Bach's and Davis's eyes. He was amused at the contrast between their reactions.

Davis couldn't believe what he was seeing. He was overwhelmed by the sheer wonder of it all. Bach, on the other hand, was trying to figure things out. There had to be an incredibly sophisticated technology at work here, he thought. He wanted to find out how it was all happening. They watched the moving abundance of light, and they began to smile. They had seen nothing like it before. Neither Bach nor Davis had anything in their experience to compare it with.

Suddenly both Bach and Davis broke out into laughter, loud, rolling laughter that echoed throughout the Great Meeting Hall. Anton himself was chuckling like a mischievous boy. Soon Bach and Davis were on the floor doubling over with laughter. A part of Bach was observing the experience, amazed at the way things were happening, at the sight of the elliptical patterns of light that were providing such delight. He hadn't experienced anything even remotely similar since he was a child. Davis was totally absorbed in the experience. The laughter and the light intermingled until both of them were delirious with the joy of the experience.

In the weeks that followed, Anton introduced Bach and Davis into the world of the colonists, and in the process of explaining his world to them, he grew to understand their own. What they learned was altogether unexpected from what they had thought of the colonists' world and culture. Bach and Davis discovered that their own dome science and technology, had continued on a straight line of development, admitting no deviations from the strict series of logical, developmental events. This was altogether different from Anton's world. The colonists' technology had circled in upon itself, assuming elegant shapes that were not fixed but fluid and alive, transformed in their own evolution so that each stage of technological development became a cause for celebration, for delight, for imaginative recreation.

Whenever there was an opportunity for it, Bach would press Anton for information on the light source. How was Anton able to make the light move? What was the light made up of? What was the source of it? Anton would bring them to the Great Hall and show them the beauty of the moving light.

"Anton," exclaimed Bach, "You have tremendous will-power. I'm amazed at what you can make these mysterious particles do."

Davis just stood there, open-mouthed, incredulous at what he had just seen.

"But Bach, it is not will that makes it happen so. It is here," he said touching his chest with his forefinger, "here, in the human heart, the desire to make things happen so, the vision to make it so, the desire to have it be."

The light continued to move in patterns of great delicacy and beauty high over the marble floor of the Great Hall. There were times when the light seemed to slow somewhat, stopping here or there at some whim of Anton's.

"Teach us how you do it Anton, show us how," Davis asked.

"These are not tricks," Anton said, emphasizing the word tricks as if they were missing the point of it all somehow.

"The way to begin is not with trickery or even a method, but with the poetry of images. That is how things happen. Not with will, but with desire. I do this because it is a way of showing my love and my joy."

Bach studied Anton's broad beaming face, the eyes bright and lustrous. "Anton, I'm curious about the light. What is the source? Where is it coming from?" Anton looked up into Bach's lean, hardened face.

"Neutrinos," he said succinctly.

Bach was obviously at a loss to understand the significance of the word. Davis was trying hard to remember what little science he had without much luck.

Anton chuckled. "Neutrinos. They are bits of energy from beyond the skies that we have harnessed for our use. Sun use. I am simplifying this, but you will come to understand. I will show you the place where we have them... in our observatory. There, that is where the great discovery was made. You see, in the first days after the terrible destruction of the nuclear wars, all of the heavy water was sealed deep within the earth. One of the first Elders, a man named Tezlar, a man of great vision and science both, hit upon the idea.

Anton brought them to the observatory. It was housed within a hollowed-out cavern and consisted of a huge tank filled with water.

"In the early days," Anton explained, "our scientists would study the subatomic particles known as neutrinos, which originate in the sun and the stars. They wanted to determine if these invisible particles were the basic kind of matter in the universe. They found that heavy water interacts more efficiently with neutrinos than ordinary water. Located here, deep underground, there was no danger from interference by natural radiation. You see, light was produced when the neutrinos penetrated the underground chamber and collided with the nuclei of the heavy water atoms. This is where it all began. Tezlar positioned sensitive photo-multiplier cells around the tank to record the amount of light produced. It was an exciting time. He discovered that neutrinos exist everywhere. They are the very stuff of the universe."

Anton smiled. "Here, right here, in this very place, the universe showed itself to us. At first, we watched. It was a marvellous time of rich discovery. And then, much later, after the hard discoveries had been made, we played. And that's where the magic, the poetry comes in."

T he Infanta ran splashing through the water, making faces at one of the guardians. Suddenly the low drone of an aircraft could be heard overhead. The sound of it instantly galvanized the attention of the men surrounding the small boy. One of the men raced to the trapdoor hidden beneath some shrubs. He scrambled to lift the heavy lid that led to the underground chambers below. He held it open while he gestured to the others to hurry over. The Infanta chuckled and pointed to the aircraft in the sky above them. His joy in sighting the craft made him oblivious to the concern and fear the guardians felt.

The Infanta, surprised at all the commotion, looked into the eyes of Petar, the protector cradling him against the sudden rush of sound and motion. Petar carried the Infanta to the safety of the nearest brush. He reckoned that he was too far away from the trapdoor to make it before they were sighted by the aircraft. It was nearing sunset. He prayed for it to fall quickly. He glanced at the Infanta. Petar was startled by the look in the child's eyes. There was such sweet consolation in them, such gentle consideration for Petar's own sake that Petar's eyes welled up with emotion despite his anxieties over the situation they were in. He felt a lump deep down in his throat. The child raised his right arm and softly caressed Petar's cheek. There was something altogether wonderful about this child whose subtle influence seemed to evoke such great tenderness in any that came near to him.

The light had almost gone from the sky. The sun fell into the sea, and Petar caught a glimpse of a sharp green light against the horizon and then it was gone.

The sounds of muffled explosions could be heard about them. The guardians scattered. That was the strategy followed in the first moments after an attack. The priority was to keep the Infanta safe. Everything else was secondary. Petar and the Infanta were safe in the scrub bush, at least for the moment.

Petar could hear the sounds of small aircraft landing nearby, and then, after a few minutes, nothing but silence. Petar was keenly alert for any clue that would tell him what was happening. He pressed the child closer to him. Suddenly a staccato burst of laser shots whizzed by them. The attackers were firing at random about three feet off the ground, aimless shots meant to flush out anyone hiding in the bushes. Petar could feel his heart pounding. His body curved over the child in an arc of safety. His weight rested on his elbows. The child was quiet, very still, as if he apprehended the danger of their situation.

Petar heard something like a gasp and then the dying cry of one of the guardians. Petar lay very still hearing only the light breathing of the child. Several of the laser shots came very close, but they were safe. Oddly, after each of the laser shots, the coloured tracers lingered in the night air for a full minute before dissolving. There was a criss-cross pattern of greens, blues, reds, and yellows around them. Petar knew the purpose of the coloured tracers. If there was a hit, the victim could be found by following the tracer colour. The Infanta, looking up through the opening of Petar's massive arms, saw the cat's cradle network of colours. He smiled and cooed in Petar's ear.

"Pretty colours, Petar, pretty."

Petar nestled the child in closer to him and whispered softly, "Shh… shh . . . shh . . . ."

The child looked up in wonder at the netted rainbow and smiled. Petar waited until not a sound could be heard and everything was completely motionless. Then, with the sleeping Infanta in his arms, he crawled out of the scrub brush. He almost stumbled over the two bodies of the other protectors. He was glad the child was asleep. He made his way towards the distant place where a safe haven could be found for the child. For himself he did not care, but the Infanta must be safe. Petar was not afraid of death, but the precious child must be protected and kept safe and alive. He jogged lightly to the place several miles distant to where another trapdoor led to the subterranean world of the colonists, where the child would be safe.

The child was still asleep when Petar opened the trapdoor and descended the ladder to the place where there was a cache of food and other necessities for just such an emergency. The Infanta was safe. Within moments he placed the child in a small bed and covered him with warm blankets. He looked around the small room and noticed that everything was in place just as he remembered. The child began to snore softly and Petar smiled. He went to one of the monitors near the foot of the ladder and, as he had been instructed, entered a special code word on the keyboard... Olympia. The word would signal that the Infanta was safe. Too exhausted to enter what had happened to the others, he simply went over to the sleeping child, made him comfortable, and then lay on the floor beside him.

A nton looked steadily at Davis while Davis was in trance. He recognized that Davis was in a medium-level trance by the respiratory pattern and by Davis's lack of normal facial expression. His facial muscles were completely relaxed. Anton touched Davis lightly on the shoulder and Davis slowly roused.

"You enjoy trance wandering," Anton said softly.

"Yes," Davis said. "I like it because it's as comfortable and as good as it gets. But you said 'wandering'. What do you mean by 'trance wandering'?"

Anton laughed mischievously. "In trance," he answered, "it is the wandering that takes you here, there, everywhere. It is not the same you that travels and that wanders. You leave behind the parts that can't wander. I myself have wandered far, but unlike you, I've never seen the dance of Chi!"

Anton was very impressed with Davis's recent experience of having witnessed the lost dance performed by the master Chi. Davis had informed him of every detail of the event, and now, the colonists could re-create the legacy that had brought such joy to the people in earlier times. Anton was grateful and wished to give something precious, in return, to Davis.

"Davis," Anton asked, "would you like to wander? If you wish, I can assist you. You may discover something of value on this journey."

"Sure," Davis replied. "I'd like to do that. I've only done it on my own so far, but I've never gone as deeply as I've wanted to go. I'd like to go further. Do you think I'm ready?"

"Yes, yes." Anton said. "Already, you have seen the great dance. Like a gift, it fell upon you because you were receptive to it, open to it, open to an experience that was waiting for the right person to receive it. Oh yes, you are ready to wander."

Very slowly, very gradually, Davis went into trance and then came out of it again. He did this, at Anton's request, several times successively, each time going a little deeper, but never further than a medium-level trance. Anton watched Davis's every movement carefully, attending to the slightest change, the smallest motion, observing everything.

And then Anton began, "Yes Davis, yes. You are sitting comfortably and now, now you can begin to relax as you have done so many times before... by simply waiting to see where the first movement in your hand will occur. Will it be your right hand or your left hand? You may feel a warm sensation perhaps. Perhaps a finger will twitch or move or want to move or twitch. I don't know what will happen, or when it will happen, but something will happen. Yes, there. The finger moved. And now I'm as curious as you are to know where the next movement will be, or will there be no movement at all for a while until everything is ready for it to happen, with everything taking its time, ah yes, the fingers are spreading apart now and moving ever so slightly upwards... yes, yes, moving upwards. And that sensation, does it feel pleasant or just barely so, as your arm rises now, this very moment, and now as it is at eye level, the wrist turns, the elbow bends, and everything is so comfortable as it all happens, and your eyes begin to close, everything in movement, the fingers moving as if to touch your face, but where will they touch your face? I don't know, do you? Or will they touch your face at all? Could you even stop the fingers from touching your face, or would you even want to as everything is so relaxed, so comfortable, and now, just now, as the fingers touch your nose and the arm gently falls to your lap again, do you even want to make anything happen as you go deeper and deeper into a wandering that is so much a part and apart from you."

Anton continued in this manner, observing Davis closely, until he was certain that Davis was deeply in trance. Once this was done, Anton began to speak with a new and quiet intensity.

"Hear now Davis, there will appear in the utmost clarity, in deeply penetrating reality, in a confusion of actual events, that which once truly was, but which now, now in the depths of trance will meet you in such a way that all of your memories and understandings and dome experiences will be confronted and challenged... and you are ready, readier for this experience than you have ever been."

Davis could hear Anton's voice droning on and on, some of it confusing to him, but all of it so reassuring, so comfortable. There was such a comfort in forgetting for him, forgetting to remember and remembering to forget. He could hear Anton, but Anton seemed distant somehow. But something was changing before him now, something unexpected, and all of it was happening just as the monotonous, repetitious drone of Anton's voice continued on and on. Davis was terribly annoyed at the distraction.

"Will you please keep quiet! What's happening here is absolutely fantastic. I can't concentrate with you talking so much," Davis said.

For the next three hours Anton watched Davis sitting with his eyes open and staring directly in front of him, in rapt attention. Davis was totally absorbed in whatever he was seeing. Suddenly he turned to one side with his head slightly raised as if Anton was there, above him.

"Anton, this is really confusing. I don't know why you're peering at us over that balcony. Neither of us knows you. Why you're here I don't know. We're standing on this patio, and I don't know who is talking to you. Is it him or me? We know that you can tell us who is real and who is just a projected image of the past or future. You have to help us determine what is real. What is happening here? This is fascinating Anton, absolutely fascinating."

Anton began to speak with a quiet earnestness again. "And now you can continue to do whatever you're doing, listening to me closely as you're doing it, and in your own way, taking the time that is available to you to do what you want to do, as you listen to what is being said and choose to act upon what is said. And all this time, feel a growing need to link up with my voice, with me, and with returning with me to the familiar beginning and know that you will find it comfortable to remember everything that is comfortable to remember. And now, just now, that's it, you're there, sitting there with me here, and you're feeling so comfortable, so relaxed, so rested."

Anton watched as Davis rubbed his eyes and calmly remarked that nothing of any interest to him had taken place during the trance. Davis even doubted that he had been in a deep trance or had had any trance wandering experience whatsoever. Anton spoke about different matters for quite some time, matters unrelated to the trance experience.

And then Anton said to Davis, "If you were to make a speech, which balcony would you use?"

Davis sat up in his chair instantly. "That's the strangest question Anton. But that word, balcony, has such an odd effect on me. Anton continued on talking, and then finally levelled his gaze upon Davis and said quietly, "Davis, and which patio were you sitting on while I was on the balcony?"

Davis felt a warm, fluid feeling pass through his body. The feeling puzzled him. He was unable to determine why he should feel this way. He concentrated intently on the words Anton had spoken but nothing meaningful was associated with the words. He was confused. He rubbed his forehead, perplexed.

And then Anton touched Davis on the shoulder, saying "Now you will find it comfortable to remember everything."

Davis perked up immediately, completely startled, and in an avalanche of words began recounting his trance experience.

"Anton, Anton..." Davis said excitedly, "it's incredible. I remember it all. Fascinating! I was standing on the patio, and there, right there in front of me was an infant on a straw mat. I watched it, and I had the most incredible sensation of being the child too...actually being it at the same time as I was watching it. I watched it growing, struggling to crawl, to walk. It was as if time were compressed and distorted somehow. When the child was beginning to speak, I could feel the struggle in pronouncing words, the elation when the word matched the thing it represented. Anton, it was the most incredible experience. The infant grew in front of me, and then, at the age of about thirteen, the boy...grown from an infant looked at me closely. And I looked at it... I mean him. It was me, Anton, me, at that age. The boy was me, and I could sense him wondering if I was real in the same way that I was wondering if he was real! Each time I began to speak, the boy began to speak, uttering the same words that I was saying. Exactly the same words. I could sense his wonderment at seeing himself, me, at thirty-three years of age, just as I was marvelling at how I looked and felt at thirteen years of age. Amazing! Totally amazing! Anton, we could see you there, peering over the balcony, and we knew instinctively somehow that you were the only one who could solve the mystery. Who was real? Was it the boy or me? I can remember how angry I was with you for droning on and on... but somehow we both knew you could help us find out the truth."

"Yes, Davis," Anton interrupted, "and there is comfort in remembering to forget."

As soon as Anton had uttered those words Davis stared blankly at him.

"Anton, nothing happened in the trance. It was relaxing, very relaxing, but nothing happened." Anton went on to recount what Davis had just told him about his experience on the patio with Anton peering over a balcony, but Davis remembered nothing of it.

Several moments passed with Anton noting everything Davis had said to him, and then Anton touched Davis's shoulder saying, "You will find it comfortable to remember everything that is comfortable to remember."

Instantly Davis remembered his trance experience in detail, but he hadn't any recollection of having expressed his wonder and surprise to Anton. Davis asked for an explanation of why this was so.

"Davis, the little I did was simply to rearrange things comfortably for you to explore and wander in... you are a curious man, open to experience from within. You did it yourself. Your potential to trance wander is very great indeed. We'll talk more of this later, but now let's walk over to the gardens."

Davis found the experience totally exhilarating. He knew that he wanted to learn more about life in the colonies, this strange new world beneath the world. Anton smiled at him, his eyes dancing merrily.

Devlin cried out, "That's it, that's it. They have power... somehow they've harnessed power. Ha! That's the way we can convince the League to strike them in force. This is too good! We've got them now. You, my boy, are about to be rewarded. Dawkins, take the good man to my own private harmonizer- give him the full treatment, stint on nothing. He has solved my biggest problem. He's given me the lever I needed. Now I can finish them and become a hero to boot. Ha! Send for Tara. Tell her I need to speak to her at once. They'll be one glorious celebration."

Devlin placed his arm around the trooper, smacking him on the back heartily. Devlin was ecstatic. Dawkins and the trooper left while Devlin waited for Tara. He remembered their last encounter and felt a pang of regret. But then his mind raced with the anticipation of desire: images, sensations, not of Tara, but of certain parts of her only. Body parts: her lips, an image and a sensation of lush softness. Reducing her to so many parts in his mind, that was how he saw her, in parts. He sat down enthralled by the vivid images his lust had created.

There were times when Davis felt homesick for the Dome. Here he was, he thought, living the adventure of a lifetime, and he was thinking of his apartment and the places he knew: longing for home. He wondered if this feeling was a weakness in himself.

What he was seeing around him was in no way inferior to dome living. Certainly, it was underground living but even the quality of light was surcharged with a glowing intensity that he had never experienced in the Dome. There, he remembered, energy was becoming more and more of a problem. Shortages, not frequent, but occurring nevertheless. He thought of Anton and his facility with light. The Dome citizens would never believe that. How could they? There was nothing in the Dome, or any of the domes for that matter, that could even come close to duplicating it. People there couldn't even imagine it.

And then he thought with a start of the renegade troopers. What they would do if they realized that the so-called nulls, had harnessed the energy of the cosmos, and even played with it.

Anton the magnificent. The dance of Chi. What imaginative power these people had! He speculated on the different ways the dome citizens and the colonists had gone. He knew in his heart the way of the colonists was the better way, but he was from the domes and loved the domes. He wondered if there could be peace between the domes and the colonies. Was it possible both worlds could share a new, brighter life together?

Davis caught Bach's startled reaction when he saw the surveillance vehicle. It was one of their own. It had the special markings, the brand that designated it as one of Devlin's military craft. They both knew what its mission had been. Flying at cruiser speed with its scanners fully activated, it would have been after nulls. The ideal search and destroy vehicle.

Franco knew he could trust the two of them. He had an instinct for people and felt comfortable with them. He watched as they walked about the vehicle, Bach examining every inch of it so keenly while Davis followed behind him, curious about it, wondering how Franco could have downed the aircraft with only an antique hoe, a tool from a museum. Bach was sitting on his haunches, fingering the rent in the hull. He looked up at Franco and Davis and smiled, saying nothing. He went from there to the side of the vehicle and stood for the longest while in front of the door panel, examining it in detail. He ran the palm of his right hand along the tiny crack distinguishing the door from the rest of the body until he stopped at about the mid-center of the door's bottom section. He then reached into his pocket and pulled out a very thin, triangular-shaped piece of plastic, no bigger than a thumbnail. He inserted it at the very spot where his palm had rested earlier and then worked away at it, probing and pushing with the piece he held between his thumb and forefinger. Suddenly there was a little clicking sound followed by a whirring noise from behind the door. Bach motioned to Franco and Davis to stand clear. Three seconds passed, and then the door sprang open.

"An old outrider trick," Bach said, "for when you've forgotten the door remote." Franco looked at Bach appreciatively.

"Bach," Davis said, "you're just full of surprises." Bach chuckled. Franco liked the friendship between the two, the easy good humour. They were like colonists he thought. It was odd to him that he could once have thought of them as enemies.

But he didn't know them before. Franco winced at the thought, the irony of it. He hadn't taken the time to know them. But for the Elder who intervened, they might have been killed.

Franco followed Bach and Davis into the ship. He hesitated for a moment at the door. It was an alien space, and he feared entering into it. Davis, already sitting in the rear of the craft, motioned to him to come in. Franco marvelled at the plush interior of the craft. The seats at the rear and in the cockpit were made of a soft, flexible material that conformed to the shape, dimension, and weight of anyone or anything settling within them. Bach saw his interest and encouraged him to try out one of the seats. Franco did so, laughing when he sprang to his feet and could still see the indentation his body had made upon it. Bach winked at Davis. Then Bach set about inspecting the intricate controls and the very heart of the ship. A couple of hours passed before Bach came out of the ship and stretched. Davis wondered if it was serviceable.

"Well boys, we'll soon be airborne," Bach said as he stretched after leaving the airship. There was much to be done, he thought, pressing one of his thighs against his chest. He knew that he would have to obtain permission from the Elders to fly the craft, particularly for what he had in mind. He wanted to return to the Dome and tell them what he had seen. The stretching relaxed him. Bach knew that the League would not sanction the slaughter of innocent colonists. Colonists or nulls, whatever name was used, the league would never condone what Devlin's troops were doing, in going out of their way to seek nulls beyond the established defensive perimeters of the domes. Senseless murder in the name of security. As an outrider he knew that the patrols had gone far beyond the outer limits of dome territory. There was no need for defensive patrols hundreds of miles away from the outer periphery of dome lands.

"Bach... do you think we can go up today?" Davis asked.

"No, it's not quite ready," Bach replied. "But a little more work, and if the powers that be are agreeable, I think in about a week or so we can do it. All the way, I mean... back to the domes."

"Just the two of us?" asked Davis.

"No," Bach said, "a full crew. I'd like some of the colonists to join us. We'd need the ship we came in too, for parts to use in repairing this larger ship. I'm surprised Devlin hasn't sent a mission out here... to find out what happened to the fallen crew."

Franco smiled. He liked the way Bach approached things. The two of them were much alike. He knew too that Davis was the follower in all of this, deferring to Bach when any decisions had to be made. Franco took them aside and showed them the cache of weapons, boots, and clothing that he and his men had salvaged. He did it shyly, a little hesitant to show them. Bach nodded quietly when he saw the stash of familiar dome uniforms and insignias. There was a spattering of dried blood on the collar of one of the uniforms. Bach studied it grimly.

"Where did you find these?" Davis asked Franco. Bach winced. Franco turned aside, walking away from the two for a moment.

Bach raised his eyebrows, looking intently at Davis. Davis breathed in sharply, pursing his lips with the sudden realization of what had happened.

They made their way back to the underground colony in silence, savouring the cool freshness of the day. Not a cloud was in the sky. Franco brightened when he showed them the fields that had been worked by him and his men. Overhead, a lone pigeon was flying southward. Soon they were making plans, talking about a crew, about the Elders, about the journey to the Dome. Davis wondered if he would see Rachel, the thought of her providing warm comfort in the back of his mind.

The Elders decided that the first flight out would not be to the domes, but southward, to the Southern Colonies. Bach was disappointed at first. He thought they would lose valuable time, time that could be better used flying directly to the domes. Devlin's troopers could make additional strikes at any moment. Bach wanted desperately to report to the League Committee about the clandestine operations. He even feared strikes against the Southern Colonies.

A few days later the group of them were flying towards the Southern Colonies. Marta had insisted on going. The Elders, Anton and Mayerling, were chatting excitedly over the novelty of the experience of flight. Dirk and Jak tried to conceal their own excitement initially, but the exhilaration they felt proved too much for them. They pointed to the miniature ghost towns dotting the surface above the underground colonies. They recognized some of the landmarks and laughed, never having dreamt they would see them from such an unusual perspective. Bach and Davis were a little amused by it all. Mayerling was impressed by the deep, rich green of the landscape and the way it contrasted against the sands that dominated so much of it.

"So many different shades," he exclaimed, pointing to a dark, thick line of green running along the shoreline of a meandering river. "It's just wonderful," he said, offering his window seat to Marta for a better look.

Marta flashed a smile at Bach. Everything was so exciting. The world could be so tiny she thought as she looked upon the crooked finger of a river that stretched across the landscape below them. The Southern Colonies held such ripe promise for her. She loved knowing that she would be sharing the experience of it with Bach. The anticipation of it gave her such a thrill. Only now and then, when she chanced to think of her brothers, was her adventure soured. The memory of them was like a long, dark feather tracing a line under each of her closed eyelids until there were only a few brief tears to mark the passage of it. She smiled through the tears, her liquid vision, and down onto the sunny landscape below. The past was prologue to a new adventure, and she was determined to move on into life. Her grief would not undermine her, not now, not as before. She breathed deeply, and looked with love at Bach's profile as he was speaking to Dirk.

As Davis concentrated on the easy, rhythmic movements of his breathing, he began to relax more and more deeply. There was a curious heavy sensation in his limbs and then a sudden, effortless lightness of being. He had a sense of his body, heavy and relaxed and totally still. He heard laughter. The voice was familiar. It echoed round and round. With a shock he discovered it was his own voice, high above his own body. He had an image of himself laughing and in a sitting position about forty feet off the ground, in mid-air. There was nothing supporting him. For the first time in his life he had a sense of having two distinct selves, one heavy and gravity-bound, and the other light and laughing and insouciant. It was rollicking laughter that he heard, great swells of laughter giving him the clue to this other self.

There was also the memory of a similar experience, or had he just dreamt it? There was an ache of remembrance to the feeling. He knew he had heard this laughter before, but he hadn't realized that it was his own, or like his own. He felt a surge of power and then with a great sigh, he found himself drifting back, back to the everyday consciousness of his resting self.

It was so odd for him to have been in this state. An altogether detached feeling. He had felt as if he were apart from himself, from his very body. He marvelled at the experience. Initially, when he was entering into a trance state he had been afraid, with the fear of losing himself in it. The trance experience was impersonal and quite apart from his conscious sense of himself. Gradually though, he began to let go of the effort of keeping aware of himself as a distinct personality, and he began to like it. He felt a freedom deep and untrammelled, distinct from his personal identity. Eventually he trusted to this experience and savoured it for it always left him refreshed and invigorated.

Anton marvelled at the Infanta's playfulness and energy. In that, he was like other children, Anton reflected, but there was something different about him: prescience, precociousness? He wasn't quite sure how best to term it. But it was wonderful to behold such a bright spark of life. He smiled at the Infanta who was making faces at one of the matriarchs. She extended her hand, wanting to touch him. But immediately, he jumped to one side and then ran over to one of his new guardians and hid behind him, shrieking in delight. Anton chuckled at his antics.

The Infanta then looked over to Anton, curious about him. He walked over to him and looked at him closely. He saw a round, happy-looking man who had a small pouch attached to his belt. The Infanta looked at the pouch and then smiled at Anton. There was a warm twinkle in Anton's eyes as he looked down upon the Infanta. He didn't know quite what to expect.

The boy slowly reached up to take the pouch. Anton offered him no resistance, only smiles. Anton released the pouch from his belt and gave it to the Infanta. He stood looking down upon the child in silent, amused wonder. The Infanta placed his hand inside the bag and moved it about, trying to find something inside. At first he seemed disappointed. But as he continued the movement, his face brightened into a smile, and he tossed his head back with glee. Anton's eyebrows lifted momentarily in speculation.

The Infanta gave Anton a glance from the corner of his eye. He opened and closed his hand several times, and each time he showed the palm of his hand to Anton. He was smiling mischievously.

Anton turned to one of the matriarchs. "You have been instructing him?" he asked.

"A little," she replied, "but why do you ask?"

"He seems to have an awareness of what my pouch contains." Anton offered it to her. The matriarch loosened the drawstring around the opening and examined it.

"But there's nothing inside. It's empty."

"Nothing visible," Anton said, "but there is something inside the pouch. Of that you can be sure. You see, it contains refined neutrinos, invisible to the naked eye. The Infanta has a sense of what is there... he has a very subtle and accurate vision." Anton beamed at the child, wondering over him.

Petar was permitted to be present when the matriarchs worked with the Infanta. Theirs was a special bond, with the child looking to Petar whenever he accomplished a task that the matriarchs had set for him. A smile from Petar was more to the Infanta than the pineapple juice given to him as a reward for his excellent learning skills. With Anton's help too, the child was gaining in power. He would reach into Anton's pouch and move his hand about and then withdraw it. Anton would move deftly then, touching the back of the Infanta's head and hand, smiling all the while. The Infanta would close his eyes, entranced and empowered.

Afterwards, in the cavern of the summer god, where the child would use his healing touch to cure some of those brought before him, he would often urge Anton to give him the pouch of neutrinos. Then, the child would reach into the bag with his hand and become very still. After a moment he would slowly remove his hand from the bag, and with his arm extended, he would point to the smooth face of their summer god. Incredibly, the huge stone face appeared to light up from within, translucent and glowing. And then the child would laugh, and with his small arms encourage the gathered colonists filling the cavern to join him. Laughter would reverberate throughout the cavern, spilling light and mirth everywhere and all about in a privileged moment.

Anton and the matriarchs wondered over the Infanta's healing powers. There were many whom he was not able to cure. Did his healing powers have limits, or was he still too young in the full realization of his powers? They speculated, and the child played. He loved the beaches of the island. So much so that Petar requested special defences to be built. After the near fatal attack, it was agreed that the guardians would be given any additional resources they felt necessary to safeguard the Infanta. Elaborate underground chutes were constructed at hundreds of beach points around the island. These chutes, hidden in sand banks and shallow caverns, would enable the Infanta and his protectors a speedy escape from the surface. They would enter the chutes, concealed under scrub brush, and slide down hundreds of feet to safety, deep within the great caverns of the colonies.

Petar's sharp eyes scanned the beach area. He knew the defences were crude, compared to the firepower of the aircraft he had seen, but they had escaped then, and he was encouraged to anticipate anything that might happen. He loved the child playing in the sand before him. The other guardians were fanned out in a wide arc around the beach area where the Infanta was playing with a conch shell. If an aircraft were sighted, they were to sound an alert and then run in previously designated random patterns to find safety.

None were to go for the child. That was Petar's responsibility first, followed then by others who would lead the child to the nearest chute if Petar were to fall. In the confusion of seeing dozens of men dashing about the beach, precious seconds would be saved allowing the Infanta to escape the laser sights of the dome pilots. It would, of course, have been much easier to simply keep the Infanta away from the beaches and deep within the confines of the underground caves, but the matriarchs believed that he needed time to develop on the beaches that he loved.

Marta loved the strange sensation of sand beneath her feet as she walked along the beach. It was all so novel and wonderful: walking in the open air on a brilliantly sunny, windswept day. Perfect. She breathed in the sea air deeply and waded, just a little way into the sea itself. How strange to feel the waters moving about her ankles. Could people have lived like this? Could they have taken these precious experiences for granted? She looked closely at the sea-grape floating in the foamy waters. These things were wondrous to her. She tasted the sea water, so salty tasting, so old and powerful. Could people have lived an entire lifetime in a paradise like this? Surely they must have been happy. These southern colonies were magnificent. Little wonder they revered a summer god.

One of the matriarchs, a woman named Delia, had spoken to her of their laughter-encouraging deity. He was there, she said, in all of us. The trick is to release him, in laughter, for he always returns. Laugh like a summer god! Marta felt the sun on her face and a cool, breeze upon her back. What a heaven it would be to live here with Bach. She smiled at the thought that was half wish.

The winds of this place must be strong, she thought, as she looked upon the twisted shapes of the trees to one side of her. Delia had told her of the attack on the Infanta. Here, even here, they had come. Would there be more attacks? How stupid, how horribly stupid.

Marta found it so difficult to believe, that just as things were changing, just as the surface lands were being cleansed, and people could dream about living on the surface of the earth and not under it, the same ancient menace of war came to explode dreams, and lives. Why? She felt such a fool for always asking herself why. As if there were a reason behind the senselessness of hate.

The sun felt so warm, and the wind and the sea air invigorating. Overhead, a white-crested pigeon winged northward. She wished it could bring these very things that she was experiencing, to her own home colony in the north: this feeling of the sun on her skin, the lingering taste of the sea on her lips, and the scent of flowers whose names she did not know.

Bach looked out over the beach and beyond to the open sea. The islands of these southern colonies were magnificent, he thought. He felt so physically content here. He was fully alive in this open sea air, standing on the earth, and by a sea whose turquoise colours he could not ever have dreamt in his wildest imaginings. He had spent his life in the domes. He preferred it to life as it was lived in the underground colonies, deep below the surface of the earth. The dome worlds were enclosed, but here, they were beginning to live above ground without any barriers between them and the skies. To even dream of living in the open air for days on end was like a miracle of fulfillment to him. And they were beginning to actually do it, here in these southern colonies. He watched a group of children as they jumped and dove into the waves crashing upon the seashore. Seabirds were flying high above them, uttering sharply pitched cries. The seashore itself seemed to augur endless worlds.

They were doing it, he thought. The colonists were effectively neutralizing the radioactive winds that had made life uninhabitable on the surface of the earth. Unprotected, human life was doomed there. But he could see what they had accomplished here. Their scientists were doing it. Somehow, they were doing it. He stooped down to look at a bunch of sea-grape washed upon the beach. This world was so full of marvels. He thought about Anton, about his control of neutrinos. What a wonder! And the child, the Infanta, with his power to heal. He tossed the sea-grape back into the water. He would love to live here with Marta. It would be paradise. It was his truest desire. But he knew he had to look to other things first. It was inevitable. Devlin would strike again soon.

The days passed in the southern colonies were idyllic for Bach. And he was discovering that the island colonists had made great strides in cleansing the environment. Their scientists had substantially reduced radioactive levels of contamination. They had perfected an air-washing process that reconstituted radioactive particles with oxygen-rich subatomic elements. Bach didn't understand the process at all, but he loved living under blue skies without a transparent dome between himself and the sun. He couldn't quite believe his good fortune to have found Marta and to be here, now, walking on a sun-swept beach with the woman he loved. They had only a few days before their return to the underground northern colonies. Soon, he thought, all of the colonists would be living on the surface of the earth. With their know-how, the colonists could show all of the dome peoples a way to leave their protective domes, and live life as it was meant to be lived. To walk on the surface of the earth breathing real air and feeling the warmth of the sun and cool, caressing breezes, this was a great privilege.

Once he was back in the northern colonies, he would fly quickly to the domes accompanied by Davis, Dirk and Jak. The attacks must be stopped. Everyone could benefit from a peace that made the world whole and clean again. He looked again at Marta. He noticed how the sun was bringing out golden highlights in her hair. She smiled at him as he casually ran his fingers through her luxuriant hair. What a world it was, and what a world it would be.

"Come on, let's race," Marta said suddenly, sprinting away from him. Bach, taking up the challenge, laughed and then darted after her.

Marta ran past the point jutting out into the sea to a sheltered bay on its leeward side. She scampered into the water, and then turned suddenly, splashing away at Bach, her face radiant in the sunshine and the sparkling water. Bach hesitated for a moment and then moved slowly into the sea.

"Wait," Bach said, "Give me a minute. It's my first time. I've never waded into sea water before, not out in the open like this. It's wonderful."

Marta looked up at him laughing. "And it's ours if we make it so." She splashed him again. Bach darted back to the beach and then slowly, cautiously, made his way back towards Marta, as playful as a child.

Marta waited for him. She reached up to embrace him and noticed that his face and shoulders were reddening. "We'd better head back soon."

Bach took her in his arms and kissed her. The water felt cool and refreshing about their legs. Bach noticed that tiny silver minnows were swimming around them. Marta jumped at first when she saw them. Marta took Bach's arm and drew him down beside her until they were all but submerged in the shallow water. Only their heads and shoulders were above the waterline. The lightness of their bodies in the water was a delight to them. They were buoyant and laughing- and when they made love, the water lapped against them, gently caressing them with each movement that they made.

D evlin was flying low over the wide expanse of beach. He enjoyed the sensation of speeding just over the beaches of these null islands, a mere ten feet above the water from the shoreline. He was flanked by two other one-man sky ships flown by his aides, Dawkins and Krvo. Both of the pilots were a little nervous about how low they were flying but pretended to enjoy it for Devlin's sake.

Devlin loved it. He knew that soon, very soon, the Infanta would be found. He had instructed his men to keep a close lookout for anything unusual, a break from the pattern of beach and scrub bush. One of the squads led by Krvo had sighted a small child on this same island several weeks before. In addition to the null child, three adult nulls had been spotted as well. Although the mission was unauthorized, Devlin had always encouraged his men to extend their operations southward from the domes. He believed that a periodic foray into unknown territory was good for morale.

It shaped men like Krvo. Devlin admired Krvo for the risks he took, admired him so much in fact, that he made a special mental note to keep close tabs on him. Risk-taking was a good thing. It was what Devlin himself was known for. But he knew too that Krvo was as ambitious as he was, and therefore a man to be watched closely. He had authorized Dawkins to accompany Krvo on all future missions.

Later, when it was discovered that the child that had been sighted might have been the Infanta, Devlin had scrutinized Krvo's log report. Two of the nulls spotted had been exterminated, possibly three. The null child had somehow escaped. Devlin tightened his grip on the controls and sped faster and lower over the brilliant, sandy beach. Suddenly, he felt an instinctive desire to stop there, just there, atop the hill overlooking a beach. Just to stand there for a moment, alone. He commanded Dawkins and Krvo to stand by. They had just flown across the island without a single sighting. On a hunch he brought his craft to a stop, leaving Dawkins and Krvo hovering above him. At least on the mainland they had large mutant rodents to hunt down. Here there was nothing, nothing but palm trees, feathery pines, and sandy beaches. Devlin remembered again, for a fleeting instant, the man he had killed, the moon poet, as he had once referred to his null kill to Dawkins.

Devlin heard a child's voice call out from the beach. Devlin jerked to attention.

The sound seemed to be coming from beneath the very spot on which he stood. He looked up at Dawkins and Krvo. From their position behind him they would have been unable to see anyone on the beach below. He signalled to them to follow him. Devlin found a spot where he could make his way down a steep slope to the beach. He scrambled down, eager to find out who might be there. He was glad that he thought to keep a light miniature laser in his belt buckle. He could hear the child's delighted cries quite clearly now. He wondered if it could be the Infanta that the null moon poet had written about. His excitement had an edge to it. He was breathing hard from his exertions. Finally, when he reached the beach, he almost tripped over the small child sitting there.

The child slowly rose to his feet. Devlin was struck by the child's beauty. The eyes were exceptionally bright and dark. It seemed to him that the child was smiling at him. Devlin found it so odd and menacing somehow that so many of these nulls were attractive. The physical reality of the child, this null, almost undermined what he knew to be true, his idea of the null threat itself. This one would not escape.

Devlin was about to activate his belt laser when he saw a huge shadowy figure leap from a depression in the sand bank. The null was holding a cutlass. He stood directly in front of the child, shielding him entirely. Devlin grinned, savouring the moment: two very exquisite and personal kills in the offing.

The defending null looked magnificent, tall and well-muscled. He showed absolutely no fear. His eyes were calm, focused. The null suddenly whipped around, and with one arm whisked the child off his feet and threw him several feet behind, deep within the sand bank. Shadows moved about the child and then disappeared.

Almost in the same instant Devlin touched his laser. The blade of the cutlass shattered and the null's hand fell to the ground, severed at the wrist. In one stunning motion, the null picked up his severed hand and flung it directly at Devlin's face. It struck him soundly under his left eye just as Devlin saw the null's body explode with the impact of several blasts from behind where Devlin himself stood. Krvo had dispatched the null.

Devlin ran forward after the child. He was gone. He had escaped. But how? Where? There was nowhere to go. Devlin scrambled vainly against the sand bank, searching for some kind of passageway. He found nothing. Frustrated, Devlin commanded Krvo and Dawkins to blast the entire beach area. They did so. There was nothing to be found.

Anton could see that the child was heartbroken. He had lost his beloved guardian, his Petar. The child had been able to explain what had taken place, about the strange, red-haired man who appeared suddenly, about Petar throwing him into one of the cleverly concealed chutes in the sand bank before the red-haired man could get to him. The Infanta was traumatized, but he had escaped. The child did not have to be told what had happened to Petar. He knew what had happened in the way that people looked at him so consolingly.

Anton removed some neutrinos from his pouch and placed them on both palms of the Infanta's hands. Then, very gently, he closed the Infanta's tiny fingers over them. The child looked up at him and smiled. He liked the game. The child had already learned that the neutrinos could be used to light things up or make things warm when you wanted them to. Anton had taught him how to play with them, how to hold them in the palm of the hand and smile, and extend them, as a kind of offering, a kind of love, to others.

And so, when the Infanta thought about Petar, the neutrinos, invisible at first, would begin to glow and sparkle in his hands, and he could direct them wherever he wanted to just by imagining it so. His love for Petar and his ability to send the neutrinos dancing in the air were one and the same. He even began to laugh, seeing the neutrinos encircle the top of Anton's head while Anton tried to duck out of the way, the way Petar would when there were seagulls about.

Davis was excited about returning home to the Dome. Everything was ready for their departure. Dirk and Jak were joining them. He worried a little about that. He knew them as friends, as colonists, but in the Dome world they would be known as nulls. He wondered about Bach's ability to protect them from Devlin. Would he be able to? Although Davis had great respect for Bach, he remembered the night Bach had been beaten. What could a few men do against the kind of force Devlin commanded? He had what amounted to a private army. More than that, he was cunningly articulate, a natural leader who had access to inner circles within the League hierarchy itself.

Davis felt light-headed. Looking out the window, he saw the familiar Dome with the bright tower gleaming within it. He glanced over at Bach, grinning. They were home. His first thought was of Rachel. How could he get in touch with her? Would she be at the Phoenix? Would she want to see him? Maybe he was making too much of the one encounter they had had. His mind raced madly. He was home, home after three months away. Had it been that long? He'd had such rich experiences in the colonies, but now he was home, home at last. He wondered if Dirk and Jak might want to join him at the Phoenix. Bach had already said that he was going directly to League headquarters to give his account of what was happening in the null lands, in the colonies.

Davis hurried to his apartment to shower and change before heading to the Phoenix. Dirk and Jak had decided to join Bach. Davis had been relieved to hear this, and a little guilty. If Rachel were at the

Phoenix he wanted to be free from any other obligations. He knew he wanted to be alone with Rachel. Dirk and Jak could stay with Bach.

Bryce was behind the bar when he entered. "Well, look who's here! Where have you been Davis? We've missed you." Bryce held out a huge hand to Davis and shook Davis's hand violently.

"Ah, just keeping a low profile Bryce. I decided to go underground for a while. Keep out of trouble. You're looking thinner Bryce."

"Thanks. I've lost a bit of weight, and I feel great." Davis stood by the bar chatting idly with Bryce, wondering if Rachel would drop by. He looked around the familiar bar and smiled.

Time passed easily for him in his familiar haunt. It was almost as if he had not been away. Everything looked the same. He drank slowly reflecting on what he had been through. It had indeed been an adventure. And now there was more to come, here, right here, in the Dome. He wondered what Dirk and Jak would think of a place like this. Would they find it interesting or boring or decadent?

"Why Davis, you're looking positively edible," Rachel said, sliding into the seat next to him. She took his breath away with her beauty.

"I hoped you would be here. I've missed you."

"Oh now, Davis," Rachel teased, "you just up and left. You didn't even leave a forwarding address. Where did you go? Did I offend you on that fateful night?"

Davis laughed. Touching her lightly on the cheek, he said, "Rachel, I was so shocked, so utterly shocked, that I couldn't stay in the Dome another second. So I lit out for the territories, the null territories."

And then Davis began to recount his adventures with Bach. Rachel was intensely curious about everything he said, asking him for all kinds of detail on what he had experienced. While he spoke, she would touch him now and again, squeezing his arm playfully. Finally, she placed two of her fingers over his lips.

"Look... I want to hear everything, but not here, let's go to your place, now, right now...O.K.?"

Davis smiled. "I thought you'd never ask," he said. "Let's go."

"Davis, tell me everything. Don't leave anything out. I want to hear about the nulls... all of it. Weren't you afraid of catching something? You're a madman Davis, crazy mad. Come here." Rachel patted the seat next to her, an invitation Davis found irresistible.

He had dreamt of being here with her in his apartment for months. And here he was, with the most attractive woman he had ever met. "I don't want to talk," he said, reaching to embrace her.

"No, no," she said. "I want to hear your stories. I want to know what it's like there. No one really knows about the null lands from the inside. Not even my soldier friends."

Davis went hollow inside. "Soldier friends?"

Rachel pushed him away. "Yes, my brother's an outrider like your friend Bach. He knows some troopers. I've met a few through him. Why, Davis, are you a little jealous? Have I made an impression? Are we in lust together?"

Davis smiled. "You know... you're really something."

"Davis, does your bedroom have a plastic coating on the walls?" Rachel raised one of her legs very slowly and then gently rested it on Davis's lap.

"I think so," Davis answered. "Why?" Davis held her leg in his arms. He ran his fingers over her ankle and along her calf.

"I have a new game for us, but it needs plastic walls. It'll be fun. Let me get it set up. Just give me a minute. Wait here."

A moment passed while Davis speculated on what she was up to.

Soon, she returned, and lay beside Davis. He heard a light buzzing sound in the background. He began to talk.

Rachel moved on top of him, urging him in to continue speaking while she caressed him and whispered incoherently in his ear. Whenever he stopped speaking, she urged him on again, pressing him to go on, to never stop. She wanted to hear it all.

"Talk to me Davis, talk to me. Make me yours." Davis babbled on. He wasn't even aware of what he was saying. He seemed to be floating.

"Rachel, what's happening?" Rachel too, seemed to be levitating in front of him. She was floating, laughing.

"Don't worry. It's the game," she said, pushing herself away from the ceiling where she hung suspended.

"It's an anti-gravity game I brought with me. The latest thing. Just relax and enjoy it. Catch me if you can."

Davis kicked away from the wall and dove towards her. Rachel twisted away, moving towards the floor. The bed and furniture floated about them. Davis pushed one of the bedside tables aside and made a mad lunge for her. Rachel continued to elude his grasp. She glided by him, laughing.

Rachel turned off the light switch and said in a whisper, "Careful of the furniture. If we stay together in one spot, we'll be all right, and we won't bump into it."

The nine members of the League Committee had listened closely as Bach had presented his case against Devlin. Bach had stated that he had evidence of the clandestine operations instigated by Devlin. He offered to present witnesses from the colonies. Devlin sat stone-faced, staring at Bach. Only once had Devlin spoken to an attendant as Bach was speaking. The man had left immediately. The meeting room was dimly lit, a fact which Devlin noted in his presentation. He had based his defence on a simple imperative: the need to secure alternative energy forms for the domes. His operations, he explained, were financed by the explorations branch of the Energy

Office. Devlin said this in a calm tone, and he hinted at a breakthrough in his team's search for new forms of energy.

"You mean to say that your operations have secured an energy source?"

Devlin had smiled when the Chairman had made this query. "No, not secured," Devlin had replied, "We have not secured the energy source as of yet. However, we are confident that we will if our operations are allowed to continue. We have encountered null resistance. But this resistance has been limited, and we have broken it. But I fear, gentlemen, that in the great null underground warrens, or colonies, as Bach has alluded to them, there is a growing conspiracy, against all of the dome worlds. We have new intelligence of a massive force being organized, and of a symbol of insurrection, a creature known as the Infanta."

Devlin effectively countered all of Bach's reports and observations in his presentation. The committee members were particularly intrigued by his talk of an energy source. But one of them, Arroyo, reminded the committee of Devlin's past transgressions.

"Devlin, you talk of insurrection in the null lands. This strikes me as a bit odd. You did say null. These lands are beyond our established boundaries. I recall that you were brought before this committee in the past for similar transgressions. Ah, but now there is energy involved, so you have a motive for disturbing the peace with a people that has not broken any of our laws, or invaded a single inch of dome territory. And yet they have been hunted by your forces, your military guard, now become your energy exploration team. Ah, yes, a motive. Gentlemen, let us reflect on this. Let us see these colonists that Bach has brought back. I'm ever so curious as to why not once has the question of diplomacy arisen. Is negotiation not a word in the null or colonist vocabulary? Have our military, no, our energy exploration teams taken the time to find out, or would that entail too much energy? Gentlemen, I'm most curious about answers to these simple questions. Your intelligence, Devlin, must certainly possess the answers. And now, an Infanta, a child, certainly a menace to our dome way of life. Yes, yes, gentlemen, let us probe a little more deeply past the surface of things. Perhaps we will discover new worlds out there, and not null lands."

Arroyo smiled at Devlin and looked over to the other members of the committee. Devlin bowed deferentially to the committee, and took his leave, just barely containing his fury before he left the meeting hall. Arroyo motioned to Bach that he wished to see him. Bach respected this grey-haired fox who had a passion for truth, and who clearly detested Devlin.

For both Dirk and Jak the Dome experience was incredible. They marvelled over the huge transparent dome that enclosed everything, and the great tower within it that afforded such majestic views of the Dome and the surrounding territories around the Dome. Everything within the Dome had such a sheen to it, a shininess, as if all of it was new and just made. It was all so functional, so impersonal in its utility. They rode the shuttle cars about the city, and they noticed, with much surprise, that no one spoke to another. Their fellow passengers simply stared ahead blankly until they reached their destination, and then left, silently. The system was very efficient, but cold.

Jak adjusted the language encoder dot that he had applied to his throat.

"Bach's description of the Dome was true to the last detail. But the feel of it is so barren." Dirk nodded.

As Jak spoke, the sound of the language to him was harsh and clipped. It was odd to him that conversation could be framed in such a tight way. The people that they saw all looked healthy enough, but something seemed to be missing. There was no hint of enthusiasm among these people. There was activity, but it was all so dessicated and sterile. It made them both a little sad.

They travelled in the shuttle system for hours before they realized that none of the people they had seen had touched one another, even when it was obvious that they knew each other. But when they looked overhead, the openness of everything was wonderful. Through the high density plastic of the Dome, they could see to the outside world. Dirk wondered if people could remain outside the Dome for prolonged periods of time. He could see nothing but sand, and the occasional splash of green. Was it really as bleak and lethal as Bach had told them? Surely the Dome people must be able to get out in the open some of the time. People needed to get out.

"Arroyo is against Devlin, we can count on that," Bach said. "But he's told me that Devlin has some very powerful friends. He's using the Dome's energy shortages to gain some support. Dirk, we'll be in danger if we stay in the Dome. Arroyo wanted to see you and Jak, but he cannot guarantee either your safety or mine. He's suggested that we leave the Dome immediately. Arroyo needs more time, time to convince the League that Devlin's bent on killing and little else. We should leave tonight."

Dirk looked hard at Bach. "I hoped we'd have a chance to speak. The warriors are assembling. We don't have much of a chance against these killers- at least not against their high-powered weapons. But we're not afraid to die." Dirk looked away after he spoke. There was no reason for any of it. Bach knew it. Others must know it too.

Jak pushed at Dirk's shoulder.

"Aw, c'mon... the Elders will find a way out of this. Look at Anton. He's hidden himself away. He's doing something that will help us all. I'm sure of it."

Dirk smiled wryly at his huge good-natured friend. Jak was a true colonist: powerful, optimistic, and compassionate.

Dirk shrugged his shoulders, "O.K., let's go then."

Their departure from the Dome signalled the end of something for Bach. He didn't know if he would return. His life there was finished. He longed to see Marta again. As they sped away he turned to see the Dome one last time. The full moon had cast an eerie sheen on the great bubble that had been his home. It looked to him like the dwelling of some fantastic mollusc. The world he wanted to live in was before him, in the colonies.

Tara was giddy with excitement. She would surprise Devlin. On the return flight from her sister's neighbouring dome, she could think of nothing but him. They seemed finally to be growing more intimate. The strong physical attraction was always there. But lately, a new delicious kind of intimacy had grown between them. She wanted so much for it to last. She wanted the other women out of his life. The overhead lights flickered on and off as the shuttle moved from station to station. It was most annoying to Tara as she daubed a light powder on her face. She was almost there.

Racing away from the shuttle, she looked up to see if there were lights on in Devlin's penthouse apartment. She could see the lights of his bedroom extension were on. She laughed excitedly. Devlin had given her the codes she needed to enter the building, and his apartment. In a moment she was there, in front of his door. She entered the apartment very quietly, wanting to surprise him. Removing her shoes, she tiptoed towards the bedroom. She stood by the bedroom door for a moment, and then pushed it open, crying "Surprise!" as she did it.

Devlin, naked, turned round desperately to see who it was. Beneath him, a woman lay still, waiting. Tara simply looked at him, struggling against her tears, against the hard lump in her throat, against everything.

"Devlin?" Tara looked at him for the longest moment, and then with an expression of ineffable sadness on her face, she left. Rachel looked up at Devlin wondering what she should do.

F or Davis, it all seemed oddly archaic. Davis's horse neighed and threw his head up. There was something in the air, an excitement that was menacing and portentous. Before them, half a mile away, ranged Devlin's elite force. A thousand strong, standing in a V-formation. They looked impressive and resplendent in their blue uniforms, the bits of silver on their collars shining in the sun. A strange calm surrounded everything, a deep, pervasive calm.

Davis looked across at his friends, Bach, Dirk and Jak, each of them on horseback. Three horsemen on the slight rise of a hill. Suddenly his skin crawled; he remembered the trance, the time when it all began. Back home at the Dome. It was a wondrous strange feeling for him to realize that in his trance he had anticipated this moment. Davis rode up the hill and joined his friends.

His friends were scrutinizing the V-formation, trying to decipher Devlin's strategy. The special headgear worn by the troopers totally concealed their features. Squirrel helmets, Bach had once called them. Dirk's horse snorted, its powerful flanks pressing against Davis's mount.

Bach looked over at Davis and smiled, "You know, they've definitely got something in mind." Davis swallowed, trying hard to manage a smile. He admired Bach's poise. Dirk chuckled.

Behind them, completely out of sight and below the hill that flanked them, the Elders had formed a circle. Just beyond the circle ten thousand colonists stood at the ready. No one spoke.

They were concentrating their attention, linking up with the Elders in the first circle. Davis caught sight of a break against the line of the horizon. Beyond the V-formation of Devlin's troops he could see growing clouds of dust obscuring something very large and moving very fast. For several moments Davis couldn't make anything out. He wondered if it might be a cyclone or a tornado. He hoped it might be one of those even as he recognized the force bearing down on them. It was what he feared most. Now he could see the vehicles, the hover-craft, the full military might of the Dome League. Davis felt sick. Devlin had convinced them. They may have had a chance against Devlin's troops, but not against the size and magnitude of the army he saw arrayed before him. So he would die then, a colonist, a null, fighting against his own people. So be it, he thought, so be it. He wheeled his horse around to see the others.

Behind him he could hear the colonists singing. He rode to the top of the hill to get a better view. Around the circle of the Elders, Davis saw larger and larger circles of colonists positioned for battle readiness. It was a moving song with a tone of finality about it. Men in each of the circles would lead the song, and then when they stopped, the others would join in. Their collective voices were very powerful and poignant. Davis felt the naked emotion of it. He looked at these brave, vulnerable men. Their weapons were almost negligible, nothing more than crude tools for the most part. What could they possibly do against the league forces that were about to meet them?

The song died down for a moment creating a lull, a moment of near silence. Davis heard it then. The inner circle of the Elders was humming. Only when the singing had died down could it be heard. The humming sound that seemed to vibrate everywhere. There was such a gathered power to the sound that Davis felt an almost fluid kind of elation move through him. He was startled by the feeling happening within him, considering the grave danger he knew they were in.

Bach surveyed the situation closely. He knew that even the bravest hearts could do little against the weapon wizardry of the League. And there they were. In a few moments the battle would begin. Devlin's troops would advance and when they were close enough, they would use their hand-held lasers, the nerve-destroying lasers that had already killed so many colonists. The fast approaching League forces might even prove to be overkill; after all, the lasers could do the job, the soldier in him analyzing the situation objectively and critically.

Bach looked again at Anton. Anton was smiling, gently rubbing the pouch he carried at his side, the pouch of refined neutrinos,

Anton's pocket of light. He remembered Anton's tremendous light show, and the way the great meeting hall had been filled with thousands and thousands of points of light moving and merging in accord with Anton's exuberant orchestration. He remembered what he had said to Anton, and what Anton had said to him.

"What's the secret,'' Bach had asked.

"Believing, just believing," Anton answered, "There's nothing more to it."

D evlin leaned against the arm rest and gazed towards the low brown hills where the null riders were positioned. Krvo was with him in his flagship. His troopers were fanned out from the point made by his flagship. He demanded precision in military movement.

Devlin knew that null warriors were behind the hills. He wondered about the Infanta, about where the child was at this very moment. The child guardian he had killed had been a brave man, the bravest Devlin had ever encountered. Only a man such as he could have saved the Infanta from death on that day he remembered so vividly. Devlin gripped the arm rest tightly. There would be another time. The Infanta couldn't hide forever. There would come a day.

But now he would see to the nulls. He couldn't fathom why they wanted to meet him here, like this, out in the open. They didn't have a chance. Behind him he could see the advance of League forces. He didn't want any interference. He knew he could finish this little operation in a few moments. The League would not stop him, not now. He had come too far. He signalled to Krvo.

Devlin had a plan. Dawkins was to offer the plan to the null forces through Bach. One man from each side would meet on the field in hand-to-hand combat, a fight to the death, as in storied ancient times. If the null's chosen warrior won, the League forces would leave, never to bother them again. If, however, the League champion won, the nulls would surrender unconditionally. Devlin thought the plan would give him some additional time, time to fully assess how best to deal with the nulls. He never intended to honour it, if the nulls were to win. He would exterminate all of them regardless of the outcome. It amused him to stage something like this. Krvo would be his champion.

Bach relayed the message from Devlin to the Elders on the field. It was accepted. Dirk would be their champion.

Mayerling, touching Dirk's forearm lightly, said, "Let the time slow for you. Your reflexes will be faster if the time you use is slowed. Be careful. They have no honour."

Dirk nodded and stepped quickly away from the colonists and on to the field.

Devlin smiled. He ordered all of his troops back into their ships. They were to be at the ready. Krvo was summoned to confer with Devlin.

"Krvo, good luck. Your victory over this null creature will bring us honour."

Krvo laughed, confidently. "There is no doubt of that. I am ready."

Devlin, glancing at Krvo's belt laser, said, "In any event, you will win... but here... take one of my personal belt lasers. You will find it very responsive."

Krvo would have preferred his own weapon, but in deference to his commander, he took it with a slight bow, and then left.

As Krvo approached him, Dirk went very still. His expression was wooden. Krvo swaggered towards Dirk, lightly touching the belt Devlin had given him. He wanted to dispatch the null quickly, without using the weapon. The null was bigger than he expected, and quiet, too quiet. He didn't appear afraid. Krvo was used to seeing fear, but this null showed no fear.

Krvo ran straight at him, and then leapt up kicking with both feet at Dirk's head. Dirk moved deftly to one side, just missing the blows. Krvo was back on his feet in a moment, feinted to the left, and then threw a side kick that caught Dirk squarely on the chest. The force of the blow knocked him to the ground. Krvo hoped to finish him then, with a fatal kick to his throat. But Dirk was quick. He whirled around in an instant, just in time to deflect the kick, and reach back to grasp Krvo's extended leg.

Time slowed for Dirk when he did it. He watched the expression on Krvo's face change from menace to fear as Dirk stepped back and drove his foot against the side of Krvo's knee. Everything was happening so slowly. Krvo cried out in pain, falling hard on his back, and realizing with a start that he had lost. He aimed his belt laser at Dirk and fired. A long moment passed before Dirk reacted. Nothing had happened. The laser was defective. In the second it took for Krvo to realize he had been duped by Devlin, Dirk smashed into his skull with the heel of his boot killing him instantly.

Devlin knew that he must act decisively. He must destroy them now while their hero was still on the field. He knew he had only a few moments before the league commanders were about him. His unauthorized attack would be grounds for a court-martial. But he had before him the best of the null warriors. If he could destroy them now, the null threat would be gone forever. A few would be spared for intelligence purposes. There was still the Infanta to be hunted down. And perhaps, just perhaps, he would learn of their energy source. It was worth the strike against them, whatever the repercussions. Their hero had won. He had defeated Krvo fairly. But a null victory was just that... null. He laughed aloud over his cunning treachery. He signalled Dawkins to initiate the plan- a broad sweep around to the right while he and several other troop ships moved to the left in a pincer movement. Dawkins signalled in acknowledgement. All weapons were activated.

Dirk stood ever Krvo's body and glanced about. Everything was too quiet. Anton and Mayerling watched as the troop ships began to surround them. Bach, seeing what they were about, cried out to the colonists to attack. Davis heard the humming sound of the warriors growing louder and louder. Anton released the neutrinos from his pouch. A series of brilliant points of light advanced and thundered over the warriors and the troop ships.

Devlin puzzled over the light movement, quite taken by the beauty of it. He hesitated for a moment before giving the final command to destroy the nulls.

Devlin waved his troopers on. Dawkins directed his lasers towards a group of warriors standing in one of the null circles. He fired. The blast killed all of the men instantly. Dawkins threw his head back in triumph.

The moving points of light were shining brilliantly and had begun to coalesce into a cone-shaped apex high above the field. Dawkins directed a laser at the spot where Bach and Davis stood with their mounts. The light from the cone grew more and more intense. The last thing that Dawkins saw in the split second after he fired was the shock of brilliant white light that tore through his ship disintegrating everything. Whenever a trooper ship fired, there was only the blinding, searing heat of the explosion that blasted their own ship.

Devlin ordered a halt to the firing. The troopers left their ships, and armed only with light hand-held lasers, they prepared to destroy the nulls on foot. But the instant they fired their small arms, they were either killed or wounded by their own fire.

Devlin, standing free of his craft, spotted an old man with a hooded cap, an empty pouch clutched in his hand. Devlin activated his belt laser and fired. The moment he did so, his right hand was severed from his arm by the force of the blast. He fell to his knees, crying out in pain.

Mayerling and Anton stood calmly in the innermost circle of the colonists concentrating their attention on the neutrinos of light high above the field. The cries of the wounded and dying filled the air. Within just a few moments the troopers had been decimated. Word was quickly passed through the elite force to discard their weapons. They were to engage in hand-to-hand combat.

Mayerling motioned to Dirk to bring his men forward. The warriors moved swiftly and silently to the front. There were no loud war cries, no outbursts. Just a collective, grim, determined movement forward. Franco and Big Tanner led the way.

The light generated by Anton's neutrinos made everything on the field sharp and distinct. Some of the horses behind the colonists' lines began neighing as the two forces approached each other.

Devlin was trying desperately to focus, to concentrate his mind through the shock and pain of his injury. An aide applied a tourniquet to stop the bleeding. The troopers surged forward, breaking into the ranks of the nulls. The colonists seemed to give way before them, then absorb them, allowing them to move past their lines, but only for a moment. All along the lines, the troopers would break through only to find themselves immediately surrounded by the colonists.

The warriors attacked them with a vengeance. Franco and Dirk rampaged over any trooper opposing them. They were merciless. Big

Tanner tore through the ranks devastating the troopers with fatal blows.

The battle was over by the time the airships of the league forces hovered over the field. The warriors knew they had no hope against such reinforcements. But they would stand, knowing it was better to die fighting on the field than to be hunted down. The league forces hung suspended over them, watching them.

The league commander, Arroyo, gave instructions to one of his lieutenants. Seconds later, white peace banners issued from atop the cockpit section of all of the league ships. It was over. Finally, it was ended. Anton fell exhausted to the ground. The Infanta was safe.

After the battle Bach met with the Elders and arranged for them to meet with Arroyo and the other league commanders. Arroyo pledged that there would be no more attacks of any kind. The marauding trooper teams were finished. Devlin, Arroyo assured them, would be banished, exiled. It was promised. The colonists were free from his menace. There were strange new powers afoot, and Arroyo, with the Elders, desired peace. He had seen enough to realize that the colonists possessed uncommon resources.

Together Arroyo told them, there was the opportunity for the dome peoples and the colonists alike, to cleanse the world, to render it whole again. The Elders listened thoughtfully to the ideas and to the feelings behind the words. They liked him. Arroyo was a man they could deal with. Davis, the Elders insisted, would be the intermediary, the first of many to light the way between their worlds.

Devlin was stunned. He was in shock, the loss of his hand had devastated him. Dome surgeons had done all they could, but the hand could not be saved. There was no pain. The surgeons had seen to that. Devlin stared at the stump of bandages where his hand had been. He murmured the word null again and again. He vowed a private vengeance under his breath.

For the first time in a long time, Davis felt comfortable, physically. His belt wasn't pinching or suffocating him. He wasn't disgusted with the shape he was in anymore. He liked the way he felt. He didn't want to go to the Phoenix. There was nothing there for him now. The place would be lonely without Bach. He looked around his apartment. It was good to be back, he thought. The replica of the tower was right where he had left it. There it was. During the entire time that everything was happening, he thought, the little tower had rested right there, in that exact spot, on his shelf. He found it so odd that things can happen to a person, and yet some things remain the same. He wished his father were still alive. So much he could tell him about a whole new world.

He settled comfortably into the chair. Easing himself into the trance, Davis wandered through his adventures with Bach in the underground colonies. Davis had learned to compress time, savoring the experiences that brought joy. Anton had taught him so much. He could almost hear that voice now, the sheer, life-affirming, exuberance of it.

And behind the familiar voice, he began to hear laughter, gentle and rich and rolling, like the laughter of a god. The laughter filled the room as Davis began thinking about another trip to the southern colonies. Bach and Marta had told him they would be waiting for him. He would go, but not to stay. His home was here in the Dome. This was where he would live. There was much to be done in linking the two worlds together, the domes and the colonies. He would be a part of that, and his place was here in the Dome.

The laughter grew so loud that Davis fell out of his chair, and waking, discovered that it was the sound of his own laughter.

ABOUT THE AUTHOR

Frank Buchar is a writer of fiction and non fiction. He lives in Hamilton, Ontario, Canada, with his wife, son, and daughter.

CPSIA information can be obtained
at www.ICGtesting.com
Printed in the USA
LVOW12s0314041016

507217LV00001B/110/P